The Second Door

The Secret of Arking Down, Volume 3

Kira Morgana

Published by Teigr Books, 2024.

THE SECOND DOOR

First edition. May 31, 2024.

ISBN: 979-8224866199

Written by Kira Morgana.

Table of Contents

For Paul T.

Prologue

The darkness behind her eyelids surrounded her. It held and caressed her body in a warm friendly, even over friendly way that made Morgana sigh. She didn't want to open her eyes yet.

"Morgana. Sweetheart." Her mother's voice seemed distant to her, the slight tremble of fear making Morgana feel a little ashamed.

"She may be a little Nyctophobic after this." That was the doctor.

He sounded young and sexy, but to tell the truth, Morgana hadn't ever seen his face. *I hope that he is young and sexy.*

"What's that?" Morgana's mother sounded more scared than before.

"Afraid of the Dark." There was a pause and Morgana imagined her doctor shrugging. "This procedure has only been tried three times before successfully and each patient has been nyctophobic."

I think it sounds romantic. Like something out of those Victorian based romances that Jules reads to me. Morgana sighed. *God, I hope he's sexy.*

"Morgana, I know you're awake." Her mother was trying to sound stern, but all she managed was worried. "Please sweetheart, open your eyes."

Morgana considered drawing it out a little longer, but as the moment lengthened, she decided that she wanted to find out if her sight really was restored.

She opened her eyes...

One

The train blared out its warning as it entered the tunnel. Morgana watched the black mouth in the hill get closer to her and bit her lip. *I hate this.* Her carriage was swallowed up and the lights came on.

It isn't dark, I am not afraid. It isn't dark, I am not afraid. Morgana repeated the phrase over and over again, pressing her right thumb into the pad below the left, using the pressure to remind herself that everything was all right.

The train emerged out of the tunnel into a valley. Morgana sighed as the sunlight hit her and smiled.

"Beautiful place isn't it?" the man in front of her said.

"Pardon?" she blinked.

"Arking Valley. I love coming here." He stretched. "It's one of the most unique habitats for wildlife in the whole of Britain. Did you know that the whole area has been declared a Global Site of Special Scientific Interest?"

Morgana shook her head.

"The border runs for miles along the outside edge of the downs. Even the government has to get special permission to build anything in Arking Valley." He sounded smug.

Morgana looked away from him, out the window. The train was curving around the edge of the hill and below the tracks, she could see marshes spreading out towards a sparkling lake. On the opposite side, the small hill that formed Arkingham rose, houses marching up towards the town centre in orderly rows.

Behind the hill was heavily forested and the leaves on the trees were a riot of autumn colour.

"They say that the trees in Arking Forest are the oldest in Britain. It has Ancient Woodland status." The man grinned as she looked back at him." I suppose you're wondering why I know so much about the Valley."

Not really. Morgana shrugged.

"I'm taking up the position of Manager at The Arkingham Grange Wildlife Reserve and Conservation Centre." he smiled again and this time, it was infectious with excitement.

Morgana smiled back. "Congratulations."

"Thank you. You're Welsh, aren't you?" he paused for a moment, and when she didn't answer, ploughed on. "This area was a hotly contested settlement during the border wars with Wales. There are a large number of people here that are of Welsh descent and the Lady of Arkingham is herself Welsh."

"I know." Morgana bit her lip. *I can feel her now. Just on the edge of my mind.*

The man frowned. "Are you all right? You went very pale inside the tunnel, and you still don't have much colour." He leaned forward, looking into her face.

"I'll be okay. I just don't like tunnels, that's all." She smiled at him, and he seemed to relax.

"Well, we're nearly to Sowthdon Station and the end of the line." He looked out the window. "In fact, we're just coming into town now. One of the things that I love the most about this journey is the fact that the train only goes this far."

"Why?" Morgana busied herself with putting her things back into her bag.

"Trains make a lot of pollution, even if they are more economical for transport. Can you imagine if there were train lines to all the towns in the Valley? The place would be an absolute mess." He stood up, balancing himself against the sway of the train as it slowed down. "Do you need any help with your luggage?"

"No, thank you. I'm fine." Morgana patted the large rucksack on the seat beside her. "My father lives in Arkingham so I don't need to bring a lot with me."

The man blinked and frowned, looking at her face carefully. She could hear his train of thought in her mind: *Platinum blonde hair, blue eyes, pale skin. Welsh accent. Father lives in Arkingham...*

Rolling her eyes she stood up, hoping to forestall his conclusion. "Well, it's been nice talking to you..."

"Lady Gwynnhafr Arkingham?" he said.

Morgana cursed her sister silently. "No, that's my sister. I'm Morgana Davis-Pendry."

The train screeched to a halt in the station, throwing the man forwards into his seat.

Morgana grabbed her rucksack, threw it over her shoulder and headed for the doors as fast as possible. As she stepped out onto the platform, she spotted her dad and Walter the Manager of the Stable yard waiting.

"Morgana Davis-Pendry!" her dad caught her up in a huge hug. "You're all grown up!"

"Da, stop it, I'm not a baba any more." Morgana blushed as she registered Walter's grin. "Hi Walter."

"Lady Morgana." Walter inclined his head to her. "I hope you had a good trip."

"Well, I could have done without all the tunnels, but otherwise it was fine." Morgana smiled. "And please don't call me Lady. I know I have a title, but I hate using it!"

"Just like your sister." Walter shook his head. "Lady Myfanwy insisted that we use your titles in public, but Jenni won't have anything of it!"

Morgana bit her lip, a surge of rage making it difficult to breathe. *She always has to be so...*

"Look, Walter, there's Angelino Berghaus." Dad pointed at the man who had been talking to her on the train. "Walter, you take him to the cottage and get him settled in. I'll take Morgana on a bit of a tour round town, before we go up to the Grange."

"All right, Artair." Walter flicked off a salute. "Mission understood. I'll see you later, Morgana."

"Bye Walter." Morgana waved slightly.

Artair shouldered her rucksack and grabbed her hand. "Come on sweetheart, I want to take you to see all the sights."

JENNI STEPPED THROUGH the Earth door as it fogged and opened, a sheaf of envelopes in her hand. "I'll see you at the New Year Ball, Rilx."

"Sure, Jenni." The reptilian humanoid stood on the other side, a small brightly coloured dragon on his shoulder. "Have fun with your sister."

"I'll try to." Jenni waved as the door fogged closed again, then turned around. Beside the white door she'd come through, was a Black Door without a handle. In the stone floor in the corner opposite the black door was a blue enamelled circle.

She stepped into the blue circle. As always, she glanced at the black door's alarm to make sure it hadn't been tampered with. *The light is still green. Good.* There was a hum, and a tube of blue light surrounded her, making her skin tingle. *I still can't get used to that.* Then she was in another small room with a spiral staircase leading out of it.

"Grandfather! I'm back." She called out, pulling a slim black mobile phone from her pocket.

"About time. How's the Kingdom?" her grandfather's voice came from the phone.

"About the same. The General is doing a good job of being steward, so I arranged the ball and left him to it." Jenni smiled at the CG face that hovered above the surface of the phone screen.

"Good. Your sister just got here. Artair just called in."

"Okay. Are they doing the ten-pence tour of town?" Jenni dashed up the stairs two at a time, paused at the top to push the small button and slipped under the door as it slid upward.

As the door shut again behind her, Jenni pushed out her mind. *There she is. With Dad at the Castle. I hope she's going to be reasonable this time.*

MORGANA COULD FEEL her sister pushing at the edges of her mind, trying to re-establish their old connection. She kept the wall she'd created against Jenni firmly in place and eventually, Jenni gave up.

I didn't want to do this. she reminded herself as Artair showed her around the castle. *Mum forced me to come.*

At the top of the tower, looking out over the town, Morgana could see other towers, all around the town and up on the hills. "What are all those?" she asked her dad.

He grinned. "The one in front of us amongst the trees in the park is the Lady's Tower. Directly behind us, on the north western tip of Arking Down is Arianrhod's Tower." He turned and pointed. "The spring that feeds the waterfall is up there. If we go around clockwise, the rest of them are the North Watchtower; the Llyn Watchtower; Sowthdon Watchtower and Yeracha Watchtower."

"Why so many?" She asked as they turned to head back downstairs.

"The local archaeologists think that this valley was considered a holy place. They've found remains of temples and sacrifices in the bogs around the lake." At the bottom of the stairs, Artair took her hand. "The Grange History books written by your grandfather detail all sorts of reasons for the towers."

"Aderyn Archington was not my grandfather." Morgana said, dropping his hand.

She stalked away into the next room.

"Morgana, we need to get a few things straight before we go up to the house, so I think we ought to go and have a snack at the café." Artair caught up with her.

"I don't want to talk about anything to do with it." She snapped.

"Too bad. I don't care if I do the talking, as long as you listen." He took her hand again and practically towed her into the café.

Once they were installed in a booth with drinks and cake, Artair looked at her. "I am your adopted father. Your birth mother died of cancer and your birth father suicided."

Huh? Mum never told me that. She blinked. "I know they're dead. I don't care, you and mum are my real parents."

"Aderyn Archington brought you and Jenni to us for adoption because he'd been unable to cure Helen's sterility." He put sugar into his tea and stirred it. "He was the father of your birth mother and thus is your grandfather. Lady Myfanwy is your aunt."

"I know!" Morgana growled. "Mum told me."

She remembered the conversation in the hotel, the evening of the funeral. She also remembered crying her eyes out because she was so jealous of Jenni's bequest. *Only it was more because she actually met our grandfather, and I didn't.*

"Good, I don't need to go into detail then." Artair sipped his tea. "Aderyn Archington didn't die."

Morgana blinked and dropped her fork onto the plate of chocolate fudge cake. "What?" her voice rose and Artair waved at her.

"Shhh. The town know him as Archie Birdenth, one of the staff who work up in the Grange."

"Does anyone else know?" Morgana frowned.

"Your Mother, Jenni, Walter, Maebh and Myfanwy. All the other staff at the Grange, the Riding School and the Conservation Centre know him as Archie."

"How did he survive? I thought he had terminal lung cancer." Morgana started eating her cake again.

"His body died, but the medical branch of Archington Industries designed and built a cybernetic body for his brain to be implanted into." Artair shrugged. "He's just like any other human, except he's a little heavier than normal and a lot stronger."

"Okay. Is that the only thing?" she could feel him holding something back.

"Um... I've met someone." Artair looked down into his teacup. "Jenni said that I shouldn't tell you, but I don't want you to get off on the wrong foot with her."

Morgana felt herself go very still inside, almost icily calm. *So much for my dreams of getting mum and dad back together.* She swallowed her mouthful of cake. "Okay. Da, I'm nearly twenty, I can take anything that Jenni can."

"It's Myfanwy." Artair looked up at her. "Your birth Aunt."

Morgana smiled. "That's wonderful!" she forced herself to relax. *At least it's someone nice, unlike...*

"We're getting married next spring." He smiled. "Would you mind being a bridesmaid with Jenni?"

She smiled again. "No problem, Da."

He looked relieved. "Thank you. I was hoping you would. Shall we go up to the house now? Your sister should be back from Monaco by now."

Morgana shrugged. "Well, I have to see her sometime. Better sooner than later."

Two

As they pulled up on the gravel in the front of the house, Morgana's twin sister came flying out of the front door, followed by Maebh, Walter and a tall man with dark blond hair.

Morgana looked out the window at them. *I can do this, I am not afraid.* She chanted silently, pressing her thumb into her palm.

"It'll be fine, Morgana." Artair said as he opened his door. "Come on."

Jenni dashed up to Artair and flung her arms around him. "Dad! I'm so happy to see you."

"Jenni, you're twenty this year, try and act like a young lady, instead of a hooligan." Artair hugged his eldest daughter back and set her back down on the ground.

Jenni smiled and turned to Morgana. "Hello Morgana. It's been a while."

"Hello Gwynnhafr." Morgana replied. She pushed her thumb into her palm until it ached. "Yes, it has been a while. Five years or so."

"How are you feeling?" Jenni tilted her head a little to the left, her long platinum blonde fringe falling across her eyes.

"Tired. Where am I staying?" Morgana looked up at the house. "Dad and I usually use his house in town when you're away."

"I thought you could stay upstairs with me. I have several guest bedrooms in my private apartment." Jenni turned to Artair. "Is that okay, Dad?"

Her accent has changed. It's not exactly Welsh, but not English either. Morgana looked at Artair as well.

11

"It's okay with me. Just be careful with her, Jenni. She only got out of hospital a week ago." Artair laughed as identical disgusted expressions crossed the twins faces.

"Da! I'm not fragile." Morgana protested.

"No, *you* aren't, but the device used to bring your sight back is and if you over stress yourself, you might go blind again." The tall man said.

"Morgana, this is..." Jenni looked at their father again. He nodded so she continued. "...Archie Birdenth. He runs Archington Industries for me, so he knows a lot about the procedure that you had done."

Morgana stared at the man. *This is my grandfather?*

Archie held his hand out. "I'm delighted to meet you, Lady Morgana. Lady Gwynnhafr has told me so much about you."

Shaking his hand, Morgana smiled politely. *I'm sure she has.*

"Shall we go inside?" Maebh asked. "I've laid out some tea and refreshments in the Orangery."

They followed Maebh into the house. Walter took Morgana's rucksack off of Artair. "I'll put this in the Family Quarters."

"Thanks, Walter." Jenni said.

Morgana echoed the salutation and followed her sister into the warmth of the huge glass and iron conservatory. *I like it in here. It's so soothing and with the others around, Jenni and I won't argue.* She pushed her thumb into her palm absently.

Maebh poured tea for everyone except Archie.

Morgana found herself staring at the man who was supposed to be her grandfather but looked nothing like the picture she had been given. *Except for the eyes. They're the same. Green and piercing.*

Jenni looked at her sharply and opened her mouth. Archie waved a hand and Jenni shut it again.

Walter came in and shut the door behind him, turning the key in the lock. "All secure." He announced, sitting down. "The last of the staff have gone home and I've locked up for the night."

"Good." Artair turned to Archie. "Aderyn, how long will it take the implant to embed properly?"

"Considering she's had it in for almost a month, I'd say a few more days." Archie looked at Morgana. "No riding or strenuous exercise for you until I've had the med techs do an MRI Scan on you to check it."

"How long is that going to take, Grandfather?" Jenni asked, looking upset. "I was going to suggest going riding tomorrow."

"Hold off on that until Monday, Jen." Archie smiled. "I'll arrange it for Friday, so take it easy until then."

Morgana bit her lip. *They're talking about me as if I'm invisible!* She stood up, drawing all eyes to her. "Gwynnhafr, I'm really tired from the journey and Dad's tour. Can you show me where I'm going to sleep, please."

Jenni stood up. "Of course, Morgana." She unlocked the Orangery door and led Morgana out.

"I'll come up to say goodnight later." Artair called.

Morgana acknowledged him with a wave and followed her sister down the corridor to the massive stairs in the main hall.

"Do you want to go the scenic route or the quick route?" Jenni asked.

"Quick please. I really am tired."

"Okay then." Jenni opened a concealed door in the panelling beside the stairs. "This way."

They walked in silence. Every footfall on the uncarpeted tiles echoed and Morgana began to wonder if Jenni was going to say anything at all.

"I'll get you your own set of keys tomorrow. The ones for the Orangery, the front door, the library and the door to my apartment.

That one opens the door to the Family Quarters as well." Jenni led her up a set of scuffed wooden stairs, the handrail's wood smooth and warm under Morgana's hand.

When they reached the landing, Morgana saw two white painted doors. One had a brass horse on it, the other a house.

"That's Maebh and Walter's apartments. The family quarters are on the other side." Jenni smiled. "Myfanwy was determined to give us all a bit of privacy when she refurbished the house."

"What's she like?" Morgana asked, glancing out the windows that over looked the forecourt. The sun was setting over the forest that surrounded the grounds and the leaves flamed in the reddening light.

"Myfanwy? She's nice. Has Dad told you about the wedding?" Jenni paused in front of another white painted door with a brass tree on it. Pulling a bunch of keys out of her hoodie pocket, Jenni unlocked the door.

"Yes. I said I'd be happy to be a bridesmaid." Morgana looked around the room they stepped into. It was a nice room, with dark red leather sofa and chairs covered with cream scatter cushions. "Did Myfanwy pick things out in here?"

"No. Dad did." Jenni smiled. "I suspect that Van had a hand in it though. Ah there's your rucksack." She shouldered it and staggered. "Good goddess, 'Gana, what have you got in here?"

"The usual." Morgana followed Jenni through a frosted glass door and up a spiral staircase. By the time she made it to the top, Jenni had opened the door and was waiting inside.

"Take your pick." Jenni gestured to three open doors.

Morgana looked through each door and the view out of the third of them caught her eye. "This one will do."

Jenni put the rucksack on the bad. "Okay. You've got an ensuite bathroom through that door and there's a small walk-in wardrobe behind the next one."

Morgana felt the rage again. It bubbled up inside her, making her chest tighten. "How long has dad's new girlfriend been *Van* to you, *Gwynnhafr*?"

Jenni frowned. "I've known her for five years, *Morgana*. I think that entitles me to call her by her nickname. Besides, they only admitted what they felt for each other about six months ago."

"And where were you?" Morgana stared at her sister. "I bet you were swanning off round America with those daft friends of yours, weren't you."

"What if I was? I can afford to." Jenni leaned against the door jamb. "You could have come, I sent you an email about it through mum."

"Six months ago, I was blind, Gwynnhafr. How would I have enjoyed it?"

"That's right, throw that in my face. "Jenni bit her lower lip.

Morgana stared at her, also biting her lip. The silence lengthened.

"It wasn't me that made you go to school with Meningitis." Jenni snapped, her Welsh accent strengthening. "You should have stayed home; you were ill!"

"I had an exam that morning. And I needed to get my DT coursework finished." Morgana said calmly. "You would have done the same."

"Mam said you had a temperature of 40 degrees! It's your own fault that you got blinded, so don't blame anyone else." Jenni stood up. "It's also not my fault that I was born first and inherited the Arkingham estate or..."

"Or what?" Morgana sneered. Inside her mind a small voice said: *Don't do it, you'll regret it forever.* "Or got all the money and could afford to go to whichever University you wanted? Or introduced Dad to Myfanwy and stopped any chance of him and mam getting back together?"

"I didn't do that! Van is our birth Aunt, you know that. She's our Legal Guardian until we're twenty-one as well." Jenni clenched her fists. "Besides, Mam and Da are adults and entitled to their own lives without us interfering."

"Well, if you'd helped me when mum started dating that bastard Holewinski, we might have managed it." Morgana spat.

"It was none of our business!" Jenni shouted.

Morgana could sense that her sister was holding something back, but she couldn't get a sense of what it was. *Her mind is stronger. I used to be able to force my way in. Now I can't even make a dent in her privacy wall.*

"Stop that." Jenni was the calm one now. "You're being rude."

"What?"

"Trying to force your way into my mind is rude. You have to knock and ask to be let in." She tilted her head to the right.

Morgana heard a definite knocking sound in her mind. "Was that you?"

Jenni raised an eyebrow. "What do you think?"

"I think that you've become arrogant and nasty, Gwynnhafr Pendry. Ever since you inherited Aderyn Archington's money and title, you have been mean and I am disgusted with the way you've treated me." Morgana growled.

"And I'm disgusted to hear the bile in your voice, Morgana Pendry." Artair said as he moved Jenni gently to one side. "You will apologise to your sister now."

Morgana pressed her thumb into her palm. "No. It's time she heard the truth and as her twin sister, that's my right."

"What on earth are you talking about, 'Gana?" Jenni's eyes filled with tears.

"In the last five years you have not visited me once. You've not emailed me or called me." She glared at her sister. "You say you emailed me through mum, but I never heard anything about a trip to America. You're lying through your teeth."

There was silence.

"Jenni, go downstairs, Aderyn wants to talk to you about something." Artair said. "I can see that I need to talk to your sister."

Jenni left the room, wiping her eyes on her hoodie sleeve. Artair beckoned to Morgana. "Come out to the living room where we can sit down properly."

Three

M organa sat down opposite her father. *He's never been this serious before. What's going on?*

"Mum called me after you caught the train. She told me a few things that have surprised and dismayed, no, disappointed me." He said.

I haven't done anything wrong have I? Mum would have said something. Morgana started to get worried.

"I asked her if she'd spoken to you about it and she told me that you've been very difficult to talk to since regaining your sight." He paused and fiddled with his watch.

"What did she say about me?" Morgana asked.

"Well, firstly that you've been trying to disrupt her relationship with her current boyfriend. Why? I thought you'd grown out of that."

"To be honest, Da, I'm not exactly sure." Morgana bit her bottom lip and flushed. "I have this vague notion that you'll get back together if neither of you is attached to anyone."

"Did you lie to me about being happy for Myfanwy and me?" he frowned.

"No... yes... No, not really." She stopped, flustered by her own emotions. "I don't know how to feel about it, Da. Mum hasn't married any of the men she's gone out with."

"She's never been able to trust you with meeting them." He sighed. "Let alone consider an engagement."

Mum doesn't trust me? The pain that bloomed in her heart threatened to cut off her breathing. *I didn't think that sabotaging her boyfriend's interest in her would do that.*

"Another thing she told me is that you refused point blank to have any contact with your sister, even after your accident. It got to the point that Helen couldn't even mention your sister's name without you having a break down and she got so worried for your health that she started censoring the news from here." He levelled a glare at her. "That's why you've not heard from Jenni for five years. Your poor sister has been beside herself with worry for you the entire time and all you could do when you two finally get a moment alone together, was pour vitriol into her ears."

Morgana looked out the window behind her, trying to rationalise what she was hearing.

"I don't care if you're not looking at me, I'm going to tell you these things and you are damn well going to listen." Artair's voice hardened. "Since Jenni has left school, she's been unable to go to university because of her responsibilities here. You might think that her life is all having fun and spending money, but she works twice as hard as anyone else on this estate, sometimes harder."

Morgana turned back. "Now that I can't believe. What could she do that she can't pay someone else to do?"

"At eighteen, your sister took over the running of the House and estate. She assigned Aderyn to head Archington Industries because he has the best knowledge for the post. She engaged Angelino Berghaus to manage the Conservation work. The rest of it, she does herself. All the publicity work as well as give tours around the estate."

"She always did like being centre of attention." Morgana muttered.

That seemed to ignite something. Artair stood up. "That is enough. You've been catered to and spoiled for the last five years. I brought you to Arkingham to recuperate from your operation, not argue with your sister."

Morgana felt her jaw drop open. *Even Da has changed. What is it about his place? Everyone who comes here is ruined forever.* She clenched her jaw shut. *I will not let it happen to me.*

THE PULSING, BUZZING noise of the MRI Scanner made it impossible for Morgana to hear anything clearly. She kept her thumb firmly pressed into her palm for the whole thing and shut her eyes tight, not wanting to see the huge doughnut shaped machine pass over her.

"Relax, Morgana, nothing is going to hurt you." Aderyn's voice said from the speaker.

All Morgana heard was; *...Morgana...going...to...hurt...* and she felt the panic begin to sweep over her. *I can do this. I am not afraid.* She chanted.

Then all of a sudden, it was over and the platform she lay on slid out of the now quiet machine. Sitting up she looked over towards the glassed in booth where her father and Aderyn sat with the technicians.

"You can come out here now." Aderyn said. "We've managed to get what we needed."

Good, because I wasn't going through that thing for a fourth time. She pulled her trainers on and left the Scanner room. Another technician entered and began fiddling with the machine behind her.

Aderyn and Artair came out of the room with the Doctor handling her case. He'd been brought in from Bristol for his expert opinion and Morgana was very glad to see him.

I was right to think he was young and sexy when I woke up from the operation. She thought as she followed the men down the corridor to Aderyn's office. *I can't keep my eyes off that tight butt of his.*

They sat down and Aderyn's PA brought coffee in. The doctor went through the scans one at a time, checking each one minutely with an eyeglass.

After about half an hour of silence, he sat back. "As far as I can tell there is no rejection of the implant and no damage to the brain at all." He smiled at Morgana and her heart did a flip-flop of excitement. "I'd say that you're healed completely, Morgana."

"Excellent news." Artair smiled as well. "You'll be able to go riding now."

"Just as long as you wear a proper safety helmet." The doctor cautioned. "It's just possible; about a one in thirty thousand chance that a fall from a height could undo all the good that the implant has done."

Morgana sighed. "Good, I've been dying to try that new Arab gelding out." She stood up. "Can I go now?"

Aderyn smiled. "Of course you can. Be careful."

The three men watched the teenager leave.

"She has recovered quite remarkably from such an invasive operation." The doctor said. "And in such a short time too."

"It's the air here, everyone who lives in Arking Valley goes away in better health than they arrived in." Artair said.

"If you could bottle it, you'd make millions." The young doctor grinned. "As it is, I'm sure that's the reason for the number of tourists and health spas in the valley."

"Well, let's just hope she keeps on soaking up the good health." Aderyn remarked. "You can keep those files for your records, Dr. Green."

"Thank you." The doctor paused. "Have there been any significant mental difficulties since she arrived here?"

"We've had a few temper tantrums and arguments with her sister, but as they haven't seen each other for over five years, I'd expect that." Artair shrugged.

"I mean things like hallucinations or claiming to hear voices? The last patient to have the implant complained of hallucinations. He said he could see thermal images and lots of lines in all different colours running over the ground like roads." Dr. Green handed a file from his case to Aderyn. "Here's the copy of his data. I was hoping that you could get your guys to analyse our findings. He's deteriorating rapidly and has had to be sedated."

"Will that happen to Morgana?" Artair blinked.

"I hope not. He's the oldest patient to survive the operation, so I do suspect dementia." Dr Green put the films into his case and stood up. "Thank you for allowing me to see your facility here, Mr. Birdenth, it's an excellent place and I hope that we can make use of it in the future."

"For selected cases, certainly." Aderyn pressed a button on his desk. His PA appeared. "Ellie, would you see Dr. Green out to his car, please."

She nodded and waited while the doctor shook Artair and Aderyn's hands. "It's been a pleasure, Mr. Birdenth, Mr. Pendry."

The two men made polite noises back and once he'd gone, Aderyn brought the scans up on his monitor. "I'm worried, Artair."

"Oh." Artair came around the desk to lean over Aderyn's shoulder. "About Morgana?"

"Yes." Aderyn pointed at the scans of her brain. "See these dark areas? Well, they shouldn't be there, Dr. Green pointed them out and realised that I saw something similar when Angharad had her scans."

"I thought the twins mother died of Bowel Cancer." Artair said softly. He knew that Aderyn blamed himself for his daughter's death.

"That was the cancer they found in the biopsy. After she died, I arranged an autopsy and they found tumours in her brain as well." Aderyn took a deep breath. "These shadows are still very small, so we have a chance to catch it."

"What would the cancer treatment do to the implant?" Artair moved back to his chair and sat down heavily. "Sod, that, I don't care. I don't want to lose my daughter."

"We won't lose her, Artair, I promise you that. If they can bring me back from death's door, then I'm sure that we can save her." Aderyn sighed. "Don't treat her any differently though, or she'll realise something is wrong."

THE CHILL WIND THAT swept over Arking Down was invigorating as Jenni and Morgana emerged from the trees near to the stone circle.

Morgana a took a deep breath and smiled. "It feels good to be out in the fresh air."

"Shall we go down to the Gallops and try out Kedar's paces?" Jenni asked, pointing out a pale oval carved into the down. The stallion she was riding stamped and snorted. "All right, boy, we'll run in a minute."

Morgana grinned. "Sounds like fun." She tapped the Kedar's flanks and leaned forward as he seemed to fly forward over the heathland.

"Hey! Wait for us." Jenni yelled.

No chance. I want to be on my own for a bit and if I have to out ride you, I will. Morgana laughed and urged the Arab grey into a gallop.

Jenni watched her sister race off with a smile. *I'm glad that she's feeling better. I just wish that she'd talk to me properly. Maybe the ball will help her loosen up.* She clicked her tongue and the stallion moved off at a walk, quivering with enthusiasm. "Oh, all right. Let's go!"

The horse went from a walk to a run in one smooth transition and Jenni found herself laughing as she caught up with Morgana.

For several long moments, the twins raced side by side over the short grass and sandy chalk of the down, laughing and smiling.

They slowed as they reached the sand covered Gallop and Jenni sighed happily. "You have no idea how long I have been waiting to do that with you."

"Really." Morgana barely looked at her as she swung out of the saddle and checked Kedar over. "You can do this whenever you want, why would you wait to do it with me?"

"I meant I'd been waiting to go riding with you..." Jenni frowned. "You were being sarcastic, weren't you?"

Morgana just shrugged. "Take it how you want to."

"What's wrong with you?" Jenni demanded. "You got your sight back, you're allowed to do what you like and you're being really miserable about it."

"Leave me alone." Morgana glared at her. "Just leave me alone. I can get back to the stables by myself."

"And how many times have you been out here by yourself? Do you know the way?" Jenni shook her head. "No. We go back together."

Morgana swung herself up into the saddle again. "Fine." She set off the way they'd come.

"Not that way. There's a shorter route that I need to show you." She turned her horse toward the woodland at the edge of the down.

Morgana followed her sister, seething. *Why won't anyone leave me alone? I want to be by myself, but they all keep checking up on me. I'm not even allowed to go into town by myself.*

At the edge of the woodland, Jenni touched the trunk of a lightening split oak. "There's a button here, disguised as a knot." She pressed it.

What's she doing? Morgana felt queasy.

With barely a sound, part of the down opened up in front of them. Jenny waited silently and neither horse reacted.

It's a tunnel entrance. Morgana glanced into the gaping maw and shivered. "We're not going in there are we?"

"It's the fastest and safest way back to the house in the evening." Jenni shrugged. "It doesn't take long. Come on."

Jenni started her mount moving and Kedar followed the stallion. Morgana felt panic rise in her chest as the Arab carried her inside. She held the reins with a death grip, her right thumb finding the palm of her left hand. *I can do this. I am not afraid*

The tunnel entrance closed behind them; simultaneously the interior lit up. Jenni kept moving, and it was only Kedar's instinct to follow his stable mate that kept them moving. Morgana shut her eyes tightly and concentrated on breathing.

"Morgana. Are you okay?" Jenni's voice echoed slightly.

"I'm fine, let's just get out of here, please." Morgana replied, trying hard to stay in control of herself.

She let the gelding have his head and after a while when they emerged into the cool autumn sunlight by the waterfall, she took a deep breath, feeling the panic subside slowly as Kedar moved further away from the cave entrance.

Jenni reined in beside the pool. "Are you sure you're, okay? You're very pale. Do you want me to call dad to come and pick you up?"

Morgana shook her head. "I told you, I'm fine. Stop worrying would you." Tapping Kedar's flanks she followed the path away from the pool.

Jenni followed. *At least she can't get lost here, the track only goes back to the estate. I think I need to talk to Dad though, she definitely wasn't all right in the tunnel.*

Four

After lunch, Jenni disappeared into town. Morgana decided to wander around the house. *I might as well find out what this place looks like, rather than how it sounds or feels.*

The public area took a relatively short while to explore. There were some interesting exhibits and a few interactive things that seemed popular with the kids in the tours. She tagged along on the end of one tour to listen to the story the guide was telling.

It seemed to be some kind of medieval love story, but long before he got to the end, Morgana got bored and wandered away toward the conference rooms.

Maebh stopped her before she got to them though. "There are meetings in there all day. Why don't you go upstairs and watch TV or something?"

"I've been cooped up for too long, but Da won't let me go into town by myself and I don't want to go swimming while there are all these strangers around."

"Hmm." Maebh considered her. "What about the library? Have you been in there yet? Jenni stocked it with a lot of decent books."

Morgana shrugged. "I might as well. It's just behind Ade...Archie's office, isn't it?"

"That's right dear. Would you like me to bring you a snack in? I just made some chocolate fudge cake." The House-manager smiled as the girl's eyes lit up and she nodded. "I thought so. You go get yourself settled and I'll be over in a minute."

Morgana loved the library the moment she stepped into it. *I haven't seen this many books in one place since the last time I went to the school library.* She wandered around, looking at the titles and just breathing in the vanillary, dusty smell of stored books. *This place is wonderful.*

She sighed, and spotting a hardback copy of J. Booth's *Wizards*, slipped it off the shelf. "I haven't read this for ages."

"Well settle yourself down and read it then." Maebh said as she came into the room with a tray. "I've brought you some cake and tea." She placed the tray on a small table next to a large window.

Morgana curled up in the huge chair beside the table and opened the book; the world inside immediately snared her. Maebh, sensing that she wasn't needed, left the library smiling.

The change in the room's light interrupted her.

Putting her book down, Morgana stretched and picked her tea up. *This is cold. How long have I been reading for?*

The low light in the room made it difficult to see her watch and she was about to switch the light on the table beside her on, when a soft scraping noise from behind her stopped her from moving. *There's someone coming into the room from a secret door. Why does that not surprise me?*

Morgana carefully and quietly twisted in her chair so that she could see over the back. *That's Jenni. How did she get in here?*

Her sister pushed the door gently closed. It was one of those bookcase decorated doors, so it blended into the wall perfectly. As Jenni turned, Morgana ducked below the level of the chair back. *Did she see me?*

"Shouldn't you put a light on in here? Its difficult to read without it." Jenni said.

Morgana jumped. *I didn't think that she'd seen me. How did she know I was here?* There was a knocking at the edge of her mind and while Morgana was trying to work out how to keep Jenni out, her sister entered it anyway.

"Morgana Davis-Pendry, I can hear every single word you've been thinking, so is it any wonder that I know you're in here?" Jenni walked

over and sat down in the chair opposite Morgana, turning the side light on at the same time.

Morgana blinked furiously as the light sent a stab of pain through her head. *Ouch.*

"Sorry 'Gana. I didn't think about that. Dad did say the implant made you sensitive to sudden light." Jenni sounded ashamed.

"I'm fine. What do you want?" Morgana refused to be drawn into a telepathic conversation when they were sat so close together.

"Nothing. I just came back from town. It's raining so I caught a lift up with Walter and used the tunnel from the tack room to the library." Jenni grinned as she caught the expression on her face. "This house is full of tunnels. There is even a way of getting down to town without needing to drive or walk."

"Really? Where?" Morgana looked around. "In here?"

"Look, I'm glad I found you in here actually. I wanted to..."

"Wanted to what? Snipe at me? Baby me some more?" Morgana snapped.

"Apologise actually. You're the baby of the family, so I get a little jealous of the way that dad and everyone else is walking on knife edges around you. They don't want to jeopardise your recovery and I suppose I've been a little envious of all the attention recently." Jenni tilted her head. "Will you forgive me?"

Morgana stared at her. *She wants me to forgive her? For being selfish? After everything I have said to her?*

Jenni smiled. "You've not been well, and you're allowed to get angry at me. After all, when we were little, we both assumed that you were the older, so it must have been a shock when you didn't inherit the estate."

Morgana found herself speechless.

Jenni seemed to sense that her sister had been struck dumb and stood up. "Dinner will probably be ready soon, so I'm going to go and get changed. I'll see you in the dining room."

For a full five minutes after her sister had left, Morgana mulled over what Jenni had said, her book lying forgotten on the arm of the chair. *When did Jenni get so grown up?* She distracted herself from the accompanying thought that, as they were twins, she ought to be that grown up as well, by moving over to the wall where the bookcase door had been.

"So where is this tunnel to the stables then?" she muttered. Looking along the cases of books, she found one set that had double edges and shelves. *It must be here. Now, how to open it?*

After considering the matter for several minutes, she looked at the eye level shelf. Along this were the complete works of Dickens, Hardy and the Austen sisters, all bound in different colours of leather. Dickens was red, Hardy blue and the Austen's yellow. Between Dickens and Hardy was a book bound in white leather. *It doesn't have any writing on the spine.*

Morgana put her hand up to the white book and pulled it a little. There was a gentle rumble and the boor swung open. A light came on inside the revealed space to show a spiral staircase. *I wonder what's down there?*

Stepping inside she looked down over the edge of the rail. Her stomach seemed to wobble, and the panic rose in her chest. *I can do this. I'm not afraid.* Moving carefully, she followed the stairs down. Shutting her eyes seemed to calm the panic and it was almost as if the operation had never taken place; she could sense where everything was around her.

At the bottom she opened her eyes to find a junction of three passageways, all of them fairly well lit. Closing her eyes again, she extended her senses. From one direction came a distinct horsey smell. *That would be the stables.* From another direction she felt a slight breeze and the smell of rain. *I'd say that came out in the gardens somewhere.* The third direction had a damp and musty smell, almost earthy scent. *Don't know where that one comes out, but it's a long one by the feel of it.*

There came a soft knocking at her mind's door. *"'Gana, dinner will be ready soon."* Her sister told her quietly.

Morgana didn't answer and Jenni's presence withdrew, leaving a slightly sad feeling behind. *She really is sorry for being selfish and having so much money.*

Closing her eyes again, Morgana retraced her steps up into the library. Once in the darkened room, she pushed the bookcase shut and retrieved the novel she'd been reading, marking her place carefully before she left the room for dinner.

"I'M NOT SURE SHE SHOULD be allowed to come to the ball, Myfanwy. Her attitude towards Jenni is atrocious." Aderyn said. "And that's just because Jenni inherited the estates here. Can you imagine what it'd be like if she found out about Llanirstyr?"

"Father, she can't be that bad. Besides, Jenni is bringing Caoimhe and Mike with her and she'll be worse if she gets left behind." Myfanwy's voice over the internet connection sounded worried.

"I don't know. I mean we haven't even told Helen and Artair where the girls came from originally. The knowledge might flip Morgana over the edge." Aderyn leaned back. "This is just not a good time for this particular revelation."

"Father, I'll be over in a couple of days. Let me assess her." Myfanwy snorted suddenly. "Besides, Artair will need to find out about Llanirstyr soon enough, we have to have the betrothal ceremony here, remember?"

"Don't remind me. I still haven't figured that one out." Aderyn groaned.

"We'll talk about it after I arrive. I need to check what Jenni and Caoimhe will be wearing after all." Myfanwy giggled like a schoolchild. "I'm looking forward to designing their clothes."

Aderyn shrugged and grinned at his daughter. "And you became a doctor? I'll see you when you get here."

"Farewell Father."

Aderyn shut the window down as Artair came in looking more worried than normal. "All right, Artair. What has Morgana done now?"

"It's not so much what she's done, but how she's been reacting to some things." Artair sat down. "Jenni told me that when they went riding this morning, Morgana had a panic attack in the tunnel down from the Gallops. Jenni also said that Morgana sleeps with the bedside light on and the curtains open, but still has quite strong nightmares, sometimes screaming in her sleep."

Aderyn frowned. "Dr. Green said that she's showing signs of being both Nyctophobic and Claustrophobic. What has Helen said?"

"How did you guess that I'd called her about this?" Artair shook his head. "She said that the hospital had to sedate Morgana every night to stop her disturbing the other patients and that it was good that they lived in a detached house with a large garden, because if her neighbours had heard Morgana at night, Helen would have had Social Services called on her."

"That's not good. All right, Artair. I'll call Dr. Green and see what he suggests. I'll also schedule some tests and ask Myfanwy if she can assess the child when she arrives."

"Van is coming?" Artair grinned foolishly. "Why?"

"She wants to look at what Jenni and Caoimhe are wearing for Jenni's Ball." Aderyn ignored the little bite of jealousy that occurred whenever Artair and Myfanwy talked about each other. *She's a big girl now, she doesn't need an overprotective father anymore.*

Artair laughed. "The girls will enjoy that. Maybe the ball will help Morgana to relax a little."

"About that. I'm not sure it would be a good idea for Morgana to go. Especially with these problems that are now surfacing." Aderyn sighed. "Well, we won't mention it to her for now. Let's get the tests done and make sure that Morgana is a hundred percent all right first."

Artair nodded. "I don't want anything to happen to her, Aderyn."

"I know, Artair." Aderyn pushed back from his desk. "It's time for dinner. You have to eat even if I don't, so I'll walk you to the dining room."

THE NEXT MORNING, MORGANA decided to try out the idea she'd come up with overnight. *When I closed my eyes, I could stay calm. Maybe if I blindfold myself...*

After breakfast, she went back upstairs and rummaged around in her bag until she found the thick black silk scarf her mum had given her for her birthday. Then she went back to the library. Her book was still on the table where she'd left it, so she sat down and finished the story. *Now I can concentrate.* She thought as she put the book back in the shelf.

Morgana moved to the shelf with the white book. *I can do this. It might even help cure me of this fear.* Thinking about it seemed to trigger something inside of her; her palms got sweaty, and her breathing quickened. *I can do this, I am not afraid.*

Pulling the white book opened the door and Morgana stepped into the tiny room beyond. Taking a deep breath, she walked down the stairs calmly, trying not to give into the fear that bubbled up inside.

Halfway down she closed her eyes, the fear receding. *Why does that help? I lived in darkness for five years, why am I scared of the dark?*

She got to the bottom of the stairs and opened her eyes to orientate herself with the scent of horses. Then she tied the silk scarf around her eyes, opening them to make sure she couldn't see anything. *Well so far, so good. Now, let's see if I can navigate the tunnel to the stables.*

Taking a deep breath, she placed one hand on the tunnel wall and followed the warm, sweet animal scent, counting her steps as she went. *This feels like I'm blind again. I can smell and hear and feel everything so much clearer. This wall feels like brick, the mortar's slightly smoother than the brick and I think it's been painted with something, because the roughness of the brick feels plastic.*

She could feel a change in the air, the horsey smell intermingled with a manure scent that was so strong now, it made her wrinkle her nose a little. *I think I must have reached the end of the passageway.* She put one hand out in front of her and took one more careful step forward. The outstretched hand came into contact with a cool metal hand rail. *I need to take the blindfold off now.*

Opening her eyes, she saw a short set of steps leading up to a wooden door with an ordinary latch handle. There was a peephole in the door, letting a beam of bright light into the gloom of the tunnel.

Hurrying up the steps, Morgana peered through the peephole. *It's the tack room. I remember this door. There's no handle on the other side and Walter said it was an old store cupboard that had been bricked up years ago.* She checked that the coast was clear before lifting the latch and letting herself out into the room.

Once she'd shut the door, the enormity of what she'd just done hit her. *I did it. I braved an enclosed, dark space and made it through without panicking once.* A huge grin spread across her face, and she felt like cheering. *I really can do it. I can beat the fear of the dark now!*

Standing up, Morgana looked back at the entrance to the tunnel and shivered. *I think I'll walk back to the house through the silver birch wood. One step at a time!*

Five

S plashing around in the pool idly, Morgana heard the doorbell ring, but ignored it. *Jenni said her friend Caoimhe was coming over this weekend and Dad said that Myfanwy would be visiting too.*

So, she wasn't surprised when Jenni walked in with Caoimhe behind her.

"Hello again, Caoimhe." Morgana pulled herself up to sit on the side of the pool.

"Hi Morgana." The red headed girl smiled, and Morgana felt instantly at home with her. "Glad to see you well again."

Jenni sat at the table. "Maebh will be bringing some drinks and stuff in a minute."

Caoimhe headed towards the little hut which served as a changing room. Morgana slipped back into the water and swam a few lengths.

"Van is coming over this weekend as well." Jenni said, leaning forward as Morgana drew level with her.

"I know. Dad said this morning." Morgana flipped herself under and swam the next length under water.

"She's designing us dresses for my Samhain Ball." Jenni told her after knocking politely.

"Samhain Ball?" Morgana surfaced at the other end and swam back to tread water so she could talk. "You're having a ball here?"

"No. In... France. I went to school there for a while, so I have a lot of friends. Caoimhe and her boyfriend, Mike, are coming too, so I was hoping you'd join us?"

Morgana looked at her sister. "I'll think about it."

"Well don't think too loud." Jenni said. *"Caoimhe is telepathic too."*

"I heard that!" Caoimhe called from the hut. She emerged wearing a green one piece swimming costume that suited her perfectly. "Fancy a race, Morgana?"

Morgana grinned. "Why not. Four lengths?"

"And the winner gets the first piece of cake." Jenni laughed.

Morgana swam back to the end of the pool while Caoimhe slipped into the water.

"Ready, steady, Go!" Jenni called, her voice echoing from the Orangery's high ceiling.

Artair, Maebh and Myfanwy entered as Morgana just beat Caoimhe to the finishing line. All three girls were laughing as if they had no care in the world.

"Now that is a lovely sight." Myfanwy smiled.

"Van!" Jenni scrambled up to throw her arms around her aunt. Caoimhe and Morgana pulled themselves out of the pool and wrapped robes around themselves.

"Come on Jenni, let Van breathe." Artair laughed.

Maebh smiled as she laid out cake and drinks on the table. "Call me when you're finished, and I'll clear up."

"Thanks, Maebh. You should get one of the staff to do this, you're House Manager now." Myfanwy extracted herself from Jenni's grip and hugged the woman.

"I wouldn't trust them with serving you anything, Vannie." Maebh said. "I've been with your family since your sister died and I'm not about to give the duty to anyone else." She hugged the younger woman back for a few seconds before leaving the room.

"I'll just go get dressed." Morgana said, feeling a little uncomfortable. *I know that Myfanwy is my birth aunt, but I still don't know her very well.*

"You're fine as you are, Morgana. I saw you the day you were born, all wrinkly, red and crying, so seeing you in a swimming costume is nothing." Myfanwy embraced her and for a moment, Morgana felt oddly happy.

"So, is everything in France ready for the ball?" Artair asked, pouring Myfanwy a cup of tea.

"Oh yes. The venue is to be decorated like a medieval castle, complete with guards in dress uniform and the invitations have all been RSVP'd so the caterer's now have their numbers for the buffet." She took the mug he passed her and sat down. "Have you girls got your dresses sorted out yet?"

"Well, I thought..." Jenni paused for a second, then carried on in a rush. "...that you'd like to design our dresses for us."

Caoimhe giggled at Jenni's face.

"I thought you might say that. We'll start after lunch." Myfanwy smiled, then laughed. Caoimhe started giggling again and the sound was so infectious that Jenni and Morgana joined in.

Artair sighed. "You girls are all the same. I thought I might have you to myself this weekend, Van."

"No chance, Dad." Jenni grinned at him as she sipped her tea. "Designing our costumes is far more important than you two snuggling."

"Jenni!" Caoimhe gasped.

Morgana just laughed. *They do make a nice couple. Van's hair is beautiful, all red-gold and silver; she'd look nice in photographs with da and his black and silver hair.*

Myfanwy glanced at Morgana and then Jenni. Jenni shrugged and shook her head. "Artair, do you mind if the girls and I get started on their dresses now?"

"Do I have a choice?" Artair smiled. "Go on, Love."

Caoimhe grinned and picked up her bag. "Up to Jenni's rooms then?"

"I'd say so." Morgana answered. "Race you!"

The two girls shot out of the orangery through the side door and Jenni started to follow.

"Hang on Gwynnhafr, I'll walk with you. We need to have a chat." Myfanwy stood up, kissed Artair on the cheek and linked arms with her niece.

"I'll see you all at lunch then." Artair said as they left by the side door.

Jenni and Myfanwy walked slowly along the corridor.

"How long has she been broadcasting like that?" Van asked. "She's worse than you were when I first met you."

"I don't think she knows how to control it. I've been trying to teach her, little things, but her hostility towards me gets in the way." Jenni sighed. "I honestly don't know if she really ought to come to the ball. It might cause problems if the guests hear her ranting about me."

"As far as I can tell, she's single directional." Van frowned. "Can Caoimhe hear or talk to her?"

"I don't know. I'll ask." Jenni knocked gently on Caoimhe's mind. *"Kee, can you hear my sister?"*

"Yes. I told you that when we were at the funeral remember." Caoimhe replied.

"Can you speak to her?"

"I don't know. Hang on I'll try." There was silence for a moment. Then Caoimhe came back to Jenni. *"No. She doesn't respond to me."*

Jenni reported the conversation to her aunt as they rounded the first floor landing.

"Hmm. Ask your sister if she can hear Caoimhe." Van said. "I heard you tell her that Caoimhe was one of us."

"Okay." Jenni knocked on Morgana's mind.

"What do you want?" the anger in Morgana's mind voice made Jenni wince.

"Caoimhe just tried to mind link with you. Did you hear her?" Jenni felt the shock and disappointment in her sister's mind.

"No, I like her, and I would have answered." Morgana said finally.

Jenni pulled away. "She didn't hear Caoimhe at all."

"Father asked me to do an assessment of her mental condition, so I'll test her tomorrow, but I'm pretty certain that she'll only be able to respond to members of her blood family."

They reached the second floor and paused in the Family room.

"Jenni, have you really forgiven Morgana for cutting you out of her life when you inherited?" Myfanwy asked, her face serious.

"Yes. I think so." Jenni looked at her bare feet.

"I don't think you really have. I can still sense resentment in you when Morgana is mentioned and there was an air of jealousy about you while she and Caoimhe were racing." Myfanwy laid one hand on Jenni's shoulder. "It may be that Morgana is sensing these things too, that may be why she's being so hostile."

Jenni nodded.

"Look, let's go design your dresses. I brought plenty of fabrics, ribbons and things with me."

I HAD SUCH A WONDERFUL time yesterday, and now I have to go through all these tests again? I really hate this. Morgana tried hard to ignore the MRI noise. *With the blind fold I can almost relax in this thing, but why do I have to have all these tests done?*

In the booth, Aderyn and Myfanwy winced.

"Does she know she's broadcasting so loudly?" Aderyn asked his daughter.

"Jenni and I roped Caoimhe in to test her yesterday while we were designing dresses, and it seems that the only people who can speak to her are blood family members." Myfanwy sighed.

Dr. Green frowned at the screens in front of the technicians. "I don't like what I'm seeing here. I thought those shadows last time were just my eyes playing tricks, but it would seem that they're getting bigger."

"Could they be affecting the implant?" Aderyn asked. "She's exhibiting a great deal of hostility and her nyctophobia seems to be getting worse as well."

"There is a shadow near to the implant. It's tiny still, so I can't see how it would affect the device." Dr. Green said.

"Were the shadows present before the device was implanted?" Myfanwy asked. The two men stared at her. "I thought you might have checked that already, Father, really."

Aderyn dashed out of the booth as the MRI powered down. "Bring Morgana down to my office. I need to check something in her records."

Dr. Green looked at Myfanwy. "We did EEG and EMG this morning. The EMG was negative for any nerve damage or muscle problems that may have been caused by her initial accident. The EEG is showing up some abnormalities."

Myfanwy nodded. "Would going through a strong electrical current damage the circuitry of the implant?"

"I have no idea. Archie would have a better idea about that than I." Dr. Green shrugged. "I'll bring the film down with me."

Myfanwy smiled and left the booth, just in time to catch Morgana as she came out of the MRI room. "Come on, sweetheart, let's go down to Mr. Birdenth's office."

"Why isn't Da here?" Morgana asked.

"He's had to go to the doctor's himself." She laughed. "He managed to get a thorn wedged into the palm of his hand and he has to have it removed."

Morgana rolled his eyes and laughed as well. *Da always manages to get something stuck in his hand. I remember the time he was...* A wave of nostalgia and sadness swept over her, and tears filled her eyes.

"Are you all right?" Myfanwy frowned.

"Fine. I just don't like having all these tests." The girl snapped and hurried on ahead.

"Father, something has upset Morgana. I suspect it may be something to do with Artair and Helen's divorce, so tread carefully." Myfanwy said as she entered the office.

"I both heard and felt it. What is going on with this child? Angharad was never this angry about anything, even when your mother died." Aderyn looked up from the file he was leafing through. "I'm sorry that we're putting you through this, Morgana, but we need to make sure everything is all right with the implant."

"You said I was fine." Morgana all but shouted at him. "You said that I was better, and my life could go back to normal."

"Morgana, which is no way to speak to Mr. Birdenth." Myfanwy said, putting one hand on the girl's shoulder and pressing her down into a chair. "Calm down."

Dr Green came in as Myfanwy sat down. His face said it all. "Archie, your tests are conclusive."

"Do we have to remove it?" Aderyn asked.

"I think so. This data explains everything she has been experiencing. We may need to check on the other patients." Dr Green sighed. "And it was all going so well."

"There's something wrong and I want you to stop lying to me. Tell me what is going on." Morgana ground out the words through her teeth.

Aderyn looked at her then at Myfanwy. His daughter nodded. "The implant is causing some side effects that we weren't expecting. In addition, you appear to be developing brain tumours." He sighed.

"I'm going to die?" Morgana stood up. "I would prefer to be blind all my life than that. Take the damn thing out and maybe then I'll be able to be normal!"

She stormed out of the office.

Myfanwy stood up, but Aderyn shook his head. "Don't bother. Artair just arrived home, so she'll run into him shortly." He smiled. "There we go. He'll deal with it."

Dr Green looked slightly mystified. "I won't pretend to understand what you're talking about, but she does have a point. She needs to have the implant removed immediately and start cancer treatment before the tumours get any bigger."

Aderyn sighed. "Yes, and we'll have to schedule her in as soon as possible. Dr Archington, can you speak to her father, and we'll take it from there."

"Of course, Mr. Birdenth. I'll go and talk to him now." Myfanwy left the room, her heart sinking. *Poor girl.*

Six

"What?" Morgana stared at Artair. "First you say that everything will be all right, next you tell me that I have to go back into hospital?" she shook her head, eyes filling with tears. "At least tell me that I can go to Jenni's ball in France first."

Artair, Myfanwy and Aderyn exchanged a look that told her everything.

"I hate you." She stood up. "I hate everyone in this house, and I am going to go back to Cardiff on the next train."

"Morgana, sit down." Myfanwy said.

The girl sank into her chair again, tears flooding down her face. "You don't understand. I have to have something to remember before I lose my sight again."

"Morgana, you need to see this as the adult woman you are. If you are to have any prospects at all, we have to operate as soon as possible." Aderyn looked as upset as Morgana felt. "The operation to remove the implant and take a biopsy of the tumours is scheduled for three days time."

"The Ball is tomorrow." Myfanwy sighed. "Jenni, Caoimhe and Mike will leave tonight."

Morgana stared at them. *It's not fair. Jenni gets everything and I get nothing, just like always.* Artair put one hand on her arm, but she shook it off. "Leave me alone, Da. Just...leave me alone." She left the family room and went down to the library.

As she passed the Orangery, she could see Jenni and her friends in the Orangery, laughing and splashing at each other. *She looks so happy. When mam and da divorced, I thought I'd never lose my sister, no matter how far we were apart, but now I'm not so sure.* She took one more look through the orangery door. *She's not really my sister anymore.*

The library was deserted, and Morgana slipped down into the tunnels without being seen. She wound her scarf around her eyes and found her way to the stables, then she went and sat in Kedar's box, watching the gelding eat.

"You look a little down, Morgana." Walter said, leaning on the gate. "What's up?"

She sighed. "Da not told you?"

"Contrary to popular belief, I'm not the confidante of everyone in this place." He opened the gate. "Do you want a cup of tea and a chat? There's no one here at the moment. Never is this late on a Sunday."

Morgana nodded and followed him into his office on the other side of the yard.

"I see you've found the tunnels." Walter said as he filled the kettle and started it. "But why the blindfold?"

"It's a sort of test. I'm scared of the dark, so exploring the tunnels helps me. With a blindfold I can control the fear. I even turn the light off at night now."

"That's good." Walter made the tea. "Milk, Sugar?"

"No sugar; I'm sweet enough." She said automatically.

He laughed. "Jenni used to say that before she turned 18. Now she doesn't have time to have tea with me anymore."

"She doesn't have time for anyone." Morgana was surprised at the bitterness in her voice. "I bet it was her that told Myfanwy that I shouldn't go to her ball."

"Jenni? Nah, you've got that one wrong, lass." Walter placed her mug in front of her. "Why would Myfanwy tell you that you can't go to the ball."

Morgana looked at him. He was older than her father and looked a little like John Wayne. *I think I can trust him.* she took a deep breath. "I'm dying. The implant has caused brain cancer, and they have to remove it and start me on cancer treatment."

He nodded, unshed tears making his eyes shine.

"I just wanted to go to the ball so I would have one happy memory to sustain me through all the hospital stuff, but they've set the date for the operation for three days time. And Jenni is leaving for France with her friends tonight." The bitterness re-emerged.

Walter sniffed. "Ah."

She shrugged. "By the time she comes back, I'll be blind and sick again. If I survive the operation."

They sat in silence, drinking their tea, wrapped in their own thoughts. Outside the office, it started to rain, the drops drumming out a soothing pattern on the walkway roof.

"Jenni isn't going to France. She's going to Llanirstyr." Walter said softly. "It's the kingdom where you and she were born, and where she will eventually be Queen."

Morgana stared at him. "What?"

Walter looked a little ashamed. "Maebh, me, Myfanwy and Aderyn are from a Kingdom called Llanirstyr. It's in another dimension. You and your sister were the children of the last Queen, Angharad. That's why you and Jenni are so important to Aderyn."

Morgana blinked. "We're Princesses of a kingdom in another dimension? Walter have you been chewing locoweed or something?"

He laughed. "I'm telling you the truth. The two years after your accident Jenni spent hopping between dimensions using the Hall of Worlds, in an effort to save Llanirstyr."

He is telling the truth, or at least the truth as he sees it. I can tell that much. Morgana took a thoughtful breath. "I'll believe you for the moment. So how is Jenni getting to Llanirstyr?"

"She's going through the Folly. There are doors in there that lead to the Hall of The Worlds and then you go through a door into the Llanirstyr Dimension." Walter didn't look at Morgana. "I'm not supposed to be telling you this by the way. I didn't know about the cancer, but I did know that Aderyn and Myfanwy had decided you shouldn't know about Llanirstyr yet."

"Why are you telling me then?" she frowned. "Surely that's being disloyal to your employers."

"You're being treated unfairly. I think that, because you were so ill, they don't see you as an adult yet. You're nineteen and capable of making your own decisions, no matter what the situation." Walter picked her mug up. "I've told you the information you need to make a decision, that's all."

Morgana nodded, her mind whirling with possibilities. "How do I get to the Folly from the library?"

"It's in the garden, so you need to go south from there." Walter smiled. "If you take the wrong one, you'll end up in the Dragon's Cave."

"Thank you." Morgana stood up. "I need to get back to the house."

"Of course." Walter walked her back to the tack room. He opened the door for her as she tied the blindfold on. "Morgana..."

"Yes?"

"Whatever you decide to do, please be careful. We'd all be upset if you got yourself hurt."

She nodded and walked back down the tunnel.

Walter shut the door behind her, wondering if he'd done the right thing.

CAOIMHE AND MIKE FOLLOWED Jenni down through the tunnels.

"I thought your sister was coming as well?" Mike shifted his bag to a more comfortable spot.

"Dad said she wasn't allowed to come." Jenni sighed. "I argued with him, but he said she'd been too nasty to me and didn't deserve it."

"I thought it might make her loosen up a bit more if she came." Caoimhe said. "She's been quite nice recently."

"That's because she likes you." Jenni grinned at her best friend. "She's been more interested in making friends than sniping at me."

They emerged from the tunnel onto the Folly Colonnade. It was sheltered here, despite the rain that still pelted down, the Oak trees cutting the wind to almost nothing.

"It's cold out here." Caoimhe rubbed her hands together.

"We'll be inside soon." Jenni pushed on the crest carved into the limestone. There was a grating noise and a slab of limestone slid aside. She stepped inside and Caoimhe grabbed Mike's hand and pulled him inside.

"Just let me shut the door. Then we'll go down to the hall." Jenni moved to another spot and the door shut.

"Bit gloomy in here." Mike peered at the girls.

"Just come over here." Jenni motioned for them to join her. A light shot out from the wall, scanned the three of them and they disappeared.

MORGANA STEPPED OUT of the shadows. The blindfold not only helped her sense of smell and touch, her hearing was more acute as well. *Following Jenni this afternoon when she checked the route was easy. That perfume she wears is very distinctive. Hiding in here before she brought the others was a good idea.*

She stood up, pulled the blindfold off and slipped across to stand where they had. *I can do this. I am not afraid.* Looking down she saw an Arkingham Crest enamelled in blue on the floor. *Nothing has happened to me yet, so maybe I have to stand on this?*

She stepped onto the crest and a bright blue beam of light scanned her from head to foot. *Ow. What's that tingling feeling?* She blinked furiously, as her eyes began to water, and it wasn't until she'd rubbed them clear that she realised she was in a different room to the one she started in.

This one had the top of a spiral staircase leading down from the dais she stood on. Slipping her blindfold back over her eyes, Morgana carefully made her way down the stairs. As she arrived, she took the scarf off and found herself in a perfectly square room with a dais in the middle.

On the dais glowed a blue circle.

Morgana walked over to the circle. Its light illuminated the room and there was no sign of her sister or Caoimhe and her boyfriend. *So, what do I do now?* She looked around. *There's nothing else here, maybe it's a transporter circle like in Star Trek?*

With a sudden rush of bravery, she stepped up onto the dais and into the circle. The glow became a tube of light and her eyes started watering again as her skin tingled. After a second's hum of sound, the light disappeared.

In front of her was a black door with no handle. Next to it was a white door with an Arkingham crest picked out in lurid pink enamel. There was also another glowing circle in the other corner.

Morgana stepped down off the plain white marble dais she stood on, rubbing her eyes. *Maybe next time I go through those I ought to use my blindfold. It felt like the light was irritating my eyes.*

She examined both doors. The black door shimmered and shivered. *Where is that music coming from. It's like all the choirs of Wales are singing at once.* She sighed. *So beautiful.*

The white door seemed to be carved of solid marble and she felt cold standing in front of it.

Which door did they go through? Which door should I go through? Morgana bit her lip trying to decide. Then abruptly she made up her mind and moved up to the door she had chosen. As she approached the door it fogged and disappeared, so she stepped through the gap.

Seven

"Where is she?" Aderyn frowned. "Maebh can you go check her room please."

"She was very upset yesterday. I wouldn't be surprised if she'd gone to ground somewhere in the house or even in town." Walter said. He was fairly sure where the child had gone, so he wasn't too worried. *Myfanwy will help her.* he reassured himself.

"That's true. I'll go check my house, just in case she's gone there." Artair said. "I'll also do a quick run around town to see if I can spot her."

"We need to find her as quickly as possible." Aderyn huffed. "Walter, can you look around the grounds and the riding trails she was familiar with, please."

"Of course." Walter left the office.

Aderyn's Personal Assistant appeared in the doorway. "Is there anything I can do to help, Mr. Birdenth?"

Aderyn smiled. "No thank you, Julia. We'll find her in time for the tests, I'm sure."

THE DARKNESS WAS SO thick around her that Morgana stopped moving on her second step through the door. *Have I gone blind again? No, I could always see a little light in front of me. This is pitch black.*

The voices sang and whispered to her. One voice sounded so familiar that she felt tears begin to run down her cheeks. Rubbing her eyes clear she tried to see where she was. *I honestly cannot see a*

53

thing. I must be standing on something though. She stamped her feet and was relieved to feel a solid floor beneath her, even if there was no noise from the movement.

The whispers started getting stronger. *"Come with us, child. You are safe."*

"Come with us, soon, you'll be happy."

"Follow us, child and you'll have everything you ever wanted."

Morgana shook herself. *This music and whispering is starting to get on my nerves.* She swallowed on a dry mouth and said: "Leave me alone."

The whispers stopped. For several long moments there was just the music and the sound of Morgana's breathing.

"She heard us."

"The child can hear us."

"Help us, child, help us escape!"

Morgana bit her lip reflectively. "Where am I?"

"We can't tell you."

"You can hear us."

"You can free us."

"Is this Llanirstyr?" She asked.

"Dimensions, time, space... mean nothing...here."

"Free us."

"There is nothing here."

"Who are you?" Morgana could feel things brushing against her face, dry and cold. She shivered.

"We are waiting."

"Waiting for what?" Morgana was starting to feel just a little irritated now. "Don't dance around the subject, tell me the truth."

"The child wants the truth."

"Can she handle the truth?"

"No one can handle that much truth." There was a silvery laugh that spread around her.

Morgana concentrated for a moment and decided there were thousands of speakers around her. "Surely one of you must know where you are or the way out of here?"

"There is no way out."

"Free us, child."

"You can hear us. You can save us."

Feeling irritated and bored, Morgana put her hands out in front of her and started walking forwards.

"You can't leave."

"Only Soul-Owned can pass through here."

"Are you soul-owned?"

Morgana ignored them and kept moving. After what seemed like hours, just as she had decided to stop and rest for a moment, her right palm came into contact with something smooth and cold.

"No, child. Don't go."

"Stay with us."

"Free us."

"We love you."

She slid her hand across to the right, felt a ridge and then a dip. Bringing both hands to the same place, Morgana side-stepped to the right. Her fingers touched a flat cold surface. *Like a glass or metal door.*

"Don't go child."

"Stay with us."

Morgana carried on exploring the surface. It went up above her head further than her arms could reach and when she stretched her arms out to either side, her left fingers touched the first ridge, but the right ones didn't touch anything, but the surface. *It feels like a door.*

She leaned her cheek against it. It didn't budge, so she rested her wait against it momentarily and closed her eyes.

"That's good, child."

"Sleep, rest and sleep and dream."

Morgana could feel the dry cold things brushing against her face. She sighed and could feel herself falling asleep.

"Morgana. No." The familiar voice was back.

Morgana opened her eyes but couldn't see anything. *I want to got to sleep.* She closed her eyes again.

"Morgana don't sleep. You are almost free of this place, just a little further to go, my darling."

That made Morgana stand up and look around. *I know that voice. Why?*

"I am Angharad. I am waiting to be judged, but the line is long, and the wait is boring." The voice moved closer to her. *"We get so bored, that when someone like you comes in, it becomes a game, an entertainment to make them sleep and stay here."*

"Where is here, Angharad." Morgana asked.

"You have stepped into Limbo, my darling. If you sleep here, you will never see your sister again." Angharad sounded sad at that.

"Why? All I have to do is go back the way I came."

"The Black Door is one way. You come in through it, but you cannot leave through it." Angharad sighed and her breath blew through Morgana's hair. *"Go through this door and you will escape Limbo."*

Morgana felt a little more to the right. Her hand hit a smooth plate a few centimetres wide. *A push plate?* She moved herself over to stand in front of it.

"I will see you again only once more, my darling daughter." Angharad's voice faded away.

Morgana blinked. *Daughter? Was that my birth mother's spirit?* She swallowed back tears which threatened to swamp her. Sightlessly, she pushed on the plate.

The door swung open and the light which flowed over her was cool and damp. Morgana stepped through the door. It swung shut behind her with a thump.

"SHE'S NOT AT THE HOUSE in town or anywhere in the public places." Artair. said, sounding worried.

"She isn't in the house or the grounds." Maebh sighed. "What did you tell the girl that she would run away like this?"

"Is Walter still checking the trails?" Aderyn seemed annoyed. "This is her life we are talking about, not some childish game."

"What did you say to her, Father?" Myfanwy strode into the room.

"I told her nothing that she'd not already heard." He snapped.

"You told her that she was going to die and that she couldn't go to the ball because she was too sick." Walter entered, hair plastered to his scalp by rainwater. "She thinks that Jenni doesn't want her to go."

"What?" Myfanwy blinked. "I thought she understood how sick she was."

"She does." Walter growled. "I found her in the stables yesterday, crying her eyes out and dampening her gelding's mane."

"So why run away?" Aderyn stood up. "Do you know where she is?"

"No." Walter shook his head. "We talked about what was bothering her over a cup of tea. She's been exploring the tunnels trying to control her phobias, and I told her about the ones to the Folly and the Dragon's Cave."

"Did you..." Aderyn started.

Walter cut him off with a gesture. "You've treated her like a fourteen year old the whole time she has been here. You wouldn't let her go into town by herself or go riding by herself." His face darkened. "You kept her heritage from her, despite the fact that Jenni has known about Llanirstyr for the last five years."

"We did that to protect her." Myfanwy protested.

"She isn't a baby, Myfanwy. Actually, I have a bone to pick with you over Jenni as well."

"Huh?" Aderyn sat down again. "What's wrong with Jenni."

"She won't tell you, she's too nice to say anything, but you have to stop making her work so hard. She deserves some time to rest. This ball is the first time she's gone to Llanirstyr in a long time when it hasn't been to do with her position." Walter walked up to Myfanwy. "I know you want to go back to your hospital and Aderyn wants to remain on Earth as Head of Archington Industries but pushing her onto the throne in Llanirstyr before she is ready will not help."

There was silence as he finished speaking.

Then Artair stood up. "What are you talking about? What is Llanirstyr and what throne are you pushing my daughter towards?"

Myfanwy looked at Walter and sighed. "Now you've done it."

"Good. I hope you can all sort this out, because I am done with keeping these secrets from my own family." Walter stalked out.

Maebh stood up. "I'd better go and calm him down." She followed Walter but before she reached the door, she turned. "Aderyn, Myfanwy. Walter is right. We may only be distant cousins of yours, but we are family. Let's start being honest for a change, please?" and then she disappeared, closing the door behind her.

Artair turned toward Myfanwy. "Van, what's going on?"

She looked at Aderyn and the cyborg sighed. "It's okay, Vannie, I'll explain it to him. You go and find the other two and see if you can find out if Walter may know where Morgana has gone."

She nodded. "Thank you, father."

The two men waited until she had left the office and then Aderyn said, "Come with me Artair. I need to show you something."

"Can't you tell me about it first?"

"No." Aderyn stood up and grabbed his jacket from the back of his chair. "This is something that has to be seen to be believed."

Eight

Morgana found herself amongst black barked trees with silver leaves. The ground was covered with silver grass and when she turned back the way she had come, the door had disappeared.

"Now where am I?" she said aloud. The sound was flat with no echo. There was also no answer. *Where am I?*

A grey stag with silver antlers stepped out from the trees to stand in front of her. Morgana looked around. There were no other deer around and the stag just stood there looking at her.

She stepped forward, the stag moved away a few strides and stopped, looking back at her.

What does it want? Morgana walked toward the stag, which bounded away and stopped a few metres in front. Every time she tried to get close to the creature would move away and stop.

"Do you want me to follow you?" She asked in exasperation

The stag nodded slowly.

Morgana rolled her eyes. *What have I gone and gotten myself into, a Disney movie?* She shrugged. "Okay. Whatever it takes to catch up with my sister."

The stag led her through the forest. From time to time, she would see other animals amongst the trees, but no other people.

"Where am I?" She asked the stag. He stayed silent. "Well that confirms that I'm not in a Disney movie. The animals in those can talk."

The stag glanced back at her, then shook itself.

Morgana laughed. "I'm talking to an animal. Am I going crazy again?"

The stag led her out of the trees onto a riverbank where a white stone pier jutted out into the wide river. Here the stag bowed his head to her, turned and went back the way they'd came.

Morgana looked around. *Where did all the people come from?*

Around her stood thousands of people of all ages. Some of them had reptilian forms, others looked demonic or angelic. There were people who seemed to be made of metal and others that had grey skin, huge eyes and no nose or ears.

"Where am I?" she asked the nearest person to her, a handsome man with huge white wings. *He looks like an angel. But how? Angels aren't real.*

"We are waiting." He replied, not looking at her.

"That's what the voices in the darkness said." Morgana murmured to herself.

"The Darkness of Limbo is where we have come from." A woman with long black hair said. "We have been judged and now we wait."

"What for?" Morgana felt irritated. *Why can't I get a straight answer?*

The angel pointed at the river. "They come."

Morgana looked at the river. There was a large silver ship with a black sail approaching. It towed behind it hundreds of smaller grey boats, each with a tiny coloured banner flying from a pole at the front.

As the silver ship docked, running a grey wood plank down onto the pier, the people around her began to sort themselves into groups. There ended up being four different groups.

Morgana stood awkwardly by herself, wondering what she should do. She tried approaching the group with the angel in, but he shook his head. "You have not been judged yet. You cannot sail with us."

She watched as ravens flew out from the ship and landed, transforming into women wearing black feather dresses. Each group was collected by three women and taken towards the small boats where they were divided up into smaller groups.

Morgana stood there watching them and was startled when a white raven landed in front of her.

With a puff of white feathers, the raven transformed into a man in a white robe. "You are not dead."

"I know. I'm looking for my sister and her friends; they went to Llanirstyr." Morgana found that although she wanted to tell him something else, her mouth refused to co-operate.

"Only truth can be spoken in this world." The man frowned. "Did you step through a portal of darkness?"

Morgana thought for a moment. "The door was black when I walked up to it."

The man sighed. "I must take you to Hades. He is the only person who can decide what to do with you."

Morgana shrugged. "All right, old man. Take me to your leader."

The convoy got under way almost as soon as the ravens returned to the ship. The man stood at the helm but didn't even touch the wheel.

"Who is steering?" Morgana asked, looking around.

"The Lady is." The man smiled and stoked the railing in a way that left Morgana no doubt that it was the ship he meant. "Now. Who are you?"

"I am Lady Morgana of Arkingham, a High Princess of Llanirstyr." Morgana winced. *I hate using my title. Hang on, where did the High Princess one come from?*

"Exalted company indeed." He bowed to her. "I am Charon and with my Lady's aid, I ferry the Judged to their destinations." He waved a hand backward at the train of boats behind him.

Morgana stared at them, the end of the boats disappearing into the distance. "So how long before we get to this Hades bloke then?"

"A while. There is no hurry here. There is no time here until you start your judgement." The man sighed and looked at her. "You are still of the living and therefore there is one thing that I must warn you about."

"What?" Morgana was feeling tired.

"Whatever you do here, do not eat anything that one of the Judged give you. Eat only that which is given to you by an Immortal." Charon smiled as he realised that she wasn't really listening. "One of my assistants will show you to a cabin. All food and drink aboard the Lady are safe for you, so order what you will from my assistants and get some rest."

Morgana nodded and followed the raven woman that appeared in front of her.

She was shown to a well appointed cabin that had everything she might need, but Morgana only had eyes for the bed. "Thank you..."

The raven woman bowed and as the girl fell into bed fully clothed, withdrew silently and shut the door. Transforming, she flew back up to Charon to inform him of their guest's state.

"Thank you, Merla." Charon paused for a moment as the raven readied herself to take off again. "She will need a guide through the Lands of Hades. Merla, would you be happy to take up this post and guide Lady Morgana to the Fields of Elysium and Hades' palace?"

The raven transformed. Instead of a dress of feathers, she wore a feather cloak and trouser suit. "If it is your will master."

"It is my will, but you may say nay if you wish."

"I would never go against your will, Raven Master." Merla bowed. "I will guide the human."

"Thank you, Merla. Please keep her safe. I suspect there is something wrong in the Overworlds that the Portal let her through." Charon sighed and transformed into the white raven, perching on the rail and staring out over the river.

Morgana awoke as the ship bumped against a pier. Beside her stood the Raven Woman.

"We have arrived at the Plains of War. Lord Charon has asked me to guide you to Lord Hades safely. We will need to leave the Lady here and make our way on foot to the next river." The woman said, her black feather cloak fluttering slightly.

"Okay." Morgana sat up.

"We have time for you to break your fast and change. Lord Charon has provided you with everything you may need." The woman pointed at a neatly folded pile of clothes, a pair of boots and a cloak that were placed on the chair beside the table. There was also a shoulder bag beside the boots.

"I will leave you to change. You must leave everything that you brought from the Overworlds here, or you will be put upon." The woman bowed. "I am Merla, call me if there is anything that you require."

She left the room and Morgana looked over at the table again. It was laid with dishes that smelled delicious. *I might as well have something to eat and get changed.*

Half an hour later, Morgana was trying to decide if she wanted to leave her scarf with the rest of her clothes. *Mam gave it to me, so I'll take it with me.*

She wound the scarf around her neck and shouldered the bag, then went up onto deck.

Charon stood in the same place he'd been when she went below. He was watching the raven women herding all those from the red flagged boats onshore.

"I'm ready." Morgana said.

Charon looked at her and smiled. He reached out and unwound the scarf from her neck. "If you were to wear this on the Plains of War, you would be attacked instantly and as you are still mortal, you would soon join your birth mother in the Darkness of Limbo."

"Do you know everything about me?" Morgana sighed as he folded the scarf and placed it in his pocket.

"I know everything about everyone, as do Thanatos, Hades and Hecate." Charon bowed. "Thank you for placing your trust in me. I shall see that your items are sent back to Earth."

Morgana nodded. *That might not go down well. They'll have noticed that I've disappeared by now.*

"Worry not about the timing or your illness. As I said before, Chronos only grants time's ravages to those who are living out their punishments. You will not be affected." Charon led her down the gangplank to the shore. "Farewell Lady Morgana. Merla will join you momentarily."

She watched him return to the ship and as the ravens returned to the ship, one of them dropped out of the sky to land on the pier beside her.

"I will remain in bird form, Lady Morgana. May I ride on your shoulder?" the raven woman's voice sounded clearly in her mind.

Morgana nodded and the bird flapped her way up to the shoulder without the bag.

The two of them watched the ships leave and then Morgana turned inland. "So, where now, Merla?"

"Follow the white sand path and you will be safe. Do not stray from it."

Morgana took a deep breath and started walking.

Nine

Nex and Morbus sat either side of Apollyon's throne. The great hall flickered with reds and golds from the braziers lining the walls and illuminated the banners of black and red hanging from the rafters.

On the polished onyx marble gathered the assorted Demidaemon and Quadaemon beings of Apollyon's realm. Skin, scales and fur; wind and fire; water and earth; all of these were represented amongst the crowd. On a roped off dais to the left of the throne stood the full daemons, wearing formal robes of scarlet, gold and black. A similar dais on the right held the human Demidaemons, also dressed in formal robes.

"These formal audiences get so boring." Morbus complained, shaking his head.

Nex scratched her ear reflectively. *"Think of it this way. We learn a lot more about the Master's plans when we are allowed to guard him."*

"You are kidding, aren't you? Whenever we get ordered to support one of the Master's mission specialists, we end up taking the blame. Or don't you remember Master Jezebeath?" Morbus snorted.

"If you're going to pull up old missions, why not throw the Earth Dimension in my face." Nex snapped at Morbus. *"Besides, after that one, I doubt the Master will trust us with anything so important ever again."*

A fanfare blared through the hall and the massive gold plated doors swung open. The Daemon's Guard in their red enamelled armour marched in, black and gold cloaks flowing behind them. They lined the aisle created for them by the creatures in the crowd and drew their black steel swords, bringing them up to their noses in salute.

"All Hail Prince Apollyon, Lord of The Lake of Flame and Protector of the Gates of Hell." The guards chanted, the sound of their gravelly voices drowning out the last murmurs of the assembled Daemons.

Apollyon swept in, his white linen suit and blue shirt and tie accented with a white hat and spats. He wore a white woollen coat over his shoulders and blue kid leather gloves.

"Does he know how ridiculous he looks?" Nex asked her brother on their private connection.

"He likes the gangster look from the 1920's." Morbus shrugged as they watched Apollyon make his way up the aisle. *"It looks good on him."*

Nex glared at her brother and sniffed in annoyance, then ignored him as their master mounted the steps to his throne.

Apollyon turned, shrugged his coat off into the hands of Dolor, his page, who appeared instantly to catch it and fold it neatly over his red silk clad arm.

Formido appeared just in time to be handed the hat and gloves. The two pages bowed and retreated behind Nex and Morbus.

"Show offs." Morbus snapped at Dolor as he slipped around the back of him.

Nex rolled her red glowing eyes and went back to watching the crowd who had come back together in one group, behind the line of Daemon Guard who had surrounded the base of the throne.

Apollyon stroked Nex and Morbus' black heads as he sat down. *"Steady, my pets."* He told them.

Morbus growled softly. *"I hate him doing that."*

"Behave yourself." Nex growled at her brother.

Their performance just made Apollyon smile. He turned to his audience. "I have some important news to impart. There will be the chance for one of you to gain my favour."

The crowd murmured.

"High Prince Lucifer has granted me a favour. The Shield of Courage is essential to our Lord's plan to overthrow Balorn and he has granted me the power to be able to collect it from the Underworld. I require the services of a highly intelligent and capable Daemon to complete this mission, someone who will not falter, no matter what the threat." Apollyon scanned the daemons assembled. "Who will take up this challenge?"

Nex shook herself. *"What's the bet that we're going to get sent with whoever he sends?"*

"That's no bet at all." Morbus grumbled.

"I'll go, Gran... Your Highness." One of the human Daemons stepped forward.

Apollyon shook his head. "Sadly, Jezebeath, Lord Lucifer has requested that none of our family attempt the retrieval, as there is a small chance that the Quester will never return to the lands of the living."

"As His Highness commands." Jezebeath looked disappointed, bowed and stepped back.

"Whoops, he shouldn't have said that." Morbus laughed, his tongue lolling from the side of his mouth.

Nex looked out at the crowd. *"Bunch of cowards."*

All the creature Daemons had moved backward, leaving a growing gap between the Daemon Guard and their front row.

Apollyon's face darkened and he looked around again. "Will no one volunteer, or must I select a...candidate?"

The silence deepened and the two hounds whimpered as they felt heat begin to radiate off their master.

"Your Highness. I wish to volunteer for the mission." A woman in black and scarlet robes stepped forward from the ranks of the full daemons. "I am no craven and would gladly take on this mission for just a smile from your glorious lips."

"A smile you may have for volunteering, m'lady. You may yet gain other... honours from my lips should you succeed." Apollyon's temper cooled and he smiled as he took in her looks. "May I request the honour of your name?"

"I am Lady Deumara." She curtsied and her robed figure showed a significant amount of cleavage.

Apollyon's smile widened. "Then I would be pleased if you would join me in my private quarters later, to discuss the quest."

"I would be delighted to await your summons for this purpose, your Highness." She curtsied again and stepped back into rank.

Apollyon turned back to the hall. "I will select two others of your number to accompany Lady Deumara and send as a sign of my faith and affection, my Guardian Hounds, Nex and Morbus, to guard the Lady in her quest." He looked around. "That is all, this audience is at an end."

"What did I say?" Nex growled. *"We get sent along as bodyguards, which means he has a hidden agenda again."*

"Like we have any choice in the matter." Morbus agreed.

MORGANA FOUND WALKING on the white sand difficult, she wished that she could walk on the grass to either side. *It'd spare my ankles and knees, at least.* She thought as her ankle twisted in the sand again. "Ow."

"Young Lady?" A voice came from her right. Standing on the grass just off the path was a man wearing normal everyday clothes, with a steel roman helm on his head and sword in his hand. "Do you need any help?"

"Don't talk to him." Merla said and squawked angrily at the man. *"If he gets onto this path, he'll wreak havoc among the others treading it."*

"What others?" Morgana glanced behind her.

A whole crowd of Judged were walking that path behind her, having as many problems as she was by the looks on their faces.

"Why are they on the path?" she asked the crow, ignoring the man with the sword and slogging on through the ankle deep sand.

"Their punishment is not here, it is over the bridge in the Hills of Treachery or beyond." Merla told her.

"So, they have to walk through this muck to get there? That's hardly fair." Morgana protested.

"If they lived a violent life without cause, then they join the Plains of War. If they have to go to the Land of Fear or Grasslands of Apathy, they walk the Tiring Path. If they are destined for the Hills of Treachery, they walk the path." The crow shrugged and took off, circling above her. *"Death and the Afterlife isn't meant to be fair, it's a learning experience."*

Morgana trudged through the sand, glad that she'd left her trainers on Charon's ship now. *I'd have sand in my socks if I weren't wearing these boots.*

Stopping for a rest by a tree, Morgana ate some of the food Charon had given her and swallowed some water. Merla landed nearby and transformed.

"Would you like something to eat?" Morgana offered the raven woman an apple.

"I ate well of a dead horse an hour ago but thank you for the offer." The woman smiled.

Morgana hid her shudder. "Okay." She looked around. "When will the fighting stop for the warriors to sleep?"

"It never stops. There is no day or night outside the Elysium Fields." Merla shrugged. "It is punishment. If they are mortally wounded and cannot fight any more, they lie still until they are whole again and then just carry on."

Morgana stood up, brushing sand off her trousers. "So, if you are violent without a cause in life, you get to keep fighting in the afterlife without stopping? Isn't that a reward for those kind of people?"

"Ask them." Merla gestured toward a group of teenagers who were battling nearby. One of them had been cut in half and his head and torso lay close to where Morgana sat.

Holding her breath against the stench, Morgana knelt on the path close to him. "Are you enjoying all this fighting?"

The teenager turned his head and smiled. "I did, when I first got here. It was fun to smash someone's head in and see them get up again and keep fighting. "His smiled faded. "But now, I just want to be able to sleep."

A shimmer appeared around the boy and his body re-knitted itself. Gasping he pulled himself up on to his knees. "Every time I get hurt, I have to keep fighting. I can't rest until I can no longer fight, and I still get the pain." He stood up and turned back to the battle, sword in hand.

Morgana started walking again, desperate to get away from all the violence around her. "Will he ever leave the Plains of War?"

Merla flew up to her shoulder again. *"Only when he sees that violence is unnecessary and unwanted. He has to refuse to fight back three times. Then he'll be released and be able to continue on his journey to the Elysium Fields."*

Morgana thought about that for while as she trudged through the sand on the Tiring Path. *I haven't been violent toward anyone, even at my angriest, I never hit anyone.*

Merla shook herself, the black feathers tickling Morgana's ear. *"I can hear your thoughts, young one. I have just been ignoring them."*

Morgana blushed. "Sorry."

"*There is such a thing as Mental Violence, you know.*" The Raven remarked. "*But those who lash out verbally and cause mental violence usually have a deep seated reason for it and so they rarely end up in the Plains of War.*"

Morgana nodded.

They came over the brow of a rise in the plain and looked down on another river. Steam rose from its surface and the water bubbled as if boiling.

"What's making the river do that?" Morgana asked Merla.

"*This is Phlegethon, the River of Flame. The water runs along a stream of Lava from the planet's core and the heat boils it. No one can cross it unless they use the bridge.*"

Morgana saw a high arching stone bridge beside what looked like a massive kennel. As they got closer, she could see that everyone who sought to pass the kennel and go over the bridge paused for a moment in front of the opening. "What's in there?"

"*You'll find out shortly.*" Merla took off. "*I'll meet you on the other side.*"

"Great, sure." Morgana said, fear bubbling up in her chest. *I can do this, I am not afraid.* She chanted to herself as she watched the Raven swoop over the kennel and perch on the far side of the river.

Ten

S topping on the Tiring path to watch the Judged who passed the giant kennel, Morgana began to see a pattern emerge.

Those who had obviously passed whatever test they were going through stopped, bowed, presented something to the creature inside which was whisked off their hands in an instant and were allowed to carry on over the bridge.

Those who didn't pass disappeared almost instantly. Morgana couldn't see what it was that was doing this, but something was sorting the Judged.

Then she spotted the man who had spoken to her. *How did he get on the path? And how did he get in front of me?* Moving as fast as the sand would allow, she followed him until he reached the kennel.

Morgana stopped, close enough to hear what was going on, but far away enough that whatever it was inside wouldn't spot her. *Maybe I can find out what is going on and if I'm going to be in any danger.*

The man stopped in front of the kennel bowed and held out his hands, a large joint of meat on them. Morgana swallowed bile as she realised the meat was actually a human thigh.

"Mighty Kerberus, Guard of the Bridge of Phlegethon, receive my offering and grant me passage over the bridge." He waited and there came a great in rush of air from inside the kennel. The man's hair and clothing were drawn toward the kennel, and he had to brace himself to stay still. The meat disappeared on the air current.

So that's what they're giving it and how its receiving the gift. But what is inside? Morgana frowned.

A growl echoed out of the kennel and the biggest animal that Morgana had ever seen appeared in the entrance. It was bigger than

Jenni's prize Andalusian stallion and covered in olive green scales that ran all over its body with pale yellow stripes. The creature's tail ended in a King Cobra which as it emerged, hissed loudly and showed very long sharp fangs, extending its hood.

That wasn't the real shock though.

Morgana backed away as the creature emerged from the kennel fully to tower over the man. *It's got three heads. And it's most definitely female...look at all those nipples!*

The heads resembled bull mastiffs but with the intelligence of a Malamute in the glint of her eye and the stand of her ears... all six of them.

The middle head dropped down to glare at the man. "Your time in the Plains of Punishment is not up, or you would not have insulted me with such a disgusting offering."

The other two heads growled briefly then went back to keeping watch on the other sides. The middle head took a deep breath and blew the man into the river where he screamed and thrashed. "You'll stay in there until Charon can be bothered to fish you out and take you back to the Plains."

Morgana retched.

The noise attracted the middle head's attention. Kerberus sniffed and growled. "You are alive! How did you get in here?"

Morgana held herself as still as she could. *Maybe if I don't move, she'll forget about me.*

A small group of Judged waited to see Kerberus and the massive creature dealt with them, with the third head staring at Morgana all the while. Once that group was done with, the middle head turned back to her. "Hah! Not tried to run away or get over the bridge. That's a point in your favour at least." Kerberus sniffed again, dragging Morgana toward her through the sand. "You smell like Charon. Did you come over on the Lady?"

Morgana nodded. "He said that I had to see Lord Hades and gave me clothes and food for the journey."

The first head looked across the bridge and whimpered. "Ah, I see Merla is guiding you. That is a sign of Charon's favour, that he would ask his personal assistant to escort you."

Morgana smiled. "Can I go across now then?"

"No." the middle head snapped. "My duty is to stop living beings from invading the Underworld and you are still living. As much as it will pain me to cross Charon, I must eat you."

"Why? Surely you can let me through just this once."

"It is my duty." The creature growled. "Unless you have a token from Charon or Thanatos, I cannot let you pass."

Morgana rifled through the bag that Charon had given her. There was round disc about the size of a side plate in one of the pockets. It had a silver ship embossed on the front. "Is this it?"

"Yes." Kerberus inhaled and the disc flew up her nose. "Thank you. Eating living flesh is a pain, it's so messy and while humans taste good, if you have one, you end up craving another one half an hour later."

"No, thank you. I would really like to go to my sister's Samhain ball but that means I have to get out of the underworld first." Morgana checked her bag again. "Do you like gammon? There appears to be a large ham hock in here."

"Is it smoked? I love smoked gammon." Kerberus' eyes gleamed and she began to dribble from all three mouths. "It is, I can smell it from here."

Morgana moved slightly away from the waterfalls of saliva and hauled the ham hock out, throwing it up into the middle head's reach.

Kerberus snapped the morsel out of the air. "Mmm. That's good." The two other heads turned drooping eyes on Morgana.

She looked in the bag and found two more ham hocks. *How did those get in there?* Shrugging she pulled them out, throwing as best as she was able, one to each head.

Leaving a happy Kerberus behind, Morgana walked up to the bridge.

The stones started out as pleasantly warm under her feet, but as Morgana climbed the huge arch, they grew hotter until at the top she realised her feet felt like they were burning. She shrieked and ran down the other side and off onto the frost covered sand of the path.

While her feet cooled down, she turned to see the reaction of the Judged as they came over the bridge. "Why are none of them reacting to the temperature?" she asked Merla, who sat on a dead tree beside the path.

"They're dead. They only feel the temperature they are meant to feel." The Raven laughed.

Morgana looked around the area she stood in. All around her the Judged split off into groups. Some continued walking, obviously heading for other areas. Those that were destined for this section of the underworld moved off the path and into the hills.

"What happens to those who have been judged traitors?" Morgana looked at the people who were making their way into the hills either side of the Tiring Path. Many of them shivered and rubbed their arms. Others had already turned blue with cold and started to form frost on their hair and clothes.

Morgana was surprised to see children as young as ten amongst the Judged. She pointed at them and started to ask. "Why child..."

"Why Children that young?" Merla sighed, a difficult feat for a raven. *"Ten is the age when most cultures decide that humans should be able to know right from wrong. Most children remain innocent for a lot longer, but some, well."* She sounded unhappy.

Morgana could understand why. Something inside her insisted that ten year olds shouldn't be in this place at all. *It's not fair. They're just children.*

"I told you before. *Death isn't about fairness. It is the great leveller, for it comes to everyone.*" Merla shook her feathers. "*Can we move on please?*"

Morgana nodded. "I'm getting cold, moving will warm me up."

What felt like three hours had passed before Morgana felt she had to stop to rest. "How am I supposed to sleep here?" she asked Merla. "I'm not dead, I can't carry on walking forever."

"*Charon put something in the bag for you. You can't sleep on the Path, it'd be too dangerous here, you might freeze.*" Merla landed on a fence post while Morgana looked through her bag.

She found a wooden box with lots of tiny glass vials in it. "Is this it?"

Merla hopped onto her arm and looked at it, turning her head to one side to get a better view. "*That's it. The vials with the blue glass stoppers will heal you, the ones with the green will wash away tiredness.*"

"What about the ones with the red stoppers?" Morgana pointed. "There's only a couple of them."

"*That's usually strong magic. There's a label on the side, take a look.*" Merla suggested.

Morgana carefully picked up a red stoppered vial. "This one says Summons." She put it back and picked the other one up. "This one is Banish"

"*Ah. The first one will summon Charon to you via the nearest waterway. The second is to banish an enemy. Which is strange, because the dead will not harm you as long as you stay on the Tiring Path and get to The Elysium Fields.*" Merla hopped up to Morgana's shoulder. "*Take one of the green ones and put the rest away.*"

Morgana opened a green vial. "I must be going mad." She muttered to herself. "I'm lying somewhere in the grange tunnels hallucinating from a panic attack or something." Swallowing the contents was a pleasant surprise. The liquid tasted of raspberries, strawberries and thick Chantilly cream." That's gorgeous!"

"*You can only take one vial every four hours.*" Merla cautioned her as she put the vial back in the box and put the box away.

"Okay."

Morgana started walking again. The landscape around her was frozen into ice sculptures, the air too cold for snow. She passed through petrified forests where the only sound was the occasional explosion as trees burst.

The Damned in the Hills of Treachery seemed too cold to do much. The newer ones moved around, trying to keep their blood from freezing. The older ones sat wrapped in whatever clothing they had, piling frost rimmed branches around them to trap in as much air as possible.

"How do they get out of this place?" Morgana wondered, not really wanting to know the answer.

"*Treachery of any sort is a cold and calculated crime. It is premeditated and thought upon before it is carried out.*" Merla told her. "*Thus, the Judged who come here have to endure the same temperature that existed in their souls when they committed it.*"

"I'd figured out that much." Morgana said, thinking of the ten year olds that she'd seen heading out into the hills. "But how do they move on?"

"*It's not pretty. They have to make up for their treachery in some way. Sometimes you see children removing their clothes and wrapping them around an adult who wouldn't do it for them. The children learn their lessons a lot faster.*" Merla fluffed her feathers out.

Morgana stared at the raven. Then she shook the bird off her shoulder. "Leave me alone."

Merla flapped into the air and circled the area. "*I can't leave you alone, I'm responsible for you.*"

"Why does everyone seem to think I'm a baby!" Morgana yelled. "I'm nineteen and I can look after myself."

"I'll give you some time to calm down." Merla soared away into the hills.

Morgana watched her go, tears rolling down her face. *I'm not a child. I'm not an adult. What am I?*

It also enclosed a garden full of flowers in the most riotous colours Morgana had ever seen. "How do the flowers survive in this temperature?"

"You think that we'd live in weather like that?" A heavily pregnant woman heaved herself up from where she was weeding a border. "Come in, Child."

Morgana looked at Merla.

"Go on. You'll be safe in there. I need to report back to Master Charon." Merla swooped away.

"Not often that Charon sends us a guest." The woman smiled. "You must be important."

Morgana pushed the gate open and stepped into a warm English summer's day. She sighed with relief. "Thank you for inviting me in."

"Charon and I are pledged to the same Master. Only Thanatos has true independence and even he will bow to Lord Hades' will." The woman tilted her head. "You are Morgana of Llanirstyr and Arkingham, the daughter of Angharad and Meilyr and the Chosen of Arianrhod. I remember the day you were born…"

"Stop jabbering Clutha, bring the girl inside, she's exhausted." Another female voice floated out of the open window behind Clutha.

"Of course, Lachei. Come in dear."

Morgana followed Clutha into the cottage.

The first room that they came to inside the cottage seemed impossible. As far as the eye could see, stood loom after loom. Each one wove its own pattern, the colours varying in shade and tone. They all used one single thread of yarn, which wound its way out from a massive ball at the front of the room.

Sat beside the ball of yarn, was a slim woman with long grey hair like Clutha's. "Welcome to our home, Lady Morgana."

"Thank you for having me." Morgana replied, still in awe of the looms. "Are you controlling all those looms?"

"Sweet Hera, no!" Lachei laughed. "The looms control themselves, I just make sure that the pattern weaves smoothly with no snags or knots."

"You mean like mine?" Morgana's throat filled with tears. "I lose my birth parents within hours of being born, my adoptive parents to divorce, my sight to an illness and die before I have even got started on life?"

Clutha wrapped her arms around the girl as the tears overflowed. "Oh my. You aren't dead yet. There's always hope."

"That child needs a good meal in her." Another woman appeared in the doorway. "I can't have her leaving here looking starved, I'd never hear the end of it from Hecate."

"I was just bringing her through to the kitchen, Atropa." Clutha handed Morgana a hankie.

"Good idea, Atropa, we could all do with a meal." Lachei smiled.

Morgana could feel her eyelids drooping all the way through the simple meal of bread, cheese, fruit and water. *I really need to sleep.*

"Poor lamb. We should let her sleep for a while." Clutha sighed.

"Help me put the child to bed, Lachei." Atropa helped Morgana to stand up and in a short time, Morgana found herself horizontal under one of the softest blankets she had ever felt.

"THIS IS HERS, ATROPA." The three Moirae stood in front of one of the looms, studying the pattern. "See, it's reverted to her base colour."

"She is in temporal stasis then. Should we start time up for her again?" Clutha frowned, one hand rubbing her distended belly absently.

"Charon could have done that. He didn't, so we have to trust his judgement." Lachei shrugged. "Besides, looking at this pattern, she and sandpits as well as fields of heather. It smouldered like a damp tea towel over a chip pan fire.

"What happened down there?" she asked.

"That's the Land of Dread." Xanthus said. "It bursts aflame fairly frequently on the higher areas and there are areas that are thick bog and marsh. Dangerous place that, even for immortals."

"Those Judged who acted out of Fear end up there." Merla said in answer to Morgana's unspoken question. *"I actually think it is the second worst of all the rings."*

"Second worst? What's the worst one?" Morgana thought over what she had already seen and experienced in the Underworld. "I would have thought that the Hills of Treachery had that title."

"We're coming up on the worst one now." Merla said. *"Xanthus, land please. I'll go directly to Hades about the intrusion. You take Morgana to Thanatos."*

Xanthus immediately began to slow and circle down to the Tiring Path. He landed lightly, just beyond the bridge. "There you go, Merla."

"Thank you. Look after her." the Raven took off and soared away.

"Do you want to keep flying or would you prefer me to stay on land?" Xanthus turned his head to look back at her.

"I'd like to stretch my legs for a while." Morgana dismounted into the thick sand and watched in amazement as the Pegasoi' golden wings folded down and disappeared. Within moments he just looked like any other horse.

"Put your bag on my back. I don't mind carrying it for you." Xanthus waited while she folded her blanket up and put it in her pocket, then hooked the bag's strap over a hook that appeared from nowhere on the saddle.

"Might as well get moving then." She said.

The sand seemed extra deep here and the Judged waded through it. Either side of the path lay a lush grassland dotted with the bright red of poppies. Morgana could see copses of trees here and there, and the temperature was warm enough that she felt sleepy, even while she was walking.

"Where are- "she yawned, "-we?"

Xanthus chuckled. "This is the Grassland of Apathy. Those who end up here did nothing with their lives, weren't interested in anyone else and only looked out for themselves enough to survive."

"How do they get out of here?" Morgana yawned again.

"I'm not sure." He shrugged, the movement looking odd on a horse. "Merla would know."

"I need to sit down and rest." Morgana yawned and slumped to the ground, her eyelids drooping.

"Hmm. I didn't think it would affect you. You'd better ride." Xanthus nudged her with his nose.

Her eyes sprang open. "Was I asleep?"

"It's the Air of Apathy. It only affects those of the mortal persuasion, whether or not they are dead, by the looks of it." He nudged her again. "Put your hand on my nose and keep contact with me as you mount."

The moment Morgana touched Xanthus, the sleepiness faded. "That was scary. It felt like I would sleep forever." She mounted quickly and put the bag over her shoulder. "Thanks."

"The air shouldn't affect you if you ride." Xanthus started moving and Morgana rummaged in the food that the Moirae had given her.

She passed Xanthus an apple and munched on some Honeycake." That's better."

The path through the grassland was a long and winding one. Morgana fell asleep on Xanthus' back at one point, through sheer boredom. "Urgh. This feels like one of those long car trips Da would insist on taking us on." She said when she woke up.

"That's the idea, I think." Xanthus snorted. "Do you want me to speed up?"

"Yes please."

He broke into a smooth canter.

"You're so much faster than Kedar." Morgana patted his shoulder. "I don't suppose you'd want to come home with me? I'd be able to beat my sister on Acsenso with you."

Xanthus stopped moving. "Why would you want to beat her? Isn't riding with her enough?" he looked back at her.

Morgana frowned. "Why is everyone trying to tell me how to think? First my Da and Aderyn, then Merla now you."

"Sounds like you're ignoring something important about yourself." Xanthus started trotting then shifted back into a canter.

She ignored the comment, watching the Grassland around them. His long legs ate up distance and soon Morgana saw a column of black smoke rising from her right. "What's that?"

"Nothing you need to know about." Xanthus said and moved up into a gallop.

The column of smoke stayed on Morgana's right for a while, then on the horizon the black shadow of a building appeared in the grey half-light. As they got closer, it resolved itself into a tower.

Xanthus slowed and stopped in front of the tower. "This is Thanatos' Tower. I'll wait for you out here, I wouldn't fit in the door."

Morgana licked her lips nervously and dismounted. "What is Thanatos like?"

"Go find out." Xanthus moved away toward the grass that surrounded the tower.

Morgana walked up the short flight of steps to the huge ironbound oak door. *This thing wouldn't look out of place in a crypt.* She examined the gothic design of the ironwork, the skeletons chasing people through what looked like a petrified forest and the skulls that had been fashioned on the bolt heads. Above it all a robed figure with a scythe

"There isn't a door knocker or handle." She said out loud.

Xanthus lifted his head from his grazing. "Go on, knock. It won't hurt."

Morgana raised her hand to knock, and the door swung open before she got close enough to touch it. The creak echoed through the hall beyond, and Morgana shivered.

"Go on." Xanthus rolled his eyes. "Thanatos is so melodramatic sometimes."

Morgana stepped inside.

Fourteen

Charon held the Lady mid-stream. He watched the Judged sorting themselves out with the help of the Ravens with one eye and the five Daemons with the other. *I hope Merla gets to Lord Hades in time. I won't have the strength to contain these interlopers much longer.*

Sending the individual boats to the groups of Judged meant that his timetable would be out, but it was the safest way. *Should they get onboard a boat, we'll be in trouble.*

There was a cough behind him. Charon turned to see Hades appear as if out of thin air. On the deck stood the Lord of the Underworld's black chariot and horses. Charon bowed deeply. "I thank you for coming my lord."

"I came as soon as I could. Merla brought me up to speed with recent *developments* and went back to the Chosen One's side." Hades sighed. "I suspect we are in for a time of turmoil."

"Is Lady Morgana all right?" Charon looked back at the daemons on the bank.

"She's fine." Hades smiled, "The child has arrived at Thanatos' Tower. If I get this sorted out quickly, I should be back in time to throw her a welcoming ball."

"What are we going to do about them? I can't let them aboard, they would corrupt the Judged." Charon's gesture toward the daemons was uncharacteristically flustered.

"According to King Minos, they have the Fire of Perses." Hades said, frowning.

"Do they?" Charon was shocked. "I thought Balorn kept that under lock and key."

"So did I." Hades smiled again. This time it wasn't nice. "I contacted Balorn about this as soon as I found out from Minos what the Judges had done."

"They don't have it?"

"They don't have it. They also don't have his permission to be here." Hades' smile turned into a grin that made Charon shiver. "So, I can do what I like with them."

MORGANA JUMPED AS THE door creaked closed behind her. Looking around brought no help either; the corridor ended at a spiral staircase that disappeared into the gloom above her.

Looks like I have to go upstairs. Morgana started up the steps. Each one lit with a soft white glow as she stepped on it and turned itself off when she moved a few steps further up.

The light surrounded her and made her feel relaxed, so by the time she reached the top, she wasn't the least bit apprehensive. At the top was a small landing and another gothic themed door.

Morgana raised her hand to knock, and the door swung open.

"Come in, my dear. You're lucky to catch me, there's a tsunami due in Fiji shortly." The voice that floated out of the room beyond was rich and deep, sending shivers down Morgana's spine that previously only Gerard Butler had created."

"Thank you." She said, walking through the door into a sumptuous green and black velvet accessorised living room.

At one end of the room was a fire flickering cheerfully in a massive hearth, and at the other was a desk. The man sat behind the desk smiled at her and Morgana felt her knees go weak. *He's the most gorgeous man I have ever seen, I could die happy just looking into those golden eyes.*

"You flatter me." He rose and moved around the desk. "Shall we have some tea and discuss your situation."

Morgana nodded and followed him to a pair of comfortable looking chaise longue with a table between them.

As they reclined on the cushions, a woman appeared, floating above the carpet slightly. She wore a flowing white robe which covered her feet. "Your usual, Lord Thanatos?"

"Yes please, Agathe. Bring my guest whatever you think might satisfy her requirements."

Agathe inclined her head and disappeared again.

"Now, my dear. Charon and the Moirae have extended what time you will have in the Upperworld, but you still have to escape the Underworld and I think you might find this a little difficult." Thanatos looked at her with a concerned expression.

"Why do you think that?" Morgana frowned. "I'm capable of looking after myself you know."

"I know."

Agathe reappeared with a younger woman. They set the table in-between Thanatos and Morgana with porcelain and food. Then a third white robed person appeared, bearing a tray with a cake stand and plates of sandwiches.

Thanatos smiled and Morgana shivered. "I see you are fond of a traditional high tea, the only thing missing is warm scones and... Oh, there they are. Complete with butter, clotted cream and strawberry jam."

Agathe poured Morgana a cup of tea and passed it to her.

"Thank you." Morgana said, taking the cup and saucer. She was fascinated by the woman's floating stance. *Is she a...ghost?*

Agathe poured red liquid from a bottle beside the teapot into a glass. She added a shake of some kind of powder and stirred it before handing it to Thanatos.

The three white robes disappeared again.

"Yes, they are Ghosts, but of particularly powerful mages and seers that requested the chance to serve me." Thanatos shuddered as he sipped his drink. "This potion never tastes nice."

Morgana found that she was ravenous but wasn't sure if she could eat the food. "Um, Charon told me not to eat anything not given to me by an Immortal. Are your ghosts immortals?"

Thanatos laughed. "The food is safe. That caution is one that you should follow only for items given to you by the Judged. I'm surprised that some of them haven't attempted to trap you here before now."

"I haven't really interacted with any of them." Morgana helped herself to a smoked salmon sandwich. "Merla and Xanthus have been around most of the time."

Thanatos nodded. "Good. Sadly, with the next part of your journey, they will not be allowed to help you." He gestured to the food. "Eat your fill, you are going to need the sustenance."

"What is it with people around here? All I keep getting is cryptic dreams and even more obscure hints. Can't you just tell me?" Morgana struggled to keep her temper.

"I will take you to meet with Lord Hades and Lady Persephone." Thanatos smiled and Morgana felt slightly dizzy. "However, I cannot help you any further than that."

Feeling disappointed at the lack of a straight answer, Morgana shrugged and sipped her tea before she ate more. "Thank you. I just want to get out of the Underworld and go to my sister's ball."

He laughed. "I'm certain that you'll accomplish that. However, you will need to be stronger than you are now to fulfil your destiny, Chosen of Artemis."

Morgana rolled her eyes. "I don't believe in fate or destiny."

Thanatos just shrugged. "Sadly, it's not about you believing in the Fates; the Fates believe in you."

Fifteen

Thanatos allowed Morgana to take a bath and gave her a change of clothes. He also gifted her with armour, shield and a sword. All he said when he brought them in was:

"You'll need these."

Morgana looked over the battle accoutrements with a frown on her face. *I'm not going to fight anyone. So why do I need these? I just want to get out of here and go...* her train of thought was momentarily derailed as she looked closer at the symbol on the shield. *I've seen that moon and tree thing somewhere before.*

Agathe floated into the room. "Lord Thanatos said that you need to put them in the bag Lord Charon gave you. You won't need them immediately."

Morgana sighed and started to pack the armour in her bag. *It's amazing how much stuff this bag holds. I wouldn't be surprised if I could fit Xanthus in here and still be able to carry it easily.*

She plaited her long platinum blonde hair back, looping the plait up to secure it at the nape of her neck. *I may need a haircut at this rate.* Slinging the bag over her shoulder she retraced her steps into the living room.

Thanatos was clad in a long black robe, a sword belted at his waist. "All prepared then? Good." He snapped his fingers and suddenly they were outside the tower.

Xanthus trotted up. "You look refreshed, little one. Ready for the last leg of your journey?"

Thanatos whistled and a black horse appeared out of nowhere. "Can you keep up with Arion, Xanthus?"

Xanthus snorted. "He and I race all the time, of course I can keep up."

Morgana swung herself up into the saddle. "I'm sure you can keep up with him, but I'd prefer to take it steady please."

"The lady's wish is my command." Arion neighed.

"Well, that's a first." Thanatos laughed. "He doesn't normally talk to strangers.

Morgana shrugged. "It's my irresistible personality."

The two horses started moving as soon as their riders were in the saddle.

NEX SIGHED AS HADES walked down the pier from the grey ship. *"Here comes trouble."*

"I'm not sure that the Master actually understood what sending us here meant." Morbus sniffed. *"I just hope that Lady Deumara doesn't anger Lord Hades by pretending that she has the Fire of Perses again."*

"Well, he would be able to tell the difference." Nex agreed.

Hades halted in front of the group and motioned to Charon who had remained on the ship. Charon dropped the shield on the daemons.

"You are intruding on a domain where your kind is not welcome." Hades folded his arms.

"I have been sent by my Master to retrieve the Shield, Lord Hades." Lady Deumara curtseyed. "These others are merely my bodyguards."

Nex rolled her eyes. *"She says that as if we weren't able to hear."*

"Well, that is why we were sent with her." Morbus gave a tiny whimper as he looked up at the full daemon.

Lady Deumara absently patted him on the head and Morbus wagged his tail.

"*Control yourself brother.*" Nex growled softly. "*You're not a lap hound.*"

"You are aware of the rules?" Hades tilted his head. "All those who seek the Shield must complete three tasks."

"I am ready for anything that you require of me, Lord Hades." Deumara smiled.

Hades looked at her, casting his mind out over his realm, checking the state of each river and ring. Finding Thanatos' mind travelling toward the gate to the Fields of Elysium, he nodded. "Then you have my permission to attempt the tasks."

He looked around. All the Judged were on board their boats and Charon had moved the Lady out a little way into the river. He whistled and his horses appeared on the bank behind him.

"Your first task," he said as he climbed into the chariot they pulled. "Is to make it safely to the Fields of Elysium, losing none of your party in the process."

"That seems simple enough." Deumara moved toward the pier. "May we board Lord Charon's ship now?"

Hades shook his head and urged the horses to move, pulling the chariot into the air. "Oh no. You must complete this task without any help. I will no doubt see you in the Fields soon." He disappeared into the distance.

Lady Deumara's expression hardened and Morbus yelped as she clenched his ear in her fist, her long nails piercing the skin. "So, he thinks he can get the better of me, does he?"

Nex growled and Deumara swung round to look at her. "And what do you have to say about it, animal?"

The air shimmered red around Nex and when it had cleared, she stood there in girl form, her figure every bit as stunning as Deumara's. "Leave my brother alone. You aren't the only full daemon in this group."

"And what are you going to do about it, child. You know my mission; no one can cross the Acheron alive, except by boat."

"For a supposedly intelligent full Daemon, you're being incredibly dense." Nex snorted. "Get these dunderheads to knock down enough trees and kill a few of the stupid animals in this forest and you'll be able to make a raft."

The two minotaur daemons swung their heavy heads to look first at Nex, then at Deumara. Morbus crept of out the woman's reach, shaking his head and scattering drops of thick black blood over the frosted grey grass.

Nex raised an eyebrow. "Well, Deumara?"

The woman pursed those perfect lips and snapped at the Minotaurs. "Fell some trees and hurry up with that raft." She turned back to Nex. "You get to supervise them, child." Deumara sat down on a nearby rock and snapped her fingers. "Your brother can keep me company."

Morbus crept over to the woman, whimpering slightly. Nex rolled her eyes again and got on with the job. *The faster we get this shield, the faster we get out of here.*

WHY IS IT THAT RIDING *makes me feel so alive?* Morgana thought as they raced along the Tiring Path toward the bridge over the Lethe. Thanatos and Arion had no problem keeping up with Xanthus, and it felt more like a fun trip than an essential one.

"I will take you straight to Lord Hades Palace." Thanatos called over the noise of the equines hooves. "I'm certain that Lady Persephone will be delighted to meet you."

Xanthus slowed as they came to the bridge. "I'm going to need you to hold your breath going over the river, Morgana."

"Why?" Morgana frowned. "It's just water." She looked at the river which sparkled with sunlight from the Elysium fields, flowing calm and deep between its banks."

"If you breathe in the air over the Lethe, you may forget certain important things." Thanatos told her.

"Like what?"

"Like wanting to leave the Underworld for a start." Arion snorted. "So, I'd suggest that you do as Xanthus suggests."

"Forgetting some things about this trip might be worth it." Morgana murmured, her memory wandering back to the Plains of War and Hills of Treachery.

"We can deal with things like that later." Thanatos said, his deep voice making Morgana feel relaxed. "My brother Hypnos is good at removing selective memories."

Nodding, Morgana took a deep breath and held it. *I hope Xanthus can get me across fast.*

She needn't have worried. Xanthus was up and over the bridge before Morgana even had time to feel dizzy. Thanatos and Arion followed.

"Not far now." Thanatos said, urging Arion back to her side. "Welcome to the Fields of Elysium."

Morgana breathed out and the sweet scent of flowers and fresh grass filled her nose as she took a deep in-breath. All around her spread soft green grass that just begged to be laid down on, flowers that seemed to be perfect for making crowns and chains with and the air was that perfect warm summer temperature. *Not too hot, not too cold. Perfect.*

She smiled and for the first time since stepping through the black door, relaxed completely. "I can see why this is heaven."

"Only those who are completely innocent of wrong doing can come here straight away." Thanatos told her. "Charon brings them here directly on the Lady."

"Are you saying that *everyone* has to walk the Tiring Path and suffer something in order to get here?" Morgana turned to face the handsome death god. "But what about murderers or rapists?"

"Where they go depends on their motivation for the sins." Thanatos gave an odd one sided shrug. "Only those who are truly evil get thrown into the Depths of Tartarus."

"Oh. Where's that?"

Thanatos turned on the back of Arion and pointed at the column of black smoke. "There."

"Do they ever get a chance to redeem themselves?" Morgana wasn't sure why she wanted to know.

"They are offered the chance to follow the same path as the other Judged, once every millennia. They just have to be honest when they say they are sorry." He shrugged with the other shoulder and Morgana realised that none of the people thrown into Tartarus ever got out.

"Okay." She looked around. "Is that where we are going?" she pointed at a massive red and gold stone castle with spiralling minarets that seemed to grow out of the fields.

"Yes." Thanatos smiled at her. "what's the matter?"

"I don't know. I thought the palace of Hades, Lord of the Underworld would be gloomier."

"It was at one point. Lord Hades used to have his castle in the Land of Dread." Xanthus snorted. "Then he married Persephone, and she insisted on living somewhere nicer. Lady Hecate took over Lord Hades' old place and he built this palace for his wife."

"Wise man." Arion muttered.

The track they were following led up to the gates of the palace. There were warriors wearing shining mail on guard, their flowing red cloaks bearing the symbol of Hades on the shoulder.

Thanatos trotted Arion up to the gate. "I bring the Chosen of Artemis to visit with Lord Hades. Open the gates."

The guards saluted and the massive gilded steel gates swung open silently. Thanatos and Morgana rode through them into a courtyard of dazzling beauty, full of roses and passionfruit vines. At the top of the steps that rose up from it, stood a couple.

"Welcome to our humble abode, Lady Morgana of Llanirstyr." The man boomed out. "Feel free to make yourself at home, for we shall have some business to attend to before I can comply with your request."

Morgana dismounted and curtseyed awkwardly. "Thank you, Lord Hades, Lady Persephone."

"Thanatos, are you staying for a while?" Persephone asked as the god dismounted.

"Yes, my Lady. I must remain here for the foreseeable future. I will let you know if my plans change." Thanatos bowed.

A pair of stable hands rushed out to lead Xanthus and Arion away.

"May I escort you inside?" Thanatos offered Morgana his arm.

"Thank you." Morgana took it, feeling a little wobble of something start in her stomach at the nearness of the god. *I bet Jenni isn't having this much fun.*

Sixteen

JENNI SIGHED AS SHE watched the ball from the balcony. Below her, the young nobles of Llanirstyr celebrated the first day of the New Year with flirting, laughing and not a little drink. Caoimhe and Mike were happily ensconced in each other's arms, whirling around the ballroom.

"Why don't you go find a partner and dance?" Myfanwy asked for the third time since the ball had got underway.

Jenni shook her head. "Anyone I dance with will think I am looking for a husband. I've had enough of that sort of thing recently."

"Llanirstyr is fairly backward in that regard." Myfanwy smiled.

"It's okay for you. You've got that massive rock that Dad bought you on your finger, no one bothers you." Jenni sighed again.

"She'll be all right." Myfanwy slid one arm around the High Princess' shoulders, correctly divining the real reason for her unhappiness. "Your sister is tough. She wouldn't have coped with being blind for five years otherwise."

"I know. I can't feel her in the back of my mind though, and that's what's really worrying me." Jenni started walking toward the stairs. "If she were anywhere in the mortal realms, even if she was on another earth analogue like Llanirstyr, I would be able to feel her, even if I couldn't hear her."

"And you can't feel her." the Lady Steward sighed and followed her niece. "Your mother and I were just the same."

"You and Angharad were twins?" Jenni blinked. "You never told me that."

"Didn't I? Sorry." Myfanwy gave a Gallic one-sided shrug. "It's been such a long time since she passed over that I tend to forget small details about us."

There was a long silence.

"Well, wherever she is, I hope she is safe and well." Jenni said softly as she started down the stairs.

MORGANA FOUND HERSELF installed in a suite as large as Jenni's private apartment in Arkingham. There were two maids and a footman attached to the rooms as well. *If this is what it's like to be a High Princess, I want to live like this all the time.*

Persephone had shown her to the rooms and suggested that she rest and change before the audience with Lord Hades. Morgana held her tongue on the thought that she'd already rested enough and would rather get on with whatever business the ruler of the underworld had with her. *I don't want to upset my hosts do I?*

The maids bathed her and dressed her in a beautiful blue-green silk gown, put her hair up and added a small touch of make up to her face.

It's nice to be fussed over a little, but I just want to get out of here. Morgana swept after the footman as he led her down to the great hall for her audience.

The Hall itself was crowded with people. Morgana was led to a position at the front, next to a man in flowing white robes and the footman retired to the side of the hall.

"You are a delightful looking bit of stuff." The man said out of the blue, running his gaze up and down her figure. "And you're alive as well, most unusual."

Morgana focussed on the second half of his rhetoric. "Why is my being alive unusual?"

He laughed. "Dear Lady, I do not mean to offend. As you are in the Hall of Hades being alive is unusual enough, but recent events in the Underworld have brought the Alive flooding into the underworld."

"What on earth are you talking about?" Morgana frowned. "Who are you anyway?"

"I am Odysseus, and I am one of Lord Hades' advisors." He bowed. "You are High Princess Morgana of Llanirstyr and the Chosen of Arianrhod. Forgive me for not introducing myself earlier."

Morgana shrugged. "I just want to know what you mean about alive people flooding into the Underworld."

"I didn't say alive *people*. We spirit call those who have not suffered Thanatos' craft *Alives*. Your entry into the Underworld via the Black Portal was unusual but not unexpected. The incursion of the Daemonkind however..." Odysseus shook his head.

Morgana stared at him confused. *Daemonkind? What are they? I have more questions than answers now. What on earth is going on around here.*

A fanfare blared out.

"Ah, here he is, finally." Odysseus muttered. "I'm sure he'll clear things up for you."

Hades and Persephone entered the room from Morgana's left. Hades settled Persephone into the smaller throne of the two before turning to face the crowd.

"I would like to extend a warm welcome to Lady Morgana of Llanirstyr. We shall be having a ball later to celebrate her safe arrival. However, she and I have some serious business to conduct, so this audience is over for the moment."

"What was the point in all this ceremony then?" Morgana growled. "Couldn't he just talk to me first."

"You have to understand our Lord." Odysseus chuckled. "He likes to order the court around. So, the ceremony is essential."

"Odysseus! Bring our guest to the Summer Room." Persephone called as Hades helped her from her seat.

Odysseus smiled and bowed in the Queen's direction. "Shall we?" He gestured in the direction Hades and Persephone had vanished.

Morgana nodded and they followed them.

"Do you understand why you are here?" Hades asked Morgana as she sat down. Thanatos stood on the other side of the room talking to a woman with long black hair. Charon sat opposite Persephone and the Moirae.

"No, I don't. I was following my sister." She sighed. "I'm beginning to think that I should have just stayed home and gone in for the operations the way Da wanted me to."

"I'm afraid that Artemis wouldn't have allowed that." Hades said, steepling his hands in front of him. "Your condition was serious enough that she had to push you into following your sister. It was the only way to save you."

Morgana thought back. *I have felt an odd presence since I came to Arkingham. I just thought it was having to get used to having Jenni in my mind again.* She shook her head. "Why would Artemis, Arianrhod or whoever she is want me to do something for her anyway?"

"You have unique abilities due to your bloodline." Thanatos said, turning from the black haired woman. "Your sister has as well. Yours allowed you to use the Black Portal unharmed, where many others who ventured through it went mad in the Darkness."

"But what am I doing here?" Morgana felt tears brimming at the edges of her eyes.

The black haired woman sat beside her. "We believe you have been sent to retrieve the Shield of Courage for her."

"Why?" Morgana frowned. *I'm doing a lot of frowning at the moment. Why can't people just leave me alone?*

"That we don't know." Hades shrugged. "Artemis was always very mysterious about her plans for the Nexus."

Morgana stood up. "I'm sorry but I want to go home, so I can't do anything about this. Just point me in the right direction and I'll be out of your hair."

Silence dropped over the room like a chill blanket.

Hades stood up and faced her. "The moment you stepped through the Black Portal, your Soul Lock activated."

Morgana blinked. *What does that mean?*

"Every mortal carries a certain amount of sin around with them in their Soul Lock. When they die, that sin is considered and weighed by the judges." Charon sighed. "That's why the Judged cannot leave the area they are assigned to until they have atoned for their sins."

"Stepping through that stupid black door activated my Soul Lock? I'm nineteen, I haven't had enough time to do anything sinful." Morgana snapped.

"Dear child. The sins you have committed against your family since your parents divorced are enough to condemn you to the Hills of Treachery or the Land of Dread." Clutha told her.

"Only your status as an Alive is stopping Charon from taking you there." Atropa raised an eyebrow as Morgana opened her mouth to say something. "The facts are the facts, young lady."

Morgana dropped into the couch again. "So, what do I have to do to get out of here? Find the key to this lock or something?"

Persephone smiled gently. "Exactly that."

"The way that you atone for your sins here is to suffer for them. You've seen what the Judged have to go through, you will have to do something similar." Hades said. "Three tasks, one of which will gain you the Shield of Courage."

"Oh." Morgana felt sick and changed the subject, to give herself time to think. "What about these Daemonkind Odysseus said had turned up?"

Hades cast an annoyed look at the white robed spirit, who shrugged. "I'm sorry my lord, you know I can't do anything but tell the truth here."

"It's nothing for you to worry about." Hades stretched. "They have to follow the same rules as you do. You'll be out of here before they've even finished the first task."

Seventeen

The water of the Acheron stung Nex's skin, every time it splashed up onto her. She kept on paddling grimly though, the two Minotaurs and Morbus in boy form providing extra muscle.

Deumara sat in the middle of the raft, as far from any water droplets as she could. "Keep paddling, my gallant companions, the far shore is now the near shore, and we shall be safe shortly."

Nex gritted her teeth. *"I'm not blind, so why does she keep saying things like that?"*

"She's providing encouragement the way a leader should." Morbus said, even his mind tone sounding like an adoring puppy. *"You surely don't expect her to paddle the raft, do you?"*

Nex bit her lip and ignored her brother, using the frustration his reply caused to fuel her paddling.

As the shore bumped against the raft, the Minotaurs leapt off. Ignoring the smoke which rose from their legs and arms, the massive daemons lifted the raft slightly and dragged it onto the riverbank.

Morbus and Nex returned to hound form and leapt onto the ground, using their keen sense of smell to detect danger.

Deumara stepped daintily from the raft to land, not one hair out of place or a single piece of clothing wet. "Nex."

The female hellhound turned to look at her.

"Become a horse, there's a dear." Deumara tilted her head and batted her long red and black feathered eyelashes a little. "Morbus can scout ahead as my hound and the Minos Twins make excellent bodyguards, but you're a little out of place in our group. If you become a horse, I'll be able to ride, and you'll have a role to fulfil."

Nex growled.

"Nex, do as she says. It's a good idea; after all, I don't think she'd be able to keep up with us and the Minos Twins if we were to move as fast as possible, so if she rides you..." Morbus' voice trailed away as his sister's growl moved up a notch, from mildly irritated to seriously annoyed.

"Nex. Stop that." Deumara dropped the sugary tone and moved closer to her. "I know exactly what you think of me. I'm not stupid."

Nex squared up against the other female daemon, her growl becoming a snarl.

"I am also not weak..." Deumara sank to her knees in front of the hellhound.

Morbus watched nervously, unable for once to read his sister's intentions.

Nex projected her mind voice into Deumara's mind. *"I know what you are doing, Mara. I went to school with you, remember?"*

"Yes, I remember. I also remember that we were good friends at one point. Why are you so against me?" Deumara sighed.

"I don't like your methods. They aren't honest." Nex snapped at the woman's nose.

Morbus growled and the Minos Twins rumbled angrily.

Deumara turned to look at them. "It's all right, boys, just having a little girl chat." She turned back to Nex. *"Honesty in a Daemon? You aren't serious, are you?"*

Nex had to admit to herself that she wasn't. *"Stop working your wiles on Morbus then and I'll do as I'm told."*

"Ah, jealousy. That I can understand." Deumara laughed. *"Sweetie, you and I have much more in common than these hulking male brutes do. Besides, I'm just using all of my assets; mental and physical, to my advantage. Let me ride and I'll teach you all of my tricks on the way to the Fields of Elysium."*

Nex let her growl peter out. *"I don't trust you, Mara."*

"*I don't expect you to, but you have a lot more going for you than just the ability to change form, Nex. I'll teach you how to use it and maybe the next time you and Morbus are sent on a mission by yourselves, you won't screw it up.*"

If Nex had been human, she would have blushed seven shades of beet red. "*The Master told you about that?*"

"*He did. He didn't blame you though: he decided that it had been Dolor and Formido's fault for not hiding the Dragon Guardian well enough.*" Deumara smiled. "*He flayed them you know. It took them months to grow the skin back, and when they resumed their duties, he forced them to wear their own skin as uniforms. Dolor's is the red shirts, Formido's is the black trousers.*"

Nex couldn't help letting out a short bark of laughter. "*So that's where the uniforms came from. I had wondered.*" She sighed. "*Okay, I'll let you ride.*"

Deumara's smile widened, and she stood up, brushing the knees of her black leather riding trousers off. "Good, I'm glad we got that settled."

Nex backed off a little way and changed into her mare form. "*I'm afraid I don't have a saddle, Mara. Can you ride bareback?*"

Deumara stroked Nex's shining red coat and silky black mane as she walked around her. "Oh, darling Nex, you are as beautiful in this form as you are in girl form." She swung herself lightly onto Nex's back. "Morbus, scout out the way, we need to be at the Fields of Elysium as quickly as possible. Minos Twins, stay close. Meranus, you take point, Terius you take rear guard."

Morbus turned and disappeared into the brush. The Minos Twins always did as they were told.

Nex moved out smoothly over the uneven terrain, more than a little surprised at how good a rider, Deumara actually was.

"*Oh, and Nex?*"

"*Yes, Mara?*"

"In answer to your question, I can ride anything. It's one of my...talents."

Eighteen

Morgana woke after a very long nap. She'd eaten well at Hades' table, careful to inquire of Charon if there was anything presented that she shouldn't eat. It turned out that it was all good and after the meal, Morgana definitely felt very stuffed.

As one maid brought her some breakfast and the other helped her to dress, Merla arrived at the window.

"Ah, there you are Morgana. Hades is waiting for you in the courtyard, so hurry up and eat and I will take you down to him." The raven hopped from the window sill to the back of the chair opposite to the one that Morgana sat down in.

"Do you know what tasks I have to do to get out of here, Merla?" the girl asked, deciding that fruit and milk would be enough for the moment.

"I know what the first one is, but I am not going to tell you, child." The raven croaked with laughter. *"It is one of your strengths though and you ought to do well at it."*

Irritated, Morgana threw a grape at the raven. Merla just opened her beak, caught it and swallowed it.

"Now, now, there's no need for that. You need to have your best thinking cap on for the first task." Merla hop-flapped to Morgana's shoulder as the girl stood up.

"Thank you for the food." Morgana said to the maids who came in to clear away. "I'll see you later."

The two spirit girls bobbed tiny curtseys as Morgana left the suite.

"Why do I need servants?" Morgana asked Merla as she walked purposefully down the corridor. "I'm perfectly capable of serving myself. It's something I never understood about Jenni."

"Go down the stairs to the first landing and turn right." Merla instructed her. *"Your sister doesn't have servants."*

"Yes, she does. Maebh makes their food and brings it to them when they eat upstairs or in the Orangery. There are maids galore around the place and even Da is known as the Facilities Manager." Morgana jumped off the bottom step onto the first landing and turned right, down another long corridor. "Then there are all the stable workers and the gardeners and the tour guides."

"I think if you were to actually ask your sister about it, she would say that they work for the Arkingham Grange Trust, not for her and certainly not as servants." Merla clacked her beak. *"I'd say that Maebh takes her role as Housekeeper very seriously and as her family have worked for your family for a very long time, she considers it her duty to look after you. Of course, that doesn't mean she wouldn't mind someone else making her a cup of tea sometimes."*

At the end of the corridor was another set of stairs, stone with no carpet. Morgana clattered down them in the riding boots the maids had insisted that she wear and out the small plain door at the other end.

"That's all very well, Merla, but..." Morgana halted mid-sentence as she realised that she was being watched by a massive crowd of Souls.

"Ah, there you are, Lady Morgana." Hades boomed out, smiling. "The first task awaits you." He beckoned her over urgently. "This might take you some time to solve, so I suggest that you start as quickly as possible."

Morgana bowed, her plait falling over her shoulder. "Thank you, Lord Hades." She hurried over and looked with curiosity at the container beside him. About the size of a water butt and made of a dark wood, it had a large red and white checked cloth draped over it.

"Merla, go find somewhere else to perch, she can't have any help." Charon said.

The raven lifted off and swooped over to where Xanthus and Arion stood in the crowd.

"Lady Morgana. This is your first task." Charon said, gesturing at the barrel. "In this barrel are 32,768 grains. You have to find the sixteen red grains mixed into them and separate them out into this jar." He pointed to a glass jar on a stand. The jar looked like a small kilner jar, with the red rubber seal and the metal clips on the glass lid.

Hades pointed to four footmen in livery. "These souls will do your bidding and help you in any way that you require – except they are not allowed to touch the grains. Only you can touch the grains and only you can pick up each red grain."

"Are you ready?" Hades asked.

Morgana sighed, rubbed her head and nodded. "As I'll ever be."

"Good." With a flourish, Hades whipped the cloth off the barrel, dropping it to the floor. "You may begin."

The two gods backed away from her as she walked over to the barrel and looked inside. *This looks like half a tonne of rice. How am I supposed to find sixteen red grains in all that?*

DEUMARA CALLED A HALT to their progress when they came abreast of a massive dog kennel. "That looks like Kerberos's house. We need to watch and wait to see what happens to people coming up to it."

Morbus sat down, panting. Nex didn't feel a single bit of pity for him. *I understand Mara much better than you do brother.*

The Mino Twins sat down as well, sweat dripping down their faces. Deumara pulled a pair of water skins out from under her robe. "Eat nothing and drink nothing from the Underworld. We are Unwanted and who knows what the food here might do to us."

The Twins caught the skins and drained them dry. Morbus whimpered. Deumara dismounted. "Nex, Morbus, turn to human form and I'll give you food and drink as well."

The daemons changed form. Deumara gave them water skins before handing out wrapped packets of food. "I can't have my team getting weak, can I." she said when Nex frowned at her suspiciously. "It's bad management practise."

Deumara sat beside Nex and opened her own packet. "Kerberos is supposed to stop unwanted from getting over the next river."

"Why don't we just swim the river and bypass the inspection then?" Morbus asked.

Nex groaned inwardly. *Did you do no research into where we were going at all, Morbus?*

The Twins had looked up hopefully at Morbus' suggestion. Deumara smiled and shook her head. "Watch and learn, Morbus."

They waited there for a long while, watching streams of Judged pass Kerberos' kennel and then pass over the bridge unharmed. Nex, knowing what Deumara was doing and why she wanted the boys to watch the kennel, began to doze off.

"What the-?" Morbus' explosive comment startled her awake.

Bleary eyed, Nex looked down at the kennel just in time to see Kerberos emerge from it.

"That thing is massive..." Meranus said.

"...How in flames' name are we going to best that thing?" Terius finished.

"Oh, I don't know. It's only a three headed dog." Morbus sniffed.

Nex bit back a laugh. *Typical Alpha male, always certain that they can beat anything, even if it's larger than they are.*

Deumara looked at her and rolled her eyes. "Keep watching."

The three headed dog sniffed the soul that had triggered its emergence and growled, loud enough to be heard where they sat at the top of the adjacent hill. "Wrong offering, no passage."

The soul said something that they couldn't hear.

Kerberos growled and snarled. "You haven't completed your time in the Plains of War yet, or you would have been provided with a suitable offering."

The soul said something else, and the three headed hound pounced on him and tossed him from mouth to mouth, crunching down hard each time. Then Kerberos tossed the soul into the river.

The soul screamed and flames flashed up around him as he struggled in the water.

Morbus blinked. "He's in the water, he should be able to swim across."

"You can stay there and boil until Charon arrives and decides to fish you out. Next!" the animal growled, the sound rolling like thunder across the hills.

"Now do you see why we can't swim across?" Nex looked at her brother. "The water is heated by a stream of molten rock under the riverbed. We'd be boiled alive before we even got a metre across."

Morbus looked sulky. "I could take the heat. Just because you couldn't is no reason to drop a perfectly good plan."

"I have a better idea." Deumara smiled sympathetically at Morbus. "I have some wonderful powder with me. It makes hounds of all kinds weak as kittens for a short while."

Morbus shuddered.

"Meranus is going to go down there with you and his brother. He'll blow the powder into Kerberos' face and then you two can restrain him with a special collar I have with me." Deumara pulled a huge metal collar out of the folds of her robe. "It's impregnated with the powder on the inside, so it will keep him so weak that we'll be able to scamper across yon bridge without any hassle."

She handed the bag of powder to Meranus. "Hold a handful of this out as if you are offering him something to eat. When he sniffs it, it'll start working." She handed the collar to Terius. "Get this around his neck as fast as possible. Morbus, you'll need your full strength to subdue him long enough, so don't hold back."

The three male daemons stood up and started walking down. Deumara turned back to Nex. "Shall we ride?"

MORGANA PICKED UP A handful of rice and let it slither through her fingers to land back in the barrel. It felt dry and somehow alive.

Picking a grain up, she looked at it closely. *There's something odd about this stuff.* The grain of rice pulsed slightly in the palm of her hand, a mote of light in the centre vibrating in time with the sensation. *It's alive. What is it?*

"*I am One.*" The grain told her, it's tiny voice tickling her mind. "*You were once a One too. I can feel you as you can feel me.*"

Morgana gasped. *"Are you a soul?"*

"*I am One.*" The grain repeated.

Dropping the grain of rice back into the barrel, she looked at the space around her. "Spread the cloth out please..." She said to one of the footmen.

They did as she asked without a sound. Morgana bit back a giggle as she counted the red and white squares on the cloth. *It's like a chess board. I wonder...there was that famous maths problem that we did at school that worked with a chess board. Would that help me?*

Working quickly, she placed one grain in the first square, two on the second and so forth. By the time she'd got to the eighth square, a murmuring had started amongst the crowd watching.

One of the four footmen had a smile on his face. Morgana noticed it as she got off her knees to start counting out the grains for the next square. "What are you smiling at?"

"I am Vellalar Sessa, most honourable Lady." He bowed. "I created both the board you are covering with grains and the mathematical problem that you are demonstrating."

Morgana blinked. "Really?

"Of my past, certainly. However, I believe you are going about this the wrong way. Have you found any red grains yet?"

Morgana pulled a handful of rice out of the barrel and looked into it. There on the top lay a single red grain. "There's one here."

"What is the difference between the red and white?" Sessa asked, his gaze intent on her face.

That is a good point. Well, I am not going to drop the rest of this white rice back into the barrel. Morgana dropped the white rice onto the cloth and held the red in between her index finger and thumb, looking at it closely.

It pulsed in the same way as the white grain had; Morgana directed a cautious thought toward it. *"Hello?"*

Nothing answered her.

"What are you?" She asked it.

"We are Many." The red grain replied.

"I thought you were Souls?" She looked closer. Numerous tiny dots of light pulsated in the grain, making it glow much brighter than the white one.

"We are. We have lived many times and will live many times more." The voice was calmer and soothing, making her relax against the stress of the task.

Morgana took a deep breath and looked down at the cloth; she blinked in awe. *All the white grains have moved to white squares. I wonder...*

Kneeling again, she dropped the red grain on a white square. It slid its way to a red one. Smiling, she picked it up again and dropped it on another white square. The red grain slipped its way back to a red square and sat there, flickering as its light pulsed.

Morgana looked up at Vellalar Sessa. "Get me something to put the white grains in once I have sorted them, please."

He bowed and the four footmen disappeared into the palace, returning, a minute or so later with a barrel the same size as the first one. They placed it the other side of the jar on the table.

Morgana picked up the red grain and dropped it into the glass jar. "I'd appreciate it if you could tip all the white grains I have already sorted into the empty barrel. Then spread it out again." She waited and watched as the footmen took the corners of the cloth and carefully tipped all the white grain into the new barrel.

Once they'd laid it out again, Morgana got a double handful of grain and poured it onto the cloth. There was a moment of silence and stillness, then with a shushing noise, the grains sorted themselves into the nearest white squares, revealing three red grains that all rolled into the same red square and lay there, flickering.

Morgana retrieved the red grains and dropped them into the jar. The footmen sifted the white grains into the second barrel and Morgana repeated the process, this time pouring as large a double handful onto the cloth as she could. This time she found a single red grain.

After three more double handfuls she had found just four more grains. "Seven left." Looking into the grain barrel, Morgana groaned. *This is going to take forever, the barrel is only just down by a third.*

The red grains in the jar glowed brighter. *"Think. We are Many. The white are One."*

Staring at the jar's light a thought occurred to her.

Without looking, she plunged one hand into the barrel. *"Those who are Many, come to my hand."* She concentrated on the image of the seven red grains moving through the sea of white to slide into her open hand. There was a strange sifting sensation as the white grains shifted around her hand, then one by one, the red grains slid into her palm.

"We are here."

When Morgana brought her hand back up, several white grains slid off, leaving eight red grains pulsing gently against her skin. She tipped them into the jar and turned on Hades.

"You said there were sixteen in there, but I've counted seventeen." She closed the lid of the jar and locked it.

The crowd cheered.

"Well done." Hades shrugged. "Every so often an One becomes a Many. The number of red in white is not the issue."

"What is the issue then?" Morgana planted both hands on her hips, feeling a little annoyed.

"You learned to listen to others to solve a task. You should remember this in order to surmount the difficulties in your future."

What on Earth is going on here? Morgana's temper began to build. *Why am I being treated like I'm on some sort of training course?*

Hades glanced at Persephone, who smiled sympathetically at the teenager. "Your destiny holds a lot more than illness, Morgana. Now you should rest before the second task."

The footmen brought out refreshments and Morgana looked into the jar of gently flickering red grains while she sipped from a glass of orange juice. *"Are you happy in there? Don't you want to be free?"* she asked them.

"We are free. When it is our time, we shall be sown in the fertile soil of Elysium and return to the mortal world. Until then, we are content."

The glow brightened and Morgana could feel the satisfaction they felt at their situation.

They're happy with their lives at the moment. Why can't I ever feel like that? She thought turning her empty glass in her fingers, watching the last few drops roll around the inside.

"You have not found yourself. You are still One." The red grains told her. *"When you find yourself, you will become Many."*

One of the footmen picked up the jar and followed the other three who were carrying the two barrels of white grain back into the palace.

Hades stood and bowed to Thanatos. "Dear esteemed colleague, I shall pass Lady Morgana over to you for the next task."

The handsome god stood and offered his arm to Morgana. "Come, we must repair to the meadows."

Nineteen

Xanthus and Arion took them to the meadows just behind the palace. A rolling expanse of grass and wildflowers, dotted with copses of trees of all types, faded away into the distance of the Elysium Fields.

Morgana gasped. "How many horses are there in these fields? Are all of them immortal?"

Thanatos shrugged. "Thirty Four were created Immortal, and some two hundred others have raised themselves to immortality through their deeds. The others are the souls of those who have passed their time in the mortal realms and on death have been brought directly here."

"What happens to evil animals?" Morgana was certain that she knew the answer but wanted to ask anyway.

"There are no evil animals." Thanatos looked at the teenager with a raised eyebrow as she nodded. "There are only animals who have been driven to extremis by the actions of their caretakers. If you knew this, why did you ask?"

"I wanted to confirm it. I'd always believed it was our fault animals went mad and now I know." Morgana took in the huge herd in front of her. "What are we doing here?"

"This is your second task, m'lady." Arion huffed. "I have been Thanatos' guide on his journeys across the mortal realms for a thousand years. It is time that I gave that job to another and spent some time grazing."

"You want me to pick a new horse for Thanatos to ride? There must be thousands of animals here, why can you not pick your own replacement; you would know better than I if they were suitable."

Morgana panicked a little. "How would I know? What if I get it wrong?"

"I know you as well as your family does. I trust you, Lady Morgana; perhaps you should trust your instincts in these matters as well." Thanatos laid one strong hand on her shoulder. "Now, while you may ride Xanthus amongst the herd, you cannot ask his advice. You must choose my steed on your own judgement."

Morgana looked around. *I hope that I can do this. How am I going to choose? There are so many.* Then something occurred to her. "When I've picked one, how do I bring them to you? Do they wear halters?"

Thanatos laughed. "None of these gentle creatures need controlling. Merely touch the animal you choose on the nose and ask them to follow you. Now Arion and I will draw apart from you and watch. Good Luck." He and Arion trotted away to a copse of trees where Hades, Persephone and the other members of the Underworld's Court gathered.

Morgana glanced around. "Xanthus, do you have any words of wisdom before I start?"

The Pegasoi shook his head snorting.

Morgana sighed. "No, I suppose you can't, can you." She looked around for a place to start. "Let's go visit with that group of horses over there." She pointed to a small group of Arab breed horses.

Xanthus trotted over and Morgana slid off his back, approaching the horses quietly, making sure that they could see her, but without looking directly at them, instead she looked back at Xanthus.

One of the Arabian's, a mare sniffed at her arm. "Who are you?"

"I'm a friend." Morgana kept her voice soft and laid her palm out flat for the grey mare to explore.

"You are a real Twoleg. Not dead." The mare lipped at her fingers. "What do you want?"

"I'm looking for someone to help a friend of mine do his job." Morgana pointed at the group of Gods under the oak trees. "He's over there."

"You come on behalf of one of the Everlived?" a stallion snorted derisively. "They ignore us."

"This one doesn't. He cares for all who pass into the Underworld." Morgana ran her hand over the mare's neck.

"The Gatekeeper? He is good." The mare nodded. "I would help him."

"You are strange." The stallion tapped the mare's back with his chin. "Come away from the Twoleg."

She bared her teeth. "No. I do as I wish." The mare turned her back on the stallion. "I shall come with you, friend."

Morgana laid her hand on the mare's nose. "Come with me then. What is your name?"

"I am known as Amira." The mare waited while Morgana mounted Xanthus, then trotted alongside the Pegasoi as Morgana suggested they visit a group of Gypsy Vanners further away. "I have said that I would help The Gatekeeper. Why do you still seek?"

"I have to be certain that my choice is the correct one, or I will not be able to return to the Overworld." Morgana told her. She slid down from Xanthus. "Remain with Xanthus, please Amira, I wish to speak with these people alone."

Amira watched as Morgana approached the group of horses in the same way that she had the Arabians. It wasn't long before she returned with a chestnut mare called Aurelia.

"Why do you want so many of us?" Amira asked as they moved on toward a group of long legged Akhal-Teke, Turkoman and Barbs.

"I haven't found the right person yet." Morgana replied, "Until I am certain which of you would be the best to help Thanatos, I will collect as many as necessary."

The horses shimmered in the golden half-light of the Elysian Fields and Morgana felt drawn to a black Ahkal stallion with a white star, whose coat had a steely shimmer to it. She left the mares with Xanthus and approached him, trying hard not to show her awe. *He's bigger than any horse I've ever seen, including Jenni's Acsenso. I'd best be careful.*

"Hello." She put her right hand out, fingers flat for the stallion to sniff. "I am looking for a friend who is willing to help the Gatekeeper do his job."

The stallion sniffed her palm, his warm breath making her sleeve billow a little when he huffed. "Who are you? You don't smell like an Everliving."

"I am not. I am merely aiding the Gatekeeper in his job, the way you would be." Morgana stoked his super soft nose.

"He has Arion." The stallion shook his mane. "Arion is faster than any of us here."

"Arion wishes to give the job to another. He would like some grazing and relaxing time." She let her fingers wander amongst his mane, which was as silky as her own hair.

The stallion threw his head up to stare across at Arion who snorted and reared in some signal that Morgana did not understand. "You are right." He transferred his gaze to Xanthus, Amira and Aurelia. "Why do you have so many of the People with you?"

Morgana reined in her temper as it threatened to explode. *I wish they'd stop asking the same questions.* She sighed. "I need to make sure that I have picked the correct person for the job."

The Stallion laughed, snorting his breath out in little puffs. "You do not trust yourself enough. I believe that I am the one you are looking for. Arion has long been my friend and I understand how he feels."

How do I know that for sure? Morgana shrugged. "Okay. You can come too. What's your name?"

"I am Ghyrdepal. It means Grey Star." The stallion nudged her. "Come little one, we must return to Arion, for there is trouble brewing."

Morgana blinked. *How did he know that?* She walked over to Xanthus and was about to mount when Amira pushed in front of her.

"Ride me, Friend. We have been summoned to the Everliving."

Morgana pulled herself up onto Amira's back. "I am not used to riding bareback."

"We can get you tack later, Morgana." Xanthus said, his wings unfolding. "I must go, and Amira can carry you as well as I."

Morgana frowned and would have said something except he took off almost immediately. She shrugged, sat up straight and wound her hands in Amira's mane. "Okay, let's go then."

The three horses burst into a canter from standing, startling Morgana. She only just managed to keep her seat.

They slid to a halt in front of the group of watching Deities. Morgana slipped down and patted Amira on the withers. "Thank you, Amira."

"Lady Morgana." Thanatos smiled in greeting, but she could feel unease behind the expression. "You have three superb horses in front of me, but which is your choice for the one who will aid me in my tasks?"

Morgana looked at Thanatos, sizing him up. Then she looked at the horses. *All three of them are intelligent. All are strong and have good stamina.* She walked around the animals. Amira was a perfect example of an Arab mare, her soft brown eyes, tracking Morgana's every move, but not in an anxious way. *Kedar would like her. I like her.* She brushed aside what Jenni might have thought.

She moved on to look at Aurelia. *She's a pretty mare. All that hair is going to be a pain to keep clean and untangled though.* The mare tossed her head and her forelock flipped out of the Vanner's intelligent looking, deep brown eyes for a second. *She's sweet, but I don't think she'll be able to stand the pressure of what Thanatos has to do.*

Standing in front of Ghyrdepal, her heart surged in her chest. *He's fast, strong and intelligent. He knows about the job from talking to Arion. He even looks the part; what with his height and that steel shimmer to his coat.* She sighed and her eyes ranged across all three animals. *But Amira is eager to do the work and the breed is incredibly loyal.*

"Well, Lady Morgana?" Thanatos' voice was soft and only she seemed able to hear it. "Are you going to trust your instincts?"

Glancing back at him, she made her mind up. "I have chosen your next helper, Lord Thanatos."

"Excellent." He folded his arms, waiting.

Morgana walked up to Ghyrdepal and laid her hand on his nose. "Ghyrdepal, would you aid Lord Thanatos in his work and carry him across the mortal realms?"

The Ahkal-Teke stallion huffed, nodding. "Aye, little one. I will help the Gatekeeper."

"Then come forward and meet him." She turned and walked back to Thanatos.

Ghyrdepal kept pace with her, his nose touching her shoulder and his breath disturbing the strands of hair around her ears that had escaped her plait.

She bowed to Thanatos. "Meet Ghyrdepal. He has agreed to be your steed and is my choice."

Thanatos smiled broadly. "Well done, Lady Morgana." He turned to the stallion and held his hand out palm up. "Welcome to my service, Ghyrdepal."

The horse snuffed at the god's palm, dropped his nose into it for a moment before lifting his head to look the god in the eyes. "I choose this freely and willingly, Gatekeeper."

Morgana had stepped away as the stallion accepted Thanatos and was feeling a little sad. *He's so beautiful. I wish I could have taken him home with me. Jenni would have loved him.* She let out a long sigh and then shrieked as she was pushed from behind.

"Why are you sad? You have completed the task." Amira shook her mane. "Have you a steed of your own, Friend?"

"No. My sister Jenni has lots of horses, but I have none." Morgana smiled as she remembered all the horses in the stables. "I have always wanted a friend of my own though."

"Then I shall accompany you." Amira tossed her head again. "You have need of a steed and a friend and I am the right one for that job."

"Sounds like you have a follower." Merla swooped in and landed on Morgana's shoulder. "Good. Mount up, child. We have to return to the palace quickly."

Morgana turned toward Thanatos who was just in the act of pulling himself astride Ghyrdepal.

"Come, my Lady, your work here is done." The god called to her.

"And mine is done now." Arion called, his joy in his freedom evident from his voice. "Good running to you, Ghyrdepal and Amira, may you always find sweet water and green grass." He reared, spun and galloped away across the grasslands.

Amira moved in front of Morgana and after a moment, the teenager mounted, wrapping her hands in Amira's mane. "Come friend. We shall beat the Gatekeeper and his new steed back to the home of the Everliving." The mare whinnied.

Merla took off and described a wide circle above Morgana and Amira. "All clear."

Morgana braced herself just in time. Amira took off in a canter, racing ahead of Ghyrdepal who snorted and followed.

Twenty

The Judged streamed off the bridge and around the five daemons in the centre of the Tiring Path. This close to the Phlegethon, the air was warm enough to make the sand soft, but Nex could see the rime of frost that covered the path's surface a short distance away.

Morbus wiped Kerberos' drool from his clothes. "That was disgusting." He flicked his hands free of the thick yellowy liquid.

"You were just supposed to get the collar around his neck, not get eaten by him." Nex snorted at her brother. *"Besides, you drool when you're a hound and that's just as disgusting."* She stamped one hoof.

"Steady Nex. It's not our fault that male daemons are as stupid as they are brawny." Mara told her from where she was healing the scalds on Meranus' leg. "And splashing through the shallows of the river wasn't a brilliant idea either."

"I didn't get a choice. The three headed mutt threw me in..." The minotaur twin growled at her.

"...and I had to try and drag him out." Terius finished.

"Well at least we're across now." Nex shook her mane. *"What's next?"*

We have to get past the House of the Fates. We don't have much time either." Mara stood up, dusting crispy skin flakes free of her hands. "There, that should hold you until we get out of here."

Nex regarded Mara with suspicion. *She's gone from Daemon Queen to everyone's best friend. What's going on with her?*

Morbus changed form into a hound and shook himself, splattering more drool across the ground which raised little puffs of dust from the thick sand of the path. *"Why don't we just go cross country?"*

Nex huffed disgustedly.

"It seems you were right, Nex. Research really isn't your brother's strong point." Mara murmured. She turned to face the male daemons who drew together in a little huddle at the contempt and disgust on her face. "Next time I take on a mission for Prince Apollyon, I will not be selecting you three to work with me. Talk about incompetence. To answer your question, Morbus, if we stray off the path and 'cut' through the Hills of Treachery, we will forfeit our current lives and be trapped here until we atone for our sins."

Morbus whined and then cocked his head and lifted his ears hopefully at Mara and Nex. Mara looked at Nex, one eyebrow raised. "What did he say?"

Interpreting her brother's animal noises was second nature to Nex, even in horse form. She sighed. *"We can't just change form and pretend to be like the Judged, Morbus. No one here can lie or deceive. We are forced to show our true natures in the Underworld."*

Mara laughed. Her fangs glinted in the dull, even light pervading the underworld. "Well said, Nex. So, we need to approach the Fates carefully. After all, they know exactly who we are."

CLUTHA WATCHED THE group coming down the hill. "Daemonkind of all persuasions. Only one of them with any chance of atoning." She sighed.

"You can't save her you know. Not in this life; nor are we supposed to." Atropa appeared in the doorway to the cottage. "What do we have to do?"

"Lord Hades said to slow them down. The child needs time to rest before the next two tasks." Lachei called out as she came through the garden. "He has sent us some aid, however."

Atropa looked at the wave of monsters appearing out of the hills around them. "So, I see. Do we give them a chance?"

"I'd say that we ought to keep them talking for as long as possible." Clutha bit her lip. "How about we do the old act?"

Lachei giggled. "Already ahead of you, sister." She pulled open the bag slung over her shoulder and rummaged. "Black or Grey?"

"Grey of course." Atropa snapped. "Black is for the end of life, not the middle."

Clutha caught the grey hooded robe her sister tossed over to her and put it on. "Do we have to do that thing with the eyeball?"

Lachei rolled her eyes. "It's only an illusion, Clutha."

"I know, but it makes me feel sick."

"You always feel sick, sister." Atropa pulled the hood up on her robe. "Ready?

"I suppose you're right." Clutha grumbled.

Lachei joined her and the two of them raised their hoods.

DEUMARA SQUEEZED HER legs slightly. "Woah, Nex. We have company."

Nex stopped moving and looked at the sea of monsters that surrounded the Moirae's cottage. *"Is Hades trying to kill us?"*

The Daemoness shrugged. "Probably. He wouldn't want our lord to get the shield."

"What's the battle plan then?" Morbus barked.

"I want to see what happens first. They don't seem to be all that interested in attacking yet." Mara kneed Nex gently and the daemon horse moved forward slowly. "Take it slowly. No challenging anyone or insulting them."

"Aww. This looks like..."

"...it could be fun." The twins said, cracking their knuckles.

"It's just like home during the Neodaemon Battle Festival." Morbus growled and his eyes gleamed with battle lust.

"Behave yourselves." Mara snapped.

The group moved forward slowly. The Judged had stopped at the bottom of the hill and were gathering in a large crowd by the start of the fence surrounding the cottage. They moved aside as the daemons arrived and when they got to the front, Nex saw three grey robed figures standing together in front of the army of monsters.

"The Moirae." She shivered, remembering the stories her half human Nurse had told her when she was in the cradle.

Mara patted her shoulder. "I think it might be a good idea to do this formally in human form." The daemoness dismounted and snapped her fingers at Morbus. "You too."

Nex and Morbus shimmered back into their normal human forms, changing their usual outfits for formal robes.

Mara's robe appeared behind her as if held by a servant. She slipped her arms into the thick red wool and fastened the buckles with a snap of her fingers. "That's better." She looked at the twins, who had also put their robes on. "You two are a mess."

The twins looked as sheepish as it was possible for bull headed daemons to get. "Sorry." They chorused.

"Well, I suppose that will do." Mara sniffed and raised her hood.

The rest of them followed suit.

"Halt, Daemonkind. You have reached a fork in the path of your fates." The Moirae said together.

"Stand aside." Deumara ordered. "We are on a mission from Prince Apollyon, and no one will stand in our way."

The Moirae stepped forward, still side by side, until they only stood a couple of feet away from the Daemons.

Nex could see their faces and five empty eye sockets stared back at Mara.

The one with the single eye spoke. "You have committed too much sin against your fellow creatures in your pitiful lives thus far. I, Toparelthon, warn you to return to your own dimension and think on this." The Moirae plucked her eyeball from its socket and passed it to her sister, who took the organ and slipped it into her empty left eye.

Nex flinched and Mara raised an eyebrow.

"Your current quest will lead both you and your master to the depths of Tartarus should you continue. I, Parovsiaste, warn you to return to your own dimension and go no further." She too, removed the eyeball and passed it on to the third sister who looked at it for a long moment before putting it into one of her eye sockets.

"There are those amongst you who shall not be saved from Tartarus' grasp in the underworld, but there is one who may evade that fate. Take heed of our warnings while you still can. I, Mellantikas, warn you to return to your own dimension while you still can, lest ye perish."

The Moirae linked hands and the eyeball slipped out of Mellantikas' face and hovered in front of them, spinning.

"In the name of Lord Hades, brother of Zeus; we abjure thee, go no further. Return to thine dimension or face the wrath of Hades." The Moirae chanted.

Mara waited until they'd finished. Then she waited some more.

Nex looked at her nervously. *She's not even fazed by the warnings. I wonder what Mellantikas meant by 'there is one who may evade that fate'. What do we do now?*

The silence obviously unnerved the monsters who began to shift and mutter behind the Moirae.

"Is that all you have to say?" Mara shrugged. "I am not put off by some two bit performance with an illusory shared eyeball."

Nex blinked and stared at the eyeball. *She's right. It is an illusion. How did I miss that?*

"I didn't think you would be." The first Moirae said. "But it's always good to practise." The eyeball fuzzed out of existence and the three sisters pushed back their hoods to reveal normal looking, if slightly worried, human faces.

"What's going on? Prince Apollyon said it would be a difficult mission, but you're deliberately standing in our way." Mara frowned and tilted her head to the left. "You already know our mission, and I'm fairly certain that despite our forced entrance, Hades wouldn't be all that bothered about us trying to claim the Shield. So, there is something else afoot."

"What happens in the Realm of Hades is none of your business." The middle sister said. "Go home Deumara. Take your friends and leave here. Lord Hades has said that if you wish to depart now, you will be allowed to, with no consequences."

"Who else is here?" Nex asked, a niggle in the back of her mind irritating her. "There's someone here that you are trying to protect. That's why you are obstructing us."

Mara shot her an annoyed look before turning back to the Moirae. "Nex has the truth of it, doesn't she?"

Nex sniffed. Even in human form, her sense of smell was far more acute than a normal human's and she smelt a partially familiar scent. *Who is that? I remember something like that from Xandin.*

"There must be someone else trying to win the shield of courage." Morbus said slowly. "Why else block our progress. They know what we are after and who we are, they don't want us to succeed in our mission for Prince Apollyon."

Mara smiled at him. "That's a good summation. So, who is it?"

"Someone familiar to us." Nex took a deep breath. "Morbus and I have met her before, I think."

The Moirae looked scared.

"You must be on the right track, Nex." Mara grinned. "I can feel the apprehension rolling off them."

Morbus took a deep breath as well. "Familiar, yet different. Pale hair, blue eyes."

Nex shut her eyes, the better to concentrate. "We were with Jezebeath on Xandin, at the court of Poseidon."

"Yes. She was there at the king's right hand..." Morbus continued.

Nex's eyes shot open. "High Princess Gwynnhafr of Llanirstyr."

The three sisters sighed and moved off the Tiring Path. "If you must continue, then you must. However, you will need to defend yourselves well." They bowed and disappeared into the garden, shutting the gate behind them.

In front of the Daemons, the gathered monsters howled a challenge and stomped on the ground, making it shudder.

Mara sighed. "And yet again it comes down to violence." With a click of her fingers, her formal robe disappeared and armour once more enclosed her form. "Nex, I prefer to fight on foot. You may take what form you like."

Morbus grinned happily. "Oh, goody. I'm going to enjoy this." His body shimmered and then the massive form of the Daemon Hound stood there. *Well, sister? Shall we fight together?*

Nex considered the monsters and her brother. "I have a better form than the hound to use brother." Concentrating she slipped into a form she had been practising, larger than the hound.

Mara grinned. "Oh, my... now that is a useful form."

"Show off" Morbus sneezed.

Nex grinned. "This way I retain my human voice, but I get a few more weapons." The dragon's head beside her human one roared in agreement and she pumped her huge wings experimentally. "I'd stay out of range when I get going though. I haven't managed to control the trajectory of the spines yet."

"Well, you're terrifying them, just standing there." Mara jerked her helmeted head toward the monsters. "Terius, you're with me.

Morbus, back Meranus up. Nex, you go and wreak havoc by yourself; you'll have more fun that way."

She looked around once more, looked at the monsters who stood there growling at them and a broad grin spread across her face. Drawing her sword, Mara shouted "In the name of Apollyon! Charge!

Twenty One

Morgana lay in the bath surrounded by bubbles. *This is heaven. I feel like I've been wrung out to dry with all the thinking I've had to do. It'd be nice to just rest for a whole day, no tasks or rushing around.* She closed her eyes and sighed happily.

"You'll go all wrinkly if you stay in there, daughter." A voice said. Morgana's eyes shot open.

There floating serenely beside the bath, stood Angharad, her blonde hair almost touching the floor and bright green eyes regarding her daughter with a hint of laughter.

"Mama?" Morgana sat up, ignoring the bubbles and water that slopped over the side to soak the towels she'd laid on the floor beside the bath. "I thought you were in Limbo."

The beautiful ghost smiled. "I was judged and brought directly to the Elysium Fields by Charon. Lord Hades asked if I wished to help in the palace, rather than make a home in the Fields."

"But you deserve to rest. Why did you want to help in the palace?" Morgana frowned.

"You look so much like my beloved Meilyr when you frown, Morgana." Angharad laughed. "I told you when you were in Limbo that I would see you once more, remember?"

"And that is why you said you'd serve in the palace? Mama, you're a queen, you shouldn't be serving anyone." Morgana felt angry at the thought of her birth mother having to work in the Underworld.

"Even as a Queen of Llanirstyr, I served my people, Morgana. As your sister does in her roles of Lady Arkingham and High Princess." Angharad sat down on a chair nearby.

"Jenni doesn't have to work. She's too rich." Morgana was surprised by the bitterness she felt. "She inherited everything from Grandfather, and I get a paltry trust fund. I'm the one who is going to have to work for a living."

"Morgana, is that why are you so jealous of your sister? She is your twin, your other self, just as I am Myfanwy's twin. You have the same amount of money and property in trust for you on Llanirstyr, as she has on Earth Nexus." Angharad's smile slipped into a concerned expression. "Did you really think my father wouldn't have thought of that?"

"Mum and Dad love her more than me. She got to go with Dad, and I had to stay with Mum in boring old Cardiff. I was all by myself and she's got loads of friends in Arkingham." Morgana blurted out. "She left me and even when I was ill, then afterwards when I was blind, she never came to see me. She was always away when I came to Arkingham to see Dad."

Angharad's eyebrows shot up into her wispy fringe. "Sweet, sweet child. Did you not listen to a word Artair said to you? Your sister has been hard at work, dealing with her responsibilities. She's had to juggle two lives; one in Llanirstyr, meeting the people she will have to rule one day, learning the etiquette and laws of the land, travelling all over Llanirstyr to know as much as she can about the kingdom." Morgana's birth mother paused and looked at her, the laughter wiped out by anger. "Jenni has an easier time of it on Earth Nexus. She can be herself and ask people to help her. She understands the world better there, so she can relax."

"So, I'm a spoiled brat who cares nothing about other people?" Morgana burst into tears. "I'm not! I'm going to die of cancer just like you did, and no one will care. I'm scared and I want my sister back."

Angharad smiled sadly. "Darling, do you really think that no one cares about what is happening to you? They would never have put you in for the trials of that implant otherwise. Your sister has been busy true, but she's always been worried about you, even when she was supposed to be enjoying herself. Even now she worries about you."

Morgana fell silent, poking at the bubbles and thinking. The tears ran down her face and dripped into the bath water.

A gentle breeze wafted through the windows, blowing the pale silk curtains which obscured the view into billowing shapes and making small piles of bubbles float into the air. Angharad stood up and moved behind Morgana.

"Get your hair wet, sweetheart, I'll wash it for you."

Morgana closed her eyes tightly and dunked her head under, clearing the bubbles from her face with her hands as she surfaced. "Mama?" she said softly as she emerged from under a layer of froth.

Angharad scooped a handful of sweet smelling liquid from a nearby bowl and began to massage it into Morgana's hair. "Yes, darling?"

"Mama, what is it like to die?"

Angharad sighed. "I don't know. I remember very little of what actually happened. One minute I was lying in bed, dreaming of Meilyr, father, my sister and you two; the next I was standing in Limbo. I don't even remember Thanatos coming for me, yet he remembers entering our suite in the palace, taking my hand and leading me away, even as Meilyr collapsed on the bed beside me."

"I don't want to die." Morgana's tears had dried, but her heart felt heavy.

"Everyone dies. Life must end, in order to continue. Your soul requires rest between lives, and you have to learn the lessons that each life brings you." Angharad emptied a jug of warm clear water over Morgana's head, effectively ending the conversation. "Now get dried and dressed. You have two more tasks to complete, and the next one will test your strength, so you have to eat." She left the room as Morgana stood up, watching what was left of the bubbles disintegrate into nothing around her calves.

SURROUNDED BY MONSTERS in various states of death, Mara rolled her shoulders and head to loosen the muscles. She looked around to see how the others were doing.

Morbus and Meranus had a similar pile of dead and dying around them. They had evolved a strategy where Meranus would challenge a monster, Morbus would hamstring or disable it in some way from behind and the minotaur would finish the job when the creature fell to the floor in agony.

Terius was currently engaged hand to claw with a harpy, wrestling to remove the filthy creature's claws from the ruins of his breastplate, while she endeavoured to slice his throat with her serrated edged beak.

Eventually he gave up, grabbed her by the wing joints and pulled, his shoulders surging powerfully. The harpy shrieked and as she attempted to break free of his grip, Meranus ripped her wings from her back, blood spurting from the ruined bone and muscle to coat her body with scarlet. Meranus giggled, dropped the wings and ripped the harpy's head from her shoulders before she could scream.

Mara turned in the opposite direction to see what Nex was doing.

The corpses around Nex were mainly charred and flaming. Some boasted a forest of spines protruding from their flesh, while others looked uninjured, but a beard of frothy sputum covered their mouths and chests, testament to the venomous nature of Nex's snake tail.

Mara smiled. "Now this is what I was expecting to encounter when we came down here." She absently beheaded a werewolf as

Meranus removed the harpy's body from his armour. "But, as fun as this is, we really should be going. Nex!"

The Chimericore turned her human face toward her as her dragon head took care of a horde of Indian Ants, frying them in their own juices. "Yes Mara?"

"How many more are there?" she cleaved a catoblepas in half as it tried to poison her with its noxious breath. She waved her free hand in front of her face. "Sheesh, these things really need to clean their teeth."

Nex stretched slightly, using her forepaws to balance herself on a pile of dead monsters. "Not many more. If we join up, they might get close enough for me to deal with them from the air."

"Good plan. Morbus, Terius, Meranus! Converge on me. Nex, you get into the air." Mara slit the throat of a satyr and turned on a group of Pane that had crept up behind her. Meranus joined her and between the two of them, they reduced the goat legged men to a pile of twitching meat.

Terius and Morbus fought their way across to Mara and the four of them stood back to back.

In the meantime, Nex flattened a half dozen satyrs as she extended her wings and with a massive push of her lion haunches, she took off. The dragon head blasted a continuous stream of blue-white flame, reducing anything it touched to ash.

Flying in a circle around the small group of fighters, she took more out using her spines and her snake tail spat venom into the eyes of the taller creatures. Finally, when the pile of convulsing flesh surrounding the fighters was taller than Terius, Nex set the remainder on fire.

Dropping down into the centre of the flaming barricade, she hovered and extended one paw to each of her fellow daemons. "Grab on. I'll move you clear of this barbeque."

Morbus changed form and grabbed his sister's left forepaw. Mara took the right one and the minotaur twins grabbed a rear paw each, shooting nervous looks at Nex's snake tail which hissed and writhed above their heads.

Nex lifted up, laboriously moving higher with each down sweep of her wings. *There is no way I am going to be able to carry them like this for long.* The stench of burning tissue, fur and bone nauseated her and she concentrated hard on what she was doing.

Mara laughed at the sight of a group of minotaur running back into the hills, their flaming pelts and clothing making them seem like shooting stars as they ran through the icy undergrowth. "Well at least we warmed them up a little. Nex, can you take us to the centre of the underworld like this?"

"No. You're too heavy. I might be able to carry one person, but not all four of you." The Chimericore gasped, then she straightened her wings and glided, following the Tiring Path.

Mara nodded, but a thoughtful look settled onto her face and remained there for the rest of the flight.

HAVING SLEPT FOR AN hour and eaten, Morgana was surprised to find the armour that Thanatos had given her laid out on a stand beside the bed.

Angharad floated beside it, looking serene. "Come on, we need to get you ready. Put the tunic and leggings on that are on that chair and make sure that you lace those boots up tightly; you won't be able to fix it once you're in the armour."

"I have to fight someone?" Morgana gasped and backed away. "Mama, I've never even thrown a punch in anger, not even at Jenni. How am I supposed to fight someone?"

Angharad sighed. "I know, sweetheart, but this is one of the tasks you have to do."

Morgana shook her head. "No. I am not going to do this." She folded her arms and sat down on a stool beside the window.

Angharad laughed. "Meilyr used to do exactly that when he was being stubborn. Morgana, I know you're scared, but if you don't complete these tasks and get out of the Underworld, there will be a lot more bodies to mourn than just yours."

"What's that supposed to mean?" Morgana wriggled back into the chair. "I don't care, I'm not fighting anyone."

Angharad frowned. "I'm not sure If I'm allowed to tell you why you have to do this."

"Well unless I get some explanation, I am not going any further with this." Morgana whined. "I'm tired and I don't want to fight anyone. I just want to go to Jenni's ball on Llanirstyr. I never wanted to come here in the first place; it was an accident."

Angharad's lips thinned, and her frown deepened. She folded her arms as well but started tapping her right hand on her left arm.

Morgana was startled. *She looks just like Jenni when she's about to put her foot down.* She pushed back the memory of the last time Jenni had got her way in one of those arguments, but it slid forward again, engulfing her...

Twenty - Two

"Mam said it wasn't our fault, 'Gana." Her sister continued packing the suitcase their mother had laid out for her on her bed.

"But why do you have to go with Da? I thought you said we'd never be apart!" Morgana sat on the pillows, pulling the clothes out as fast as Jenni could fold and put them in.

"They can't separate us entirely, 'Gana. Our minds are linked, remember." Jenni smiled, sniffed and folded the pile of clothes Morgana had pulled out. She laid her hand on top of the pile. "We have to do this. The Judge has ordered it."

"We'll be sixteen this year, adults. We can live together!" Morgana grinned and grabbed Jenni's arm. "The day we turn sixteen, all you have to do is run away from Da and I'll run away from Mam, and we can meet up in Bristol and go to London together, the way we've always dreamed."

Jenni sighed and looked unhappy.

"What? Don't shut me out like that, Jen." Morgana pushed with her mind against Jenni's. *"Please, Jen. What's the matter?"*

Jenni shut her eyes, but tears still dripped through the closed lids. "Stop that 'Gana. I'm not going to let you influence me on this."

"Huh?"

"Mam knew about our plan. I don't know how, but she did." Jenni bit her lip. "She made me promise to not do it."

"How did she find out? Did you tell her?" Morgana's eyes went wide. "I'll never be your friend again if you told her."

"No, I didn't tell her. She said that one of her friends overheard us talking about it and told her." Jenni pulled her arm out of Morgana's hand.

"But they can't do this to us! I'm not going to let them." Morgana snapped her teeth together on the scream that threatened in her throat and swallowed. "Why are you letting them do this to us?"

"Mam made me swear on you, 'Gana. She knows it's the one thing I will never break; a vow made on our bond." Jenni folded her arms and frowned at Morgana, her right hand tapping on her left arm. "She said that If I do run away from Da and you run away from her, then that doctor we had to go and see two weeks ago will make sure we never see Mam and Da again."

"What? They can't do that."

"They can. It's called putting us into Foster Care."

"Then we'll run away from that as well." Morgana pursed her lips and folded her arms, leaning back into the padded headboard. "I'm not putting up with this. First Mam and Da separate, then they get divorced. We have to get them back together and I reckon running away will bring them back together"

"No, Morgana. I am not going to run away. I have too much to do with my life to waste it on the streets and in Care." Jenni took a deep breath. "I want you to swear on our bond that you won't run away from Mam."

Morgana narrowed her eyes. "No."

"Do it, Morgana or you'll never hear from me again, through our link or any other way." Jenni's hand tapped faster on her arm.

That stung. "What never ever?"

"Never ever at all. Swear."

Morgana stared into Jenni's eyes, trying her hardest to make her sister look away, to give in to what Morgana wanted. Jenni's hand stilled. *Ah, I may have taken it too far.* Morgana thought and swallowed.

"Morgana Elaina Pendry. If you do not swear on our Blood Bond as sisters that you will not run away from Mam, I swear on the Blood that runs in our veins that I will leave with Da and never contact you ever again." Jenni's tone was final. She glared at Morgana.

I've never seen her like this before. She's always given in to me when I did that before. Morgana dropped her eyes and sighed.

"Swear, Morgana." Jenni said in such a final tone that Morgana knew she'd lost.

She looked up. "I swear on the Blood that runs in both our veins that I will not run away from Mam."

Jenni grabbed a pin and jabbed herself in the thumb. "Blood Oath!" She held the pin out to Morgana.

As a bubble of blood welled up on Jenni's thumb pad, Morgana jabbed her own right thumb. "Blood Oath." She agreed.

They pressed their thumbs together and held them there.

Jenni said: "By the blood that we share and mingle this day, we swear to each other that we shall hold true to each other and remain with our respective parents until the law allows us to live as adults."

Morgana swallowed and repeated the oath. Then they kissed each other's thumbs better and hugged.

"There, that wasn't so hard, was it?" Jenni hugged Morgana tightly. "It's only until we're eighteen, 'Gana. Besides, you can always come to Arkingham for the holidays."

Morgana nodded and after the bleeding had stopped, they packed Jenni's case together.

I HATE THAT MEMORY. It wasn't fair that we were separated, and this isn't fair either... but, I have to get out of here. Morgana sighed. "Mama, I don't know the first thing about fighting. I don't even like watching martial arts movies."

"Lord Hades said he had someone who would train you." Angharad smiled. "Don't be scared little one, you can't be killed in the Underworld."

"No, you just get trapped here." Morgana stood up. "If I have to do this then I will, but I want it known that this is happening under duress."

Angharad gave the same odd one shouldered shrug that Morgana's aunt Myfanwy used. "It is a measure of your courage that you will fight for your future despite your misgivings."

Morgana nodded and put the tunic and leggings on. Then she stood still while her birth mother strapped the black and silver armour into place. It was surprisingly lightweight.

"Are you sure that this will protect me?" she asked, "It doesn't feel like it's strong enough."

"I was worried about that as well," Angharad said. "So, I asked Hades while you slept. It's made of celestial silver and is imbued with great magical power by Thanatos." She finished lacing up the back of the cuirass and strapped the ties down so that they didn't move around.

Morgana nodded, running her hands over the armour and marvelling at the flexibility of the tiny linked scales that covered her from shoulder to hip. The wide, thick leather straps over her shoulders were plated with silver and tiny owls and horses were engraved onto them, making her shoulders sparkle when she moved.

From her hips down, a skirt made of thick black leather strips embedded with silver circles fell to just above her knees. Greaves were strapped to her shins, pulling the leggings even tighter against her skin and finally, she pulled on soft short boots.

Angharad stood behind her and lifted off the floor a little, brushing and plaiting Morgana's hair, then winding it around her daughter's head. "We don't want to give your opponent a hand hold." She explained.

"Shouldn't I have a helmet of some sort?" Morgana asked as she looked at herself in the mirror.

"Ye will nae need one." A new voice said from the direction of the sitting room door.

Angharad turned around. "Lady Scathach, I didn't hear you come in." she curtseyed.

The red headed woman snorted. "Good. I thought I ha lost ma touch after such a long rest." She came into the room and circled Morgana looking over her critically. "Ye did a good job wi' t'armour, Angharad."

"One of my father's ideas was that we... that is, my sister and I... had full training with the Army and Cavalry." Morgana's mother shrugged. "I helped Myfanwy with her armour many times; it wasn't all that much different to this."

"Has ye daughter had any training at all?" Scathach frowned and ran one hand down Morgana's left arm. "She's awful weak in the upper; got good strong legs though."

"No, no training; just regular swimming and horse riding according to her memories. She was fostered on Earth Nexus and the culture is a peaceful one there. Plus, she's also recovering from a serious illness." Angharad looked worried. "Can you train her?"

"To defeat Kuklayne?" Scathach laughed. "Nay. Only Achilles and Heracles in this realm are strong enough to match ma foster son."

"Then why am I doing this? I don't want to fight anyone!" Morgana pulled away from Scathach and flopped onto the bed.

"Ye nay need ta defeat him. Just prove ye're worth the prize." Scathach laughed and sat down beside her. "I'll show ye a few things that will aid ye ta do wha' ye hae to."

Angharad sat on the other side of her daughter. "You have to do this, Morgana. After this you will have one more task to do and that is the most important one of all."

Morgana regarded her mother with irritation. "One more after this? What's it going to be after that one? Another errand or job? I'm getting tired, Mam, I want to go to Jenni's ball and then I want to go home."

Scathach stood up looking annoyed. "I didna know ye're bairn was such a wee whinger, Angharad. I thought she'd be stronger o'will than this."

"I do not whinge." Morgana snapped, standing up. She was secretly pleased when she realised that Scathach had to look up to look her in the eye. "I am tired of being told what to do."

Scathach laughed again, her eyes sparkling. "And there be the backbone o'ye're Papa. Meilyr were a decent warrior in his day, even if he be confined to t'Hills o'Treachery for now."

Morgana stared at her, then looked at Angharad who sat on the bed still. "Da is in the Hills of Treachery? Why?"

"He killed himself on the day you and your sister were born; the day I died, remember?" her birth mother looked sad. "He had a responsibility to you and your sister, as well as to the Kingdom. He ran away from that through guilt and grief and thus became a traitor to us."

Morgana blinked. *I remember that I considered killing myself when I was first blinded. Would I have ended up there as well?* She shivered and pushed the thought away.

"Come on, bairn, 't'is time for ye're training." Scathach turned to Angharad. "Hae ye the sword?"

Angharad stood up and moved over to a chest. "Yes. It's in here."

"Gie it to her."

Angharad unlocked the chest and retrieved a sword that was the length of Morgana's thigh. It's blade was an odd shape; wide and rounded next to the hilt, curving sinuously on both sides into a straight edged lower blade with a very narrow point.

"This was mine during my training. It is finely balanced, and you should find it easy to use." She laid it carefully in Morgana's hand. "May it serve you well."

Twenty Three

Nex landed on the path beside the bridge over the Cocytus. The air around them was thick with icy fog and the Judged who walked past the party of Daemons shivered and shook as they stepped up onto the crystalline structure.

"So, what's over the bridge?" Morbus asked his sister when she'd returned to human form.

She looked up at him from her exhausted sprawl on the sand with a pained look on her face. "Morbus, when we get back to the Fire Realm, I am going to suggest to our Great Grandfather that you are given tutoring on research techniques."

"Why? It's the woman's duty to be intelligent; I'm just here as muscle." He shrugged and turned back into a hound.

The two Minotaurs shook their heads. "He's giving male daemons..." Meranus said.

"...a bad reputation, Nex." Terius finished.

"Stop that you two." Deumara told them without too much heat. "You give me a headache when you start finishing each other's sentences."

The twins grinned as sheepishly as only a pair of Minotaurs could.

"Hecate is over there." Nex said, glaring at the hound, who whined and ducked his head.

"Yes, she is. We really ought to be moving on quickly." Mara said.

Nex sighed and stood up. "You'd like to ride again, I take it?"

"No, cousin. I shall walk. Morbus!" The hound looked at Deumara. "Become a horse and carry your sister carefully. She needs some rest." She snapped her fingers and before Morbus fully realised what he was doing, he'd become a black stallion.

Nex pulled herself up on his back. *"Thank you, brother."*

"I'm doing it because you're my sister. Not because she told me to." He replied, extending his mane a little and wrapping it gently around her waist to hold her safely.

The bridge arched up and away from the path, glistening in the odd twilight that covered the underworld.

"That looks..." Meranus started.

"Slippery." Terius finished.

Deumara watched some of the Judged who were making their way up the slope in front of them. They slid and fell many times before they reached the peak. "It does look a little precarious. Go test it."

Terius and Meranus exchanged a look before putting one hoof each on the crystal bridge. They pushed their weight against the bridge and began to inch carefully up the arch. The two Minotaurs got about halfway up the curve and fell over with a bump, grabbing for each other. They slid back down, snout first, and levered themselves up, snorting sand out of their nostrils.

"That could be dangerous." Morbus said to Nex.

She was too exhausted to do anything except nod with her eyes closed.

Deumara watched the Judged a little longer. As the Damned Souls got to the edge of the bridge, they stepped up out of the ankle deep sand, their feet thickly covered with the pale grains.

She leaned down to touch the bridge. The crystal was cold enough to have an aura of chill and she snatched her hand away before her skin could stick to the surface. Scooping a handful of cold sand up, she sprinkled it on the bridge. It slid back down to mound up at the edge of the path.

"You would have to wet the surface." Morbus said.

"The bridge is too cold, water would freeze." Mara said.

"The bridge is made of Ice." Nex sighed. "Send Meranus and Terius up it with their firehoof spell active and it will melt enough that you can follow on a sand trail they leave."

Deumara looked at the exhausted female daemon on the horse with new found respect. "I understand why Prince Apollyon insisted that you come along now."

She turned to the minotaur twins. "Do you two understand what Nex has suggested?"

They nodded and each of them scooped a double handful of sand up. Then with a whisper they set their hooves on fire. The sand beneath them glowed and the grains melted and began to run together.

Meranus took one step up onto the bridge. The ice began to melt, and he sprinkled sand onto it. As he stepped away, the cold of the bridge froze the melt water and ice together, leaving a rough surface. Terius did the same next to his brother. Together they made their way slowly up the arc of the bridge leaving a rough sandy surface on the bridge.

When they reached the top, Morbus followed Terius and Deumara followed Meranus. The group paused at the top to consider their next move.

"Turn your firehooves off. You'll melt through the bridge and then where will we be." Mara looked out over the land between this river and the last one, the Styx. "That's the Land of Dread. It'd be best if we get through this one as fast as possible."

Nex stirred on her brother's back. "The Grassland of Apathy is worse."

"We'll sort that problem out when we get to the next bridge." Mara shook her head. "I've heard that the Fears come onto the path here; they aren't content to wait for the Judged to come to them."

"We won't have any Fears after us though?" Terius sounded worried.

"Have you ever acted out of fear?" Deumara asked. "Killed out of fear of dying or lashed out because you were scared of the creature in front of you?"

Meranus shrugged. "Dunno."

"Well, we'll soon find out. Down there." Mara pointed. "Now, we'll slide down the other side of the bridge. Morbus take care of your sister."

SCATHACH WATCHED WHILE Morgana struggled into the saddle on Amira's back. "Come on Lass, the day may not wane here, but time is passing and ye will need all ye can get."

The mare stood so still she felt like a warm statue as Morgana fought the weight of the armour she wore. "I've never felt this heavy before." The girl complained, pushing the scabbard of her sword away from her leg.

"Aye, e'en Celestial Silver hae more weight than ye're used ta wearing. Still, if ye can nae hold its weight on horseback, what chance hae ye in battle?"

"None I suppose." Morgana patted Amira's neck. "Thank you, my friend, for staying so still."

"It was of no moment, Friend. Must we run with all these confining straps?" the mare shook her head and eyed the reins that Morgana gathered up in disgust.

"Aye, sweet animal, ye must." Scathach pulled herself up onto Aurelia's back as if the steel scale and thick leather she wore were the thinnest silk. The other mare's long mane and tail had been braided tightly so that it didn't dangle under her hooves. "If you and the lass are to fight, she must have the security of familiar strapping.

Once ye're both used to each other, then ye may try fighting together bareback."

"We have to fight on horseback?" Morgana gasped.

Scathach nudged Aurelia into movement and after a moment, Amira followed the Vanner.

"Aye lass. To begin with ye must hunt my foster son down from the forest of Elysium." The warrior woman gestured toward the dark mass of trees on the horizon. "He finds the forest soothing and loves to ride amongst the trees. So ye must find him and challenge him."

Morgana absorbed these instructions. *Why is it so important that I learn to fight? To show my courage? Haven't I done that by surviving the journey thus far?* She considered the questions as Scathach put her and Amira through their paces, changing gaits and speeds as they rode around the pasture outside the Palace.

A small audience of gods and souls gathered to watch the spectacle and applauded when Morgana and Amira pulled off a particularly difficult manoeuvre.

"Ye've done this before, child." Scathach said as she called a halt.

Morgana blinked. "What? This is just dressage. I was pretty good at that before I went blind."

The woman frowned and shook her head. "No. I think ye're recalling more than the formal dance of horse and rider as ye learned it. Your connection with Amira is deeper than that of horse and rider."

"It's my sister that is good with horses. You should see what she can get them to do with just a look." Morgana laughed. "Her blue mare, Twilight, will run beside her and let her vault over her back without flinching."

"That is her talent, Morgana." Angharad appeared beside her daughter with a glass. "All our family have a talent with particular animals. Jenni's is with Horses, dogs and dragons, although she hasn't met any true dragons yet." She passed the glass up to Morgana who drank the contents gratefully, suddenly aware of how thirsty she'd become.

Thanatos rode up on Ghyrdepal. "Is there a problem?"

"Aye, Reaper. The child appears to be more skilled than she knows."

"And this is a problem how?"

"I'm not certain yet. We'll try something a little more difficult. Can ye bring a warrior or two t'help us?"

"I'll summon some." Thanatos rode off a little way and after a few moments had passed a shimmer in front of him marked the arrival of several riders wearing similar armour to Morgana.

Scathach ignored what the god was doing and circled Aurelia around Morgana, Amira and Angharad. "Ye've never fought before, hae ye?"

"I told you that. I went to Ballet, not Kickboxing." Morgana was confused.

"That might account o'some of ye're grace, but nay as much as this. Draw ye're blade." The woman watched as Morgana slid her mother's sword from its scabbard. Then she grunted and looked over at the riders. "Defend ye're self." She rode away.

Angharad gasped as the riders thundered toward them. "Watch out, Morgana. Guard yourself." She disappeared.

The riders circled her, calling out challenges and insults.

Morgana let out a shriek as she realised what was going on. Amira trembled slightly under her, but Morgana realised it wasn't from fear. "Are you enjoying this, Amira?"

"I am. This is fun for us. You have a job to do however." The mare replied, watching the horses around her.

"What do I do?" the girl asked, trying to watch all the riders at once.

"Pick a challenge to answer." Amira told her. Then she whinnied and one of the horses answered her. "I'd go for the boy in the blue tunic. He's the least experienced warrior, he died in his first battle."

"How did you know that?"

"His steed told me. Get on with it or you'll end up fighting from a weak position." Amira tensed.

*Okay then, the blue tunic...*Morgana took a deep breath and kneed Amira forward, dropping her reins and leaning forward as they charged the boy warrior. He gasped and just about brought his shield up in time to deflect her blow. They exchanged half a dozen blows before she managed to flick the point of her sword across his knee, drawing first blood.

"Excellent, well done lass." Scathach called out. "Watch your shield arm, it's dropping a little after a round."

How did I do that? Morgana blinked as the boy blurred and disappeared. "Did I hurt him?"

"He's a soul. How could you hurt him." Amira seemed confused.

"Good point. Now what?"

"Defend yourself, oh incredulous wench!" a voice roared, and another rider charged her.

Morgana barely brought her shield up in time. "What did you call me?" she asked the man who assailed her.

"You are nothing but a harlot, wielding a table knife." He sneered.

Their horses circled, close enough for Morgana to feel the heat of the other horse on her leg.

"That's what I thought." Morgana replied and attacked, using the flat of her blade against his edge. It slid down and caught in the hand guard. Instinctively she twisted her wrist and the man's sword flew out of his hand to land point first in the grass.

"Now what are you going to do?" She enquired, flicking the point of her sword to his throat. She straightened her arm a little and

Amira took a single step toward the other horse. The point scratched the man's throat, drawing blood; he blurred and disappeared.

"Good. Try not to talk so much; you need your breath for fighting." Scathach shouted. "Pick another and try again."

They continued in the same way for another four bouts. Each one finished at first blood with the disappearance of her opponent.

Eventually, Scathach called a halt. "T'is enough for the moment. Go back to the palace and rest. We shall continue in the morning."

A page boy in Hades' livery appeared beside Morgana. "Lady Morgana, my master wishes you to attend him in the courtyard."

Scathach frowned. "What be Lord Hades up to now?"

"I suppose we should go find out." Morgana sighed. Amira began to walk toward the palace without any urging as Morgana gathered the reins.

"I think t'morra ye could fight bareback and hae the same results as today." The woman warrior said as they rode. "I wish I could work out how ye can fight so well wi 'oot training."

"I don't know. If you'd asked me to fight before I came here, then I would have run away rather than even attempt it." Morgana thought of all the times she and Jenni had argued and Jenni had won, because Morgana was too scared of losing her sister's love to fight back.

"Aye, I can believe that, child. But that is nae what I am referring to."

The horses muted hoof beats turned crisp and echoing as they entered the courtyard.

Coming to a halt in front of the steps where Hades, Persephone and Thanatos stood, Morgana and Scathach dismounted.

Grooms rushed forward to take the horses to the stables. Morgana stumbled slightly as she tried to get her bearings on the pavement.

"Steady lass." Scathach helped her stand straight.

"I'll be okay." Morgana stretched her back and legs. "I'm not used to being on horseback for so long."

"Aye, I suppose ye would nae, being a princess an' all. Ride in carriages a lot do ye?" Scathach snorted.

She wouldn't understand about cars. Morgana suppressed a giggle. "Something like that."

Hades stepped forward. "Lady Scathach, have you completed your assessment?"

"Aye, m'lord. The child has the potential." The warrior smiled at Morgana. "E'en if she dinnae know it."

"You have one more rest period to train her and then the task must take place." The god looked at Morgana. "We must hurry, there is danger approaching and should you not leave here before it arrives at the palace, you may never leave the Underworld."

Twenty - Four

"For a forest in the underworld, this place is far too relaxing." Morgana muttered as she and Scathach rode into the trees.

The warrior smiled. "That's because this is in the Elysium Fields. If ye want a creepy forest, ye need ta go inta t'Land o'Dread."

"I thought that place was full of marshes and bogs." Morgana stretched her neck. *I don't feel like I've slept. I ache more now than I did the last time I swam for the school.*

"It is. That be the clearer areas o't'land." Scathach looked around. "T'is calming here, and ma Foster Son be free of the need to prove himself amongst the trees."

"How is Kuklayne your foster son?" Morgana was starting to feel nervous. *I need to know more about him.*

"He came to me as a young man after he had made a name for himself in Eireland. I taught him the skills that he'd not gained there, and he returned to them the greatest of Eire's warriors." Scathach snorted. "He also decided he liked ma twin sister, Aife and wooed her after defeating her in battle."

"Did he marry her?" Morgana ducked under a low branch.

"Aye. T'was a wonderful ceremony. They had a son together. "Scathach smiled at the memory and Morgana had a glimpse of what the warrior woman must have been like as a girl. "But I nae think this be the right discussion for just before a challenge, Child."

They emerged into a clearing. On one side of the space lay a pond, a small steam leaving it to trickle past them into the forest. A small roundhouse with tiny round windows and a thatched roof had been constructed next to the pond and around the house, beds full of plants flourished. Smoke rose from a hole in the roof.

"It seems he has set up home here." Scathach muttered, her eyebrows drawing down into a frown. "Ye may not need to hunt for him at all."

"Now what?" Morgana asked as they dismounted.

"Call out the phrase I taught you."

Morgana sighed and stretched a little, then she loosened her sword in its scabbard and took a deep breath, running over the odd sounding words in her head.

"Siuthad!" Scathach muttered.

Morgana had heard that one a lot in the last day or so during her 'training'. *I know that means hurry up, but the thought of fighting someone like this is scary!* She sighed. For a moment she caught a movement beside the window. *He's in there and doesn't want to come out.*

"Child, if you don't hurry up and challenge him, I will." Scathach was clearly losing her patience.

Morgana nodded, and reluctantly turned toward the house, planting her feet and placing her hands on her hips. "Kuklayne! Teann a-nall agus."

There was a long moment of silence, then a voice called out. "Chan eagal dha." He sounded anxious.

"Tsk. Baoghaltachd." Scathach growled. "Say it again."

"Kuklayne! Teann a-nall agus." Morgana tried again. *I sounded more confident that time.*

"Faoin!" the voice replied.

"Try the second phrase. It's more formal and might jolt him out of whatever idiotic idea he's got this time." Scathach let Aurelia's head go and the mare wandered away to drink from the stream.

Morgana followed suit with Amira. "Don't go too far, Amira." She told her new friend.

"I won't. You might need me." Amira replied and followed Aurelia.

"Go on child."

"Kuklayne, Mi dùbhlanaich sibh." Morgana called, making it sound as serious and deadly as she could.

"Dèan as" the voice replied.

"Cuibheas!" Scathach exploded and marched up to the front door. "Òigear! You will open this door right now."

The door opened slightly. A torrent of Scottish gaelic poured out of the gap. Scathach replied more furiously with a lot of arm movement. Morgana watched as the argument through the door continued and finally, she couldn't help it any longer; she burst out laughing.

The disagreement paused and Scathach looked back at her. "What be funny, lass? Ye're on a task, nae at an entertainment."

Morgana wiped the smile from her face. "Uh... nothing, Scathach."

The woman turned back and after a final volley of gaelic turned away with a satisfied smile on her face. She marched over to Morgana. "He'll respond properly now."

Morgana nodded. "Which phrase shall I use?"

"The formal one."

"Kuklayne, Mi dùbhlanaich sibh." Morgana called

The door opened and a man stepped out, shield on one arm and sword in the other hand. "Mi Gabh." He ducked his head through the doorway and stood up straight.

Morgana blinked. *I'm not sure if it's my imagination, but he's roughly the same size as I am. I thought he was supposed to be a giant.*

"Draw your sword, lass." Scathach's voice recalled her to what she was supposed to be doing.

She did as she was bid, the hilt feeling warm and steady in her grasp. Then she stepped forward. "Siuthad, Kuklayne. Teann a-nall agus, Bodach"

"Bodach?" Kuklayne blinked. "I'm not that old."

Scathach snorted again, covering her mouth. "Aye, ye are, to this lass anyway."

"Ma!" Kuklayne hissed at her.

Morgana sighed. "Can we get on with it, please."

"Hark! listen to the child." He stepped forward, crouching slightly and holding his blade with the point toward her. He suddenly looked a lot more menacing. "Well, seeing as you're so eager, Òganach..."

Morgana dropped into the position Scathach had taught her and smiled. *I suddenly feel a lot more confident. I wonder why.*

Scathach moved back from them, watching them circle. She frowned trying to figure out why they suddenly looked so similar. *It cannae just be the training I gae her.*

A flurry of movement ended in a clash of blade and shield.

Morgana spun as Kuklayne appeared behind her and only just got her shield up again to stop the slash that descended on her shoulder. Her arm felt the weight of his blow and without thinking, she struck back under it, aiming for his legs.

He jumped her blade and struck for her shield shoulder again.

He's trying to disable me quickly. Morgana thought as she caught the blow on her shield again, feeling the blow make her arm ache a little.

"Do air thoiseach croilige a-mhàin" Scathach called. "Kuklayne, this be a task, nay a true battle, remember."

"Do you think me a fool, ma?" The warrior opposite Morgana replied. "I'm nae going to harm a leanabh tlachdmhor like this."

He's not even out of breath! Morgana felt a little more scared. Then the gaelic words he'd used translated itself in the back of her mind. *He said leanabh tlachdmhor... Cherub? He thinks I'm weak like a baby? I'll give him cherub.* She took a deep breath and began to attack instead of just defending.

Scathach laughed out loud. "Aye foster son, she's a real folainteach; folainteach cathach!"

Trainee Warrior. Morgana smiled at that. *That's a compliment.* Then her mind went blank as a red mist dropped down over her vision. She began to move automatically, as if she had been trained in combat since she was small and not just over the last two days.

"The ríastrad!" Kuklayne backed away, defending himself with sword and shield. "Who taught her to go into that?"

"I hae no idea. I certainly ne'er thought her capable o'battle frenzy." Scathach frowned. "Try not to hurt her."

"I may not hae a choice." He gasped, narrowly missing losing his ear as Morgana sliced down by swaying sideways. He blocked the blade. "The good thing about the ríastrad is that you can't think clearly in it. I just have to avoid... damn."

"Air thoiseach croilige!" Scathach crowed with delight, as blood from a long shallow slice on Kuklayne's arm dribbled across his tanned skin. "Stop Morgana, stop!"

Morgana heard Scathach's voice, but nothing registered. All she knew was that the man in front of her was attacking her and she had to kill him. She pressed her advantage as he lessened his defence and moved him backward toward a rough log bench that would impede his progress enough for her get a killing blow in.

Kuklayne moved backward. "I don't want to have to hurt her to bring her out of ríastrad."

Scathach scanned the area. The pond attracted her attention. "Drop her into the spring. The water ought to shock her out of frenzy."

The warrior nodded and changed direction with a swift side step, avoiding both Morgana's attack and being pinned up against the bench. He took a quick look around to judge how far from the pond he was, before he lured her closer to him by dropping his shield as if by accident.

"Chan eagal dha." Morgana yelled and dropped her own shield to grasp her sword with both hands.

Scathach gasped and flinched. "Such risk. She must be so deep in frenzy that she canna comprehend it."

"Don't worry, ma." Kuklayne dropped his sword and spread his arms wide as if surrendering.

Morgana screamed out in triumph and rushed in for the kill.

Kuklayne grabbed the hilt of her sword with one hand, his larger hand covering both of hers. As he put the other hand on her shoulder, he feinted with his knee, thrusting it toward her stomach.

Morgana gasped, arched her back so that her stomach moved away from his knee and felt her balance falter. She tried to correct her stance, but it was too late.

Kuklayne brought his knee down and pivoted on that foot, both hands holding her as he dragged her forward into a throw.

Morgana sailed through the air, dropping her blade point first into the soil by the spring before she plunged into the water head first. As she went under, the red mist lifted and she dove deeper into the pool, feeling the coolness of the liquid around her on her skin.

She came to a stop just above the spring's bed, hovering in the faintly blue water. *What am I doing? I was just supposed to scratch him to pass the task.*

A light sparkled in the water beside her, growing in size until it resembled a figure in shape. *Morgana.* The voice in her mind resembled that of both Jenni and Angharad.

"*Who are you?*"

"*I am she who placed thine line upon this track. Thou art but one part of the salvage of thine Realm.*" The figure stroked her face with one hand.

"*Then what am I doing in this pond?*" Morgana looked around. "*I can't help anything down here.*"

"*Thou hast one task left. Save thine sister.*"

Morgana frowned. *"She has lots of friends to save her."*

"True, she has many friends, but only one sister. In one Earth days' time, in Llanirstyr Realm, a poisoner paid by the enemies of thine sister's rule shall attack her.

Thou art the only one who can misdirect his hand, for it is in thine powers alone. The Shield of Courage shall guard thee from sight and thine mother's blade protect thee."

"So, I have to go to Llanirstyr and save Jenni from being poisoned. What about my illness? And the blindness?" Morgana shivered at the thought of living as blind again. *"If I leave here, I'll be blind again."*

"Nay, sweet daughter. Charon hath given thee the way to heal thineself and thy sister, as well as banish thine sister's attacker unharmed." The light began to fade. *"Fare thee well, mine Chosen one."*

The light disappeared completely, and Morgana realised she was about to run out of air. With a massive kick, she pushed herself back to the surface.

Twenty - Five

Kuklayne whistled and a pale bay gelding trotted out of the forest behind the roundhouse. "We have to go up to the palace."

"What about the shield?" Morgana felt confused. One minute she'd been lying on the grass drying out in the warmth of the Elysium Fields atmosphere, almost asleep; the next Scathach had been shaking her awake and looking worried.

"Lord Hades hae summoned us."

"I don't understand." The girl yawned. "I'm tired, I just want to rest."

"The lord of the underworld has summoned all the warriors of the Elysium to the palace. You have proved yourself as one of those warriors." Kuklayne glared at her. "I will not have you belittling your accomplishment this day."

Morgana sat up. "Oh, all right. Give me a moment."

Amira nudged her with her nose. "Come my friend, we must return quickly. Merla summoned us."

"She did? When?" Morgana looked around for the raven.

"Near on an hour ago, child. Ye hae been sleeping since we helped ye out o't'pond yonder." Scathach said, her voice getting rougher as she became exasperated. "Ye slept for o'er four hours!"

Four hours? It's been that long since I climbed out of the spring? Morgana stood up, using Amira as a ladder. "I didn't realise. Sorry."

"'tis nae a problem, but if we dinnae get to the palace quickly there may be one." Scathach vaulted onto Aurelia's back, gathering the reins up in both hands.

"The shield is at the palace anyway." Kuklayne mounted his gelding. "I left it there when I moved here."

Morgana pulled herself up onto Amira, feeling heavy and sleepy still. "Where's my sword and shield?"

"I put them into the bag ye carry, along wi'ye armour. I dinnae think ye'd need them." Scathach sighed. "Once we know what is happenin', we can remedy that."

The bag? Hang on. Morgana pulled the bag from its position behind the saddle and started rummaging through it. She found the wooden box and opened it.

"What are you doing? We have to go now." Kuklayne growled.

"Hang on. I've got something that might help me feel better." Morgana looked at the vials inside. *Merla said the green ones would wash away tiredness.* Plucking a green stoppered vial from the box, she opened and swallowed the contents. *Mmm, chocolate and mint this time.* The heavy feeling dropped away and she became more alert. "That's better." She murmured as she put the box away. "Come on Amira, let's race these two to the palace."

Amira threw her head up and was off at a canter almost as soon as Morgana gripped the reins.

Kuklayne and Scathach followed.

THE SCENE THAT GREETED them as they arrived at the palace was one that Morgana would never forget. Hundreds of warriors stood outside the gates, in full armour. Some were on horseback, some on foot, but all of them meant business.

This lot look scary. I thought there might be more of them though. She said as much to Scathach, who smiled wryly.

"Aye, ye'd think that. Most end up on the Plains of War and once they have done their time, the majority o'them choose the waters o't'Lethe and rebirth. Those who ye see are either heroes that the gods hae awarded immortality or are those who hae chosen to remain in Elysium."

"Are you and Kuklayne heroes then?" they had ridden through the last rank of warriors and behind them, rows of spirits stood quietly.

"Kuklayne is, aye. I decided to stay here until I were truly needed in the Mortal realms." The horses hooves clattered as they entered the front courtyard and the noise bounced off the buildings around them.

Thanatos met them at the foot of the steps. "Excellent timing. Lord Hades is holding a council of war inside and will need your input."

The grooms took the horses away as the three of them followed Thanatos inside.

"What's going on?" Kuklayne asked.

"The underworld has been invaded by a group of Daemon from the Fire Realm." Hades said in answer to Kuklayne's question.

Morgana blinked. *Daemon? Fire Realm? What on earth is going on here?* She surrendered her bag to a maid and sat beside her mother.

"Scathach, you and your son will take charge of the Celtic contingent for the battle. Ares will be taking the Greek and Roman commands, and I will handle command of the rest." Hades said, pointing out the layout of the small army on a perfectly formed model of the palace and the surrounding fields. "I will also be calling in the Monsters under Hecate's leadership. She's the one who sent word of where the Daemon are; she's currently stalling them with illusions."

"We can send them packing easily." Kuklayne exchanged a confident look with Ares. "Five Daemon against several thousand heroes and monsters; hah!"

"They are here for a reason though. We must find out what it is." Hades insisted.

Morgana felt herself sway and her mind drifted back to the pond, Arianrhod's voice echoing through her thoughts. *She has many friends, but only one sister. In a days time, in Llanirstyr Realm, a poisoner paid by the enemies of thine sister's rule shall attack her. Thou art the only one who can misdirect his hand, for it is in thine powers alone. The Shield of Courage shall guard thee from sight and thine mother's blade protect thee.*

Angharad caught her as the girl bumped into her shoulder. "Are you all right, Little One?"

"I know why they are here." Morgana murmured. She turned to Hades. "My Lord Hades, have I completed the tasks to allow me to leave the Underworld?"

"Yes. With Kuklayne's defeat in the challenge, you are free to leave when you wish." Hade smiled. "Is there anything you wish to take with you?"

"Yes. My Mother's sword and the Shield of Courage. My sister in Llanirstyr is in mortal peril and Arianrhod told me to take it to aid me in saving her." Morgana ignored her mother's gasp of fear. "The people who threaten her have sent a poisoner to her ball. I must bring them to justice as is my duty."

"Amira is waiting to carry you to the door." Charon said. "I will accompany you to ensure your safety."

Morgana shook her head. "No, Amira needs to stay here until it is time for her rebirth. I think I should leave quickly and even Amira is not fast enough."

"Very well, we shall go by boat. My lady awaits." Charon bowed.

"Hang on. Why the Shield of Courage?" Kuklayne asked. "Arianrhod told me to look after it with my life, it should stay here as well."

"Did ye nae listen to the lass?" Scathach snorted. "Arianrhod told her ta take it wi' her."

"Oh. Good point." Kuklayne shrugged. "I'll go get it." He stood and left the room.

"You said you knew why they were here, child." Hades said.

"Arianrhod said that she'd placed my line upon this path and that I was one part of the salvage of my world. If I'm one part, Jenni must be the other. I caught a glimpse of a golden cauldron in Arianrhod's mind, and I feel that the shield is bound to the cauldron and myself in some way." Morgana looked at her mother. "The invaders must be part of it as well; why else come here when I am?"

Angharad smiled and stroked her face. "It's a possibility. Either way I would feel better if you were with your sister anyway."

Kuklayne returned carrying a large round golden shield bearing a tree surmounted by a pentacle. He held it out to Morgana. "Receive the Shield of Courage, High Princess Morgana of Llanirstyr. Use it in battle to save thine sister from the evils which beset her."

"Thank you, Ser Kuklayne of Elysium." Morgana took the shield by the rim. It shrank slightly to fit her physical size.

She traced one finger over the pentacle and gasped as more figures appeared in front of the tree, glowing enamelled colour slowly spreading out from where her finger touched the metal.

Scathach chortled. "'Tis nae just the Shield o'Courage any more, lass. The Bear is strength and rebirth. Before the tree in the pond 'tis a water dragon, suggesting that ye hae strong intuition and the ability to use the power o'ye mind."

"What about the horse?" Morgana asked, touching the noble looking animal above the dragon. White touched with a silver grey filled the creature and she could have sworn that it winked at her.

"That's to help you with enduring the final trial to come." Thanatos said. "The horse symbolises power, stamina and faithfulness." He looked a little closer at it. "It even looks a little like Amira."

Morgana laughed. "It does doesn't it."

Merla fluttered in through an open window to land on Charon's shoulder. "Lady Hecate has arrived with her troops, Lord Hades. The daemons are not too far behind her."

Hades rose. "Charon, get the Princess to the Hall of Worlds door as quickly as possible. We shall entertain our 'guests' until you return."

Angharad stood as well. "May I go with my daughter, Lord Hades?"

The Lord of the Underworld looked at her. "You cannot leave the Underworld, but I will allow you to go to the exit with her." Angharad curtseyed gracefully and the God smiled. "As if I would refuse to allow a mother to say farewell to her daughter in privacy." He left the room.

Morgana watched as everyone else rose and followed him. Scathach letting the others go ahead as she hung behind, looking at the girl.

"Good Luck, Lass, it hae been a pleasure training ye." The smaller woman hugged Morgana fiercely, blinking. "Be careful and watch your left; you don't want anyone getting' t'jump on ye."

Morgana hugged her back and grinned. "I've had a lot of fun, *Muime*, I will miss you."

Scathach let go and Angharad said. "We'd best go get ready for the journey, Morgana. Lord Charon, I will bring her down to the Landing through the tunnel."

Charon nodded. "That would be safest. Make sure you bring everything you've been given with you, Princess. This is a one way trip." He gestured to Scathach. "Come Lady Scathach. I shall escort you to your command."

Morgana felt her heart plummet as they left. *I'll be all alone soon. I wish I could bring Amira with me, but she's a soul; she can't leave the Underworld.*

Sensing her daughter's mood, Angharad slipped an arm around her and guided her out of the room and up the stairs.

Twenty – Six

Deumara, Nex and the others stopped at the top of the rise overlooking the Palace of Hades.

Morbus changed back into human form "Looks like they're expecting us." The Minotaurs grunted, amusement suffusing their faces.

"Considering the show Hecate just put on for us, I had expected a welcoming party." Deumara shrugged elegantly. "I think it would be rude of us not to attend."

"Indeed, Mara." Nex agreed. "They've gone to a lot of trouble with the entertainment. See the ring of monsters around the palace walls in front of the human warriors? They think to tire us with a dance before inviting us in."

"We ought to hurry on in then." Mara grinned, starting down the hill.

Halfway down the hill, a group awaited them.

"Hold, Daemons." The lead figure boomed out. "Go no further until we have officially parlayed."

"That would be Ares then." Morbus said to his sister through their mind link.

"You think?" Nex shot back. *"Our Prince said that this would happen, remember?"*

"He also said that we had to get the shield and return as quickly as possible." Morbus rolled his neck on his shoulders. *"I hate to say this, but I don't think we're going to get it."*

"Pessimist." Nex took a deep breath as they came to a halt opposite the party, Mara carefully keeping the path between them.

"Why should we take orders from a group of second rate deities?" she asked, slouching arrogantly against Terius' shoulder.

"Your barbs are poisonless, little daemon." Ares replied. "Only the High Princes of your realm have the same level of power as I. You will do as you are told."

"He has a point." Nex pointed out to Mara silently. *"We are almost powerless here, despite our status back home."*

"I know that, cousin. I'm not stupid like the Minos Twins." Mara snapped.

"What do you want, Daemon?" Ares squared his shoulders. "If it is within my remit, I shall give it to you and allow you to depart the Underworld unharmed."

"A negotiation. They're stalling for some reason." Mara mused to Nex.

"Go along with it. Our Prince had certain commands to do with this part of our mission." Nex told her.

Mara turned surprised eyes on her cousin. *"He gave you commands that he didn't give me? Doesn't he trust me?"*

Nex gave a little bark of laughter. "Apollyon trusts no one. You were told things that we weren't. He likes to keep us off balance." She said in a low voice that only reached Mara's and Morbus' ears.

"Shhh." Mara replied, her eyes sparkling. *"Care to share?"*

"You and the twins will have to deal with the gods yourselves. We have been told to track the shield..." Nex dropped her eyes to the sand.

Deumara stiffened. *"The Minos and I are the distraction? I'm not going to accept that role."*

Morbus, who had been following the conversation while watching the gods opposite them, coughed pointedly. *"We will come back for you, Lady, I promise on my honour as a Prince of the Fire Realm. However, you have been silent too long, and our hosts are getting impatient."*

Nex sighed. *He's still infatuated with her. Damn.*

Mara flung her hair back over her shoulder and stepped forward. "We told Lord Hades what we are seeking. Do not distract us from our goal."

Ares inclined his head and smiled. "It was merely an opening, lady."

Mara smiled. "Of course, Lord Hades. Why all the distractions? We were told at the crossing of the Acheron we had three tasks to complete to win the Shield of Courage. Our first was to make it here."

"This is of course true." Ares said. "Your second task is to make your way through the forces below without losing any of your number. All five of you must arrive at the gates of the Palace."

"You think that bunch of tired, ancient heroes and ignorant monsters will make us falter?" The Daemon Princess laughed out loud. "Let us hurry to the Palace, Lord Ares and you will soon see what we are made of in the Fire Realm."

Ares joined in her laughter. "I am sure we will. Abide here a moment and allow us the courtesy of re-joining our forces for the battle ahead."

Mara swept and expansive hand down toward the gathered warriors and monsters. "We can wait that long, Lord Ares."

He bowed and the group of deities walked back to their horses, mounted and rode down the hill.

"Are you ready, my friends?" Mara said as she turned to them.

"We are always ready for battle." The Minos Twins bellowed, their voices carrying down the hill and making some of the retreating deities look back.

Morbus and Nex exchanged a look which Mara intercepted. "You are wondering how we are going to do this, aren't you." She said.

"Frankly? Yes. If we all have to arrive at the gates to the palace together, we will be observed the whole time. How can we track the shield that way?" Morbus sat down, undoing the laces of his boots and tightening them.

"I have been thinking." Mara said. "You and Nex caught the scent of the Llanirstyri Princess at the House of the Fates, yes?"

Nex nodded.

"She is the one who is our rival here. Find her and you will find the shield." Mara finished.

Nex's eyes widened, and she sat down beside her brother. "I know how to do this."

"Carry on." Mara sat opposite her, motioning to the twins to sit. "Relax you two, they aren't going anywhere, and a little rest won't hurt us." Terius and Meranus sank onto the grass, pulling food and drink out of their packs.

"Morbus and I take Hound form. We flank you on the way down the hill and in the first few moments of battle, after that we all split up and fight separately." Nex paused and took a swallow of water from her bottle.

"Risky. I assume that you and your brother will meet up and track the Princess." Mara popped a dried date into her mouth and chewed.

"Exactly. I will stay in mind contact with you and Morbus so we can find you again." Nex said.

"Good. What will you do if you find her?" Mara tossed Nex a fig.

"Kill her and take the shield. Then we'll meet up with you and head for the exit to the Hall. Once in the Hall we can slip into a world and use the portal box Prince Apollyon gave us to get home." Morbus finished his sister's train of thought smoothly aloud as she ate the fig.

Mara laughed. "We'll be celebrated throughout the fire realm if we can pull this off."

"No harm in taking a short rest then is there?" Morbus asked, stretching out on the grass of the hill."

"It would be best to be well rested before our battle, true." Mara said and one by one the daemons laid down and dozed in the grass.

High above them, a raven circled, a mere speck against the soft twilight sky of the Elysium fields. When all five of the daemons were sleeping it shot away, straight as an arrow to the Palace.

HADES RECEIVED THE Raven's report with good humour. "It seems that our guests are taking a rest before they attack." He laughed. "If I were one of their High Princes, I would have fallen on them where they lay and slaughtered them."

"Aye, 'tis a curse to be honourable." Scathach agreed. She glanced back at the palace.

"Don't worry about the *folainteach cathach*." Kuklayne said in a low voice. "She'll be fine. Charon is taking her to the exit remember."

"She hae nae left yet Lad." The warrior woman said absently. "If they break through before she does, we may lose both her and the shield."

"She is under Artemis' protection, Lady Scathach." Thanatos said as he ran a blade of grass down his scythe. "The Lady of the Moon will not allow her to be caught." The grass split into three thin slices, floating softly to the ground.

Up in the palace, Morgana gazed out at the assembled warriors, fretting. "I should be out there with them. It's my duty as a warrior."

Angharad looked up from repacking her daughter's satchel. "This from the girl who told me that she didn't even like watching Martial Arts movies?"

Morgana turned and sat down on the chaise by the window. "Mam, there is something inside of me that enjoys the Warrior's Art. I found it during the last task. I should use it for good."

"And you will be." Angharad finished folding a beautiful blue velvet gown and laid it into the satchel. She placed Morgana's blanket and the box which Charon had given her on top and did the buckles up. "You have to rescue your sister in Llanirstyr remember."

"I know." Morgana looked at the floor, feeling her throat clog up. Angharad floated over. "What's the matter, *Genethig?*" she sat down beside her daughter, laying one arm around her.

The teenager snuggled up to her mother, breathing in her scent and storing the memory of her mother's voice away for the future. The sound of Welsh made the lump in her throat harder to swallow and she struggled to breathe. *When I leave here, I'll never see you again. I don't want to lose you now I've got to know you.* She thought.

Angharad watched the tears overflow from Morgana's bright blue eyes and sighed. "You don't want to leave me, do you?"

The girl shook her head and closed her eyes, sobbing quietly.

"Your Soul Lock has been released, Morgana." Angharad reminded her. "If you make the conscious choice to remain here in the Underworld, Charon will have no choice but to take you to the beginning of the Tiring Path and you'll have to suffer for your sins before you see me again. You can't just stay here in Elysium."

"But at least I would see you again. If I leave, I'll never see you again ever." Morgana sniffed.

Angharad pulled a handkerchief out of her sleeve and flipped it open, mopping Morgana's tears up with it. "I have you in my heart, Morgana. I will treasure the time we have had together forever. I will be in Elysium until Meilyr arrives. Then once we are ready, we will choose rebirth together." She tilted her head to smile at her daughter. "We agreed when we met in Limbo that we would wait until you and your sister joined us for that, so you will see me again, I promise."

"You did?" Morgana smiled through her tears.

"Father has a gift for you and your sister. It's something I left for you when I died; so, you will always have me with you." Angharad wiped Morgana's face again and put the handkerchief away again. She kissed her cheek. "Shall we hurry up and get you to the door out of here so you can save your sister?"

Morgana nodded and stood at the same time as her mother. "I love you, Mam."

"And I love you, darling *Genethig*."

Twenty - Seven

As the Daemons charged down the hill at the combined forces of the Underworld, Angharad and Morgana slipped out of the palace compound and ran across the pasture toward a large copse of trees.

Almost as if rehearsed, those horses not taking part in the battle with their riders, moved into the path of the escaping women, hiding them from view of the battle.

Amira caught up with Morgana and kept pace with her. "Can't you take me with you?" she pleaded.

Morgana shook her head. "I'm sorry my friend. I will find you when you are reborn, I promise."

"I'll find you, you mean." The mare snorted. "No human can tell us equines apart unless we have wings on our backs or a horn on our heads."

Morgana giggled. "I'll miss you, Amira. Hurry up and be reborn please." She ran one hand down the mare's smooth coat, admiring the silvery shimmer it had. "I'll remember you though, you're on my shield."

"Good. At least I can protect you there." Amira shook her head as Arion appeared beside her.

"You are almost to the tunnel entrance, Ladies." He said. "We wish you well in your journey, Little One. We'll make sure you are safe from this end."

"Thank you, Arion." Morgana smiled as the horses turned away from them.

"You have a good friend in Amira." Angharad said.

"I know. One day she'll be reborn, and we can ride together again." Morgana looked at the black maw of the tunnel which loomed out of the trees as her mother opened the door, the fear almost paralysing her until she remembered that she'd made her way through Limbo without harm.

This is easy compared to the darkness of Limbo. It's only a tunnel. Taking a deep breath she plunged into the darkness.

THE TWINS STUCK CLOSE to Deumara as the Hounds bounded along in front of her. They sliced a few souls in half who were in the wrong place and as the monsters started to surround them, Mara gave them the signal in the form of her battle cry. "In Apollyon's Name!"

The five instantly split apart, momentarily confusing the creatures who had moved to confront them. Mara sheered left, Terius right and Meranus dove straight down the middle. The three of them hacked and slashed and generally caused mayhem while Nex and Morbus threw themselves through the attacking creatures legs without causing a single injury.

"Get to the Palace Compound." Nex told her brother. *"I imagine that the Princess is holed up in there with the shield."*

He replied with a little half bark and dodged through a group of combatants.

Nex followed, holding her amusement in as the warriors around them looked confused. One of them aimed a swipe at Morbus, but the hound avoided the man's blade and kept running.

"The Gates are just ahead, only lightly guarded." Morbus told her as she caught up.

Nex glanced ahead and saw a Hydra in the gateway. Its three heads wove a dizzying spiral as it zeroed in on the approaching Daemon Hounds. *"Lightly guarded huh? How do we get past it?"*

"Separate, snap and dodge of course." Her brother said.

Nex grinned in canine fashion as they got within striking distance of the Hydra.

Six huge red eyes glared down at the hounds. Three mouths growled draconically, the middle one leaking small flames as it did.

"Okay; if I remember correctly, the left head emits poisonous gas, the middle, fire and the right one freezes flesh instantly." Nex said as they paused to catch their breath and check the surrounding area.

"Not like the one at home then? He only has fire." Morbus sounded disappointed.

"No. I think we'll have to do a CSSD." Nex crouched as the three heads came together to attack them.

"Gotcha." Morbus crouched too and they waited until the heads were almost too close to evade. *"You give the commands this time."*

"Charge." Nex launched herself toward the Hydra. Morbus did the same. The combined movement made the Hydra flinch back violently.

Once they were under the heads far enough that the creature had to loop under its own necks to see them, they separated, Nex going right and Morbus left. The Hydra's heads separated, the gas head following Morbus and the Freeze head chasing Nex with the flame head hovering in the centre, uncertainly turning from one target to the other.

"Switch." Nex spun on the spot, her claws raking up dirt and stones from the roadway. She charged straight at Morbus who had turned at the same moment, the heads snaking around in the air and following, their targets moving too fast for them to get a shot off.

The hounds deliberately slowed as they approached each other, allowing the Hydra to zero in on them, then as all three heads decided to fire at the centre of where it thought the hounds would end up, Nex and Morbus dodged the heads and each other, circling round the creature's body to end up directly behind it.

The shots of each head scored on the other heads and as the fire hit the poisonous breath, the gas cloud exploded, giving the Hydra serious first degree burns on all three heads. The creature screeched in pain and the two daemon hounds trotted away into the Palace compound to start tracking their quarry.

Nex picked the Princess's scent up in the main hall, sniffing around one of the chairs. *"She sat here for a while, about twenty minutes ago."*

"So, while we were 'negotiating' with Ares." Morbus sniffed the chair. *"Okay, I've got her scent. Shall we continue?"*

Nex looked around at the airy white marble and soft pale silks that billowed on the breezes coming through the windows of the palace. *"Completely different feel in here to Apollyon's Throne Room."* She remarked. *"Our Prince prefers gold, red and black."*

"Well, he is a High Daemon Prince, Nex. He has to show his power in his décor." Morbus shook himself. *"Come on, we have a mission remember?"*

"Is it just a little too quiet in here or am I being paranoid?" Nex said as they paced out of the hall, following the girl's trail.

"The servants around her are more than likely souls, Nex. They probably don't appear unless you need something." Morbus shrugged.

The scent trail led upstairs into a suite that was only slightly smaller than the hall had been.

"She's been living well." Morbus yipped, his tongue lolling out in canine laughter.

"Of course she has, she's a princess. They wouldn't put her in a tiny little room with no facilities." Nex ran round the suite, checking that the girl wasn't in there anywhere. *"All clear."*

"The latest trace is going back out and down." Morbus told his sister form the top of the stairs. *"Come on. We're about ten minutes behind now."*

The two massive black hounds scraped and skidded their way back down the stairs and after a bit of confused circling in the entrance, Nex bayed and shot out of the door, her brother just behind her. The trail led out of the compound by an unguarded side gate and across a vast field full of horses.

"Why in Balor's name is this place just full of horses?" Morbus complained. *"Where are the other animals?"*

Nex snorted and dodged round a mare who had moved into her path. *"They're around here somewhere, brother. All animals come straight to the Elysium fields remember."*

Morbus growled as he was forced to slide to a stop by a shire horse and change direction. *"Well, I wish they'd all get out of the way, I keep losing the scent."*

Nex slowed and looked around. *"That's because they're herding us away from the trail. We're already about a third of a mile away from the direction the princess was heading in."*

The two stopped moving. *"Get out of our way."* They howled at the horses who had enclosed them. *"Or we'll rend your flesh from your limbs."*

A black stallion appeared in front of them. "Change form and speak properly, Daemons."

Morbus growled. *"No. We have a shield to collect, and you are in our way."*

"The Everliving shall deal with them, Arion." A silver – grey mare said.

"Besides, even if they follow the Princess to the Jetty, they won't be able to cross the river." A second mare laughed, tossing her long curled mane around.

"Good Point, ladies." Arion, the Black Stallion said. He faced the two Daemon Hounds and moved up until he was looking down his nose at them. "We have completed our task by delaying them and giving our Lady a chance to reach Charon."

Nex stared up at him. *"She's leaving the Underworld, Morbus. We have to catch up with her."*

"Agreed." Morbus growled and the horses moved away slowly, unconcerned by the noise he was making or their presence.

As soon as they could, the hounds picked the scent up again and followed it at full speed across the field and into a copse of trees. In the centre of the trees, a tunnel entrance with ornate carved marble pillars. There was a gate that barred their way.

"Down there." Nex panted and the two of them wriggled through the bars and continued their chase through the darkness, their barks and yips echoing off the dimly seen stone around and over them.

Twenty – Eight

A noise behind them made Morgana stop still, looking fearfully back up the tunnel.

"What's the matter, child?" Angharad stopped as well.

"I could have sworn that I heard dogs behind us." Morgana said, her voice trembling.

Angharad listened for a moment. "You did. It looks like the invaders have sent Daemon Hounds after us. We have to get to the jetty before they catch up with you." She started moving down the tunnel again, faster.

Morgana ran after her, not wanting to be left behind in the dark, despite the lights on the wall which lit up in front of them and turned off after they had gone past. "What happens if they catch me?"

"We know that the Daemons are here after the Shield. You are the only mortal in this realm, Morgana, if they attack and kill you for the shield you will never see your adopted home ever again." Angharad put one hand on her daughter's arm. "Run faster."

Morgana swallowed and ran as fast as she could. *I never thought I'd be running races again. Good job I kept my fitness level high during my blindness.*

An arch of light in the distance appeared and began to grow bigger, but the noise from the hounds behind her also got louder. She took a deep breath and pushed herself to run faster, Angharad keeping up with her easily.

They burst out into the light, the white stone jetty a fair distance away from the tunnel entrance.

Angharad went on ahead. "Charon. There are daemon hounds after Morgana, they must have got away from the main battle and followed her scent."

Charon looked grim. "They will not get her." He placed both hands to his mouth and whistled through his fingers in an ear splitting shriek.

Morgana heard the whistle and saw a huge cloud of black erupt from the trees on the hill over the top of the tunnel mouth. She glanced backward and saw the huge black canine shapes of the Daemon Hounds emerge from the tunnel, their eyes glowing red and gold.

"Hurry, Morgana." Angharad reappeared beside her, and Morgana realised she'd slowed almost to a walk. She sped up again, her heart pounding and her lungs beginning to burn because she couldn't seem to get air into her lungs fast enough.

A black feather drifted past Morgana's nose and she realised that the black cloud was Charon's Ravens.

"Quickly, Morgana. My Family will slow the hounds long enough for you to get aboard Lady." Merla's voice said from above her.

Too puffed out to spare breath to speak, Morgana waved one hand, focused on the beautiful boat beside the jetty and the man in the white feathered cloak on her stern, and pushed herself one last time.

The thud of her feet on the stone of the jetty startled her and Morgana almost fell over her own feet. She stumbled up the gang plank and onto Lady, dropping thankfully onto her hands and knees, chest heaving. "Mama?"

"I'm here, my darling." Angharad laid one hand on Morgana's shoulder.

Merla landed on the rail where Morgana had come aboard, pulled the plank on and called out to Charon. "She is safe, My Lord."

Morgana felt the boat slowly and gracefully slide away from the riverbank and turned over, sitting on the smooth, polished boards that made up Lady's deck. The black cloud of ravens lifted, and Morgana saw the daemon hounds standing on the jetty staring balefully over the water at her.

She stood up, feeling safe once more.

"They can't get you. If they touch the water, they will forget why they are here and what they are doing." Merla cawed, landing on the rail beside her as Morgana stared back at them.

"Water that makes you forget?" Morgana flinched as a wavelet of water splashed up the side of the boat.

"Yes, this is the river Lethe." Charon told her from the stern of the boat. "This is the water that makes souls forget who they were so they can be reborn. They have to bathe in it and drink in it three times to forget their last life."

"The Lady shields you from its effects though." Merla said. "Even if you were to drink it, standing on the Lady's decks it would no more harm you than the water you drink from your tap on Earth nexus."

Morgana thought for a moment, then looked over at Charon. "May I have three vials of Lethe water, please?"

He smiled. "All you need for your tasks now and in the future will be in the wooden case I gave you when you arrived. Including Lethe water enough to remove particular amounts of memory."

Morgana blushed. "Am I that transparent?"

"You're in the Underworld." Merla laughed. "We know what you are thinking."

Morgana rolled her eyes. "Sometimes I wish I knew what I was thinking."

Angharad floated over. "Why don't you go below and rest for a while, Morgana? The journey to the exit will take several hours and you should use the time to rest after your tasks."

Morgana sighed feeling the aches which made themselves known in every bone and fighting a huge yawn back, said, "That sounds like a wonderful idea. Wake me in an hour or so."

"I'll show you to your cabin." Merla said, flap-jumping from the rail to Morgana's shoulder. "I'll make sure she eats as well, Angharad." The raven said looking backward as Morgana started for the entrance to the cabins.

Angharad waved one hand and leaned on the rail, looking out at the banks passing by.

"Don't worry." Charon said. "We'll save them both."

NEX AND MORBUS WATCHED the boat slip away from the jetty.

"*We could go after them.*" Morbus suggested, "*It's not that far to swim.*"

"*How? It's the Lethe. One touch of that water and you forget everything.*" She growled at her brother. "*You really are stupid at times, Morbus. Didn't you do any research before we came here?*"

"*What's the point? Point me in the right direction and tell me what to do.*" He replied whining a little. "*I'm a male daemon not a leader. Not like you or Deumara.*"

Nex huffed. "*Talking of her, we'd best get back to the battle and back her up. She is not going to be happy at this turn of the tale.*"

Morbus nodded and the two of them turned their back on the river Lethe and loped back up the tunnel, the caws of the ravens following them.

They bypassed the palace compound and slunk through the battle silently until they were back at Mara's side. She spared them a glance as she decapitated three underworld Minotaurs with one blow. They disappeared into dust. "So, did you get the shield?" she panted, blood dribbling down her arm from a scratch on her shoulder.

"Does it look like we have it?" Morbus growled.

"She got away then. Any chance of us over taking her?" Mara swept her sword over his head and cut a warrior three quarters of the way through. He disappeared in a splash of dust.

"Highly unlikely." Nex said, ripping the throat out of a two headed hound that had tried to hamstring her. *"Charon has taken her aboard his boat, and we dared not pursue him."*

"What about swimming after them?" Mara destroyed the soldier behind the hound before he could behead Nex.

"In the River Lethe?" Nex shook her head, splattering blood and dust into the eyes of another warrior in front of Mara. Morbus slashed at the same warrior's guts with his claws and laughed as the gooey, blood covered intestines fell to the ground.

"Good point. We'll just have to give up and return to Prince Apollyon." Mara beheaded the groaning warrior. "Morbus, please don't play with your enemies, that's uncivil."

"But it's fun." Morbus snuffed blood out of his nose in a fine spray, shaking his head and sneezing blood and snot everywhere.

"Men." Nex sighed.

Then she became aware of the silence around them. *"Where did everyone go?"* she looked around.

Terius and Meranus wandered over. "Where did all our Opponents go?"

"We decided that we didn't need them anymore." Hades appeared a few feet away from Mara. "So, we sent them back to their rest."

Nex and Morbus growled. *"Are we attacking him?"*

Mara shook her head. "Don't bother. It's his Realm, he can do what he likes with us now."

"I think you two should return to human form now." Hades said to the hounds. He gestured and before the two could do anything, they were in their normal human forms. "In studying your actions in battle, Lady Mara, we were impressed by both yours and Lady Nexamillia's economy of action, honour and skill."

Mara exchanged a look with Nex. "Thank you, Lord Hades." She replied warily.

"However, the conduct of your male companions was reprehensible and disgusting. We concluded that when it comes to your time to be summoned by Thanatos, your male companions will have no choice, but to walk the Tiring Path and be confined to those areas which they have qualified for." Persephone appeared next to her husband, not a single golden curl out of place.

Nex felt like whimpering. *She's beautiful. In a way that I could never be.*

Persephone smiled at the Daemon Girl. "You are physically beautiful, child, but your soul needs cleaning. As does your cousin's."

"Indeed." Hades said. "In recognition of the good parts of your souls and characters we will extend a single chance to you both on the occasion that you meet with Charon."

"And that chance is?" Mara looked at the two deities in consternation.

"Your male companions will have to spend time in all the areas of the circles of the underworld for which they qualify. You on the other hand will be given the chance to pick one of the areas to be confined in." Hades' face became strong and serious and Nex felt more than a little scared. "However, in order to qualify for this chance, you two must repent of the things that are spoiling your soul. Greed, violence, killing, terrifying others. These must all be expunged from your spirits."

"Do we have to choose now?" Nex felt worried. *I'm supposed to be a Daemon with no emotions. What's wrong with me?*

"Nay child, you will have many years to clean your spirit." Persephone smiled at Nex. "

"Very well." Mara coughed. "But how can we live to clean our souls if we cannot leave here? You have already given the shield to another, and we have only completed two tasks."

"We absolve you of the need to complete the third task. There is more than one gate to the Underworld." Hades told her. "Thanatos will deliver you back to Earth Nexus that you might return home."

Mara sighed. "That is the best we can hope for then. I just hope Lord Apollyon understands our failure."

"He might punish us for it, but he will understand, I think." Nex said. "Grandfather is a practical man and will understand that we were bested by the Higher class of this realm."

Mara agreed, a mournful look in her eyes.

Thanatos appeared beside Hades. "Come with me to the exit." He said and began to walk toward the Tiring Path.

Nex and Morbus looked at Mara. She nodded and the three of them began to follow the deity.

"Come on you two." Mara called to the Minos Twins, who looked enraged at this turn of events.

"No." Terius yelled.

"We must destroy this place in our lord's name if we cannot have the shield." Meranus said. "Lord Apollyon has commanded it."

"See, I told you Apollyon didn't tell everyone everything." Nex said to Mara. "What do we do now?"

"Leave them to it. Come on Morbus." Mara snapped her fingers, and the male daemon ran to her side, grinning inanely. "Good boy." The female murmured, stroking Morbus' hair.

"I can't." Nex muttered and walked back to the Minos Twins. "This is an order to both of you. You are not to throw your lives away on one of Apollyon's nonsensical commands."

"He commanded us to lay down our lives to gain the shield." Terius said.

Meranus turned to Hades. "Give us the shield or face the destruction of your realm."

"I cannot give you what I do not have." Hades shrugged.

Nex tried again. "These people are gods. They are as powerful as Prince Lucifer. You won't be able to harm them."

"We might not, but we know the key to releasing the Incarcerated from Tartarus." Terius said.

Thanatos stopped moving and turned. "You cannot unlock the Pit of Tartarus."

"We can and we will." Meranus said, pulling a small blood red crystal from a pouch. "This crystal holds the blood of Balorn and of Zeus." He backed away.

"Drop it into the Pit and it will free those within." Terius said. "Including the Titans."

Persephone gasped.

"So, give us the shield and we will spare this realm." The twins chorused.

A chime hummed melodically through the air. Persephone relaxed and Hades smiled. "You are too late. The Shield has left the Underworld with its bearer, and you cannot have it until she lays down her burden and returns here."

Meranus spun and began to run toward the pit on the other side of the Lethe. Terius followed. Mara and Morbus watched them go with an interested expression.

Nex changed form into a Black Liger and pounded after them. *Why aren't they heading for the bridge?* She asked herself as the twins closed on the riverbank with its slow, wide, calm flow of sparkling water.

"Quickly brother, swim across and I will throw you the crystal." Meranus called out.

That's why. Did they even try to research what this place is like and the dangers? Nex swerved and attempted to head Terius off before he got to the edge of the river.

Terius dove head first into the river and swam out a few metres before stopping mid-stream.

"Why have you stopped?" Meranus screamed.

"What was it I am doing?" Terius said.

"Swim for the other shore and catch the crystal I throw you." Meranus repeated.

Nex suddenly realised her chance had come as Terius resumed swimming; his speed becoming slower and slower.

Meranus waited on the bank on this side, the crystal clutched in his hand, impatiently tapping his foot as his brother stopped moving again. "What now?"

"Why am I swimming?" Terius said.

"Because we are to unleash the Titans upon the Underworld in accordance to our Lord Apollyon's command." Meranus growled.

"Why?" Terius dragged himself out of the river on the other side and looked puzzled. "What has this place done to us?"

Meranus roared in frustration. "Just catch this. I'll be over in a moment."

As he threw the blood crystal, Nex launched herself at it, catching it delicately in her jaws and dropping it on the ground before spinning and using her full body weight to knock Meranus into the water.

He came up sputtering. "Why did you do that?"

Nex changed back to girl form, the crystal in her hand. "You asked me to." She hoped that the lie was white enough not to be included in the stains on her soul.

He blinked, treading water." Who are you? Why am I in the water?"

Nex laughed. *He looks so funny.*

Hades appeared beside her and picked the crystal up carefully. "This is a powerful magical object, Child." He swept one hand over it and the blood became blue. "Here, take this as your reward for saving the Underworld. It will function as a key for anywhere that you wish to unlock. Just touch it to the door."

Nex thanked the god with a smile as she dropped it into her belt pouch. "What will you do with those two?" She nodded at the Minos Twins who were now sat on the opposite bank playing a clapping game and singing.

"We shall find them a good home. Perhaps they too will be able to clear the dirt from their spirits." Persephone told her. "Now, you, your brother and cousin had better get going. It is time for you to leave the Underworld."

Nex nodded and caught up with Morbus and Mara.

Twenty – Nine

Angharad woke Morgana as they emerged from the tunnel between the Phlegethon and the Acheron. They ate together silently, aware that it was their last meal together for a long time.

Morgana bathed and Angharad washed her hair, lingering over the long pale strands. She combed and brushed it until her daughter's hair was smooth and shiny, before she plaited it up and secured it in a coronet across Morgana's head.

"Remind your grandfather of the gifts he holds from your Papa and I." Angharad said as they mounted the steps up to the deck. "It is important to us that you and your sister have them."

"I will, Mama." Morgana swallowed her tears. *I don't want to say goodbye yet, it's not been long enough.*

The white marble pier where the Judged gathered awaiting Charon was empty. Merla landed on the rail next to where Morgana stood with her mother. "I see the Kings have not allowed anyone else through yet." She remarked.

"Hades orders. He wanted to get the battle at the palace out of the way before we resumed our normal duties." Charon said.

Morgana nodded, remembering the grey stag that had led her there through the forest and the handsome angel she had talked to. *Do I really want to forget all this?* Pain twisted inside her heart.

The forest flowed past like a silver river itself and in the trees, Morgana caught glimpses of animals; horses, deer, rabbits, birds, all of them carrying on as if they were still alive. "I thought animals went straight to the Fields of Elysium?"

"That is the fields." Merla laughed. "The animals are brought here by Thanatos' aide, The Silver Stag and live in the forests. They have freedom from hunters here and there are many small burrows and larger caves that lead to the fields that you experienced."

"Why don't the Judged find them?" this seeming loophole made Morgana nervous. "Could the Daemon Hounds follow us using the caves?"

"Only the pure of spirit can find them, Child." Charon said.

Well that makes sense. Morgana smiled. She saw a smudge of white stone appearing in the distance. "Is that where we get off?"

Charon inclined his head. "It is. Within your bag you have everything you will need for the task ahead. You must save your sister, or the World Realms will fall to an evil far greater than you have ever experienced."

Lady slowed and bumped against the pier. Charon snapped his fingers, and the grey wood plank connected the deck with the shore.

"I cannot set foot over there, sweetheart." Angharad said, gathering Morgana into her arms. "I will miss you so much."

"I'll miss you too, Mama." Morgana allowed the tears to flow this time, holding tightly to her birth mother. "I am sorry that I was such a spoiled brat when I came here. I apologise for any pain I caused to my family, and I am desolate that I won't ever see you again." She sobbed uncontrollably into her mother's robe.

"Hush. We shall see each other remember? Once you have atoned for your sins after your physical death, we shall live in Elysium together." Angharad smiled into Morgana's hair. "This I promise to you with all my heart."

The two of them held tightly to each other for a long while until Charon gave a little cough. "Merla will show you the way to the Hall Door. It has been a pleasure to meet you Princess and I hope when we meet again you will understand more about this Realm."

Morgana let go of Angharad, sighed and sniffed.

Her mother handed her a handkerchief. "Wipe your eyes and blow your nose, Morgana. You look a sight."

Grinning, Morgana did as she was told. "There, am I presentable?"

Angharad tucked an errant strand of hair behind Morgana's right ear. "You are now. Remember that I love you and your sister equally. You should work together now, not pull apart."

"I'll try, Mam." Morgana picked up her satchel and slung it over her head, so the strap crossed her body. "I love you too." She stepped up onto the gang plank and walked lightly down it, the bounce in the wood making her concentrate on not falling into the river.

Merla flew over and perched on Morgana's shoulder.

"We shall return to the Palace now. Thanatos needs a lift." Charon called.

Merla bobbed. "Yes, my lord."

The gang plank disappeared once Morgana set foot on the pier. She moved off the white stone to stand in the grass, looking across at Angharad.

Angharad waved. Charon raised one hand and Lady set off downstream, rapidly growing smaller in the distance. Morgana waved until her arm ached and she could no longer see the boat.

Merla stroked her hair with her beak. "Come on, Morgana, we have to go."

MORGANA SET OFF INTO the trees behind the Pier. They clustered closely here, the black bark making the forest feel dark and a lot scarier than it was by the main gates to the Underworld. The even twilight of the Underworld didn't really penetrate through the silver leaves and Morgana was forced to rely on Merla for directions.

Eventually they emerged into a clearing. Opposite them, in a rock cliff that seemed to rise into the infinite, was a white marble doorway. It had a single person sized door with plain hinges and no handle.

Morgana stopped in the middle of the clearing. "How am I supposed to use it? There's no handle."

Merla launched herself off of Morgana's shoulder and swooped over to a large fallen branch, where she perched, laughing. "It's a one way door like the Black Door you came into Limbo through."

Morgana approached it. "What's on the other side?"

"The Hall of The Worlds." Merla flapped her tail a little. "It's an odd place. Time stands still and there are corridors with doors off either side of it."

"Have you been in there then?" Morgana sat down on the grass to look at the raven.

"Once, with Thanatos. Charon cannot leave the Underworld. There will be someone waiting for you in the Hall. Do not be surprised by who it is." Merla shook herself. "Now you must go through, Morgana. Your sister's life depends on it."

Morgana stood up and approached the door. It swung open silently, showing an empty room beyond the opening. She turned back to look at Merla. "Goodbye Merla. Thank you for everything you've taught me while I've been here."

The raven bobbed a little bow. "Goodbye Morgana. Fare you well."

Morgana sighed, took a deep breath and smiled. "Let's get on with this then." She stepped through the door.

One moment she stood in the black and silver forest of the underworld, the next she was in a hallway that reminded her a little of the passages at the hospital. Darkness hugged the walls and shadows flit across the floor of the hallway, luring her forward. But when she turned to look back at the door, it had gone, leaving only a smooth grey wall. She reached out to touch the space where the door had been.

From below her elbow a voice said, "There is no wall there; the door only opens outward remember." She turned to see a small person, female, dressed in breeches and a wide-sleeved white shirt. Her hair, golden, fell around her shoulders in ringlets.

Morgana blinked. "Where did you come from?" then she looked at the small girl's back. "Do you have butterfly wings?"

The girl rolled her eyes. "I come from Farinelm A. Of course I have wings." She waved one hand down the corridor.

"Farinelm? What's that?" Morgana tried to collect her wits.

"Did they not explain the Hall of the Worlds to you before they sent you through?" The butterfly girl sounded annoyed.

"Merla said that time stood still here and there are corridors with doors on either side of them."

"She got that bit right, but they didn't explain what the hall is, or who I am or where you need to go?" the girl folded her arms.

"No. All I know is that my sister is in danger, I have to get to Llanirstyr to save her and this is the fastest way to get to her." Morgana sighed. "I suppose that if time stands still here that means I don't have to worry about my illness or rushing to save her."

"Well, Llanirstyr is the first corridor next to the Earth Nexus door." The girl said.

Morgana felt even more confused. "Look, is there somewhere we can go so you can explain all this?"

The girl frowned. "I'm new to being a Hall Mentor, but the tavern is over there," she waved at the opposite wall of the corridor, "so let's go visit Madame Gilleé and sort you out."

Morgana moved across the hall to stand where the girl had indicated. "There's a tavern here? There's no door."

"Just because you can't see one, doesn't mean there isn't one." The girl grinned and stood beside her. "You just came through an invisible door, remember?"

Morgana glanced back at the other wall. *She has a point.*

The girl stepped forward into the wall and disappeared. Morgana gasped; then the girl's head poked out of the wall again. "Well, come on then."

Morgana followed.

What on earth? This place smells just like my favourite bar in Cardiff when the cherry trees are in bloom out in the beer garden. Morgana looked around. The room had a mixture of booths, formal tables and chairs, along with low, comfortable looking sofas and coffee tables. The flower scent came from potted cherry trees that were dotted around the room and a purple flower that wound its way around the bar in the centre of the room, looking for all the world like bunches of grapes.

"Ah, welcome to my bar, mes chéris." A curvaceous, red headed woman in a soft green wrap dress with a long cream pearl necklace knotted at the side as a belt entered the room from the opposite side of the bar.

She stopped, one hand rose to her mouth, and she gasped before running across the room to envelope Morgana in a hug. "Morgana. Où êtes-vous allé? We have been so worried about you. How are you feeling?"

Morgana pulled away. "Who are you? I've never met you before." She looked at the butterfly girl for some answers. The girl shook her head unable to speak through her laughter.

The woman laughed as well. "Mais oui, it was a long time ago that I held you in my arms; you were a mere bébé, you and your sister."

Morgana sat down in a nearby seat. "What is going on? First, I get trapped in the Underworld and have to fight a hero to get a stupid shield, then I'm pushed away from my mam into this place that everyone knows me, but I know no one." Tears began to run down her face.

"Cherie. It is all right." The woman sat on the chair opposite her. "I am Madame Denyse Gilleé. I am your pas grand-mère."

"You are my grandmother?" Morgana said, her French lessons coming back to her slowly.

"Oui, yes, sort of. I married your grandfather Aderyn after your real grandmother died. I live here in the Tavern because I do not age here, and I can visit him on Earth Nexus or Llanirstyr whenever I wish." She smiled.

She's got a nice smile. I feel really comfortable with her. Morgana sighed. "I have to get to Llanirstyr quickly. Jenni is in danger and I'm the only person who can..."

Madame Gilleé laid a hand on her arm. "Hush little one. You have enough time. Now, what would you like for petit dejuner? I shall make you whatever you want."

Thirty

It took Morgana a little while to get her head around everything that her grandmother and the butterfly girl told her over lunch. "So, if I've got this right, Xanthe, each corridor leads to worlds that were created when an event on the first world changes the future? And the original world of that world was created when something happened on Earth and changed the Earth's future?"

Xanthe smiled, her wings flittering a little. "Exactly right. Glad to see you're as intelligent as Jenni."

"Well, we are twins; it follows that we would have similar intelligence." Morgana soaked the last of her gravy up with a piece of bread and stuffed it in her mouth.

"Not necessarily. I'm one of sextuplets and despite being the youngest, I'm the only one intelligent enough to take Hall Classes." The other girl stretched. "So, what do you want to do now?

Morgana yawned. "I need to sleep properly. I don't feel like I've slept at all since I left home."

"That's because you haven't, ma cherie. The Underworld isn't set up for mortals, so there is no day or night." Madame Gilleé bustled over. "The potions Lord Charon gave you can only wipe the physical tiredness away."

"But I remember sleeping." Morgana protested, in spite of her body's insistence that the bar proprietor was correct. "I closed my eyes and when I opened them, time had passed."

"Time is something that man created to allow some sense of control over what was going on around him." Xanthe told her. "I learned about this in Hall Class. The Fates don't control time, just what a person experiences. They made it seem to your mind as if you had slept."

Morgana yawned again. "So, I didn't actually sleep? I was tricked?"

"Essentially, oui. And now your body, it is asserting control over your mind again, so it says you need to rest." Madame Gilleé held out her hand. "I shall show you to your room and tuck you in. Don't worry about your mission to Llanirstyr, the time here in the Tavern is as long or as short as I wish it to be."

Morgana, rose, took her grandmother's hand and followed, her eyelids growing heavy. "Okay."

XANTHE FLUTTERED DOWN the Hall to the Earth Nexus Door. She'd never been allowed to go through before, as her wings would be useless and would create too much of a fuss amongst the unaltered humans in the Nexus Realm. *But I have to tell her family that Morgana is alive. The Tavern cannot be reached by any other means than physical, so it's not as if we could just call them or anything.*

As she passed Xandin, a figure stepped out of the corridor into the Hall. "Xanthe? Is that you?"

The butterfly girl turned. "Rilx! Am I glad to see you."

"Why, what's happened?" the figure's golden eyes widened.

"We found her... Rilx have you changed skin colour? You were completely blue the last time I saw you." Xanthe's gaze wandered over the thin black and white stripes which interrupted his sky blue scales.

"I had my fiftieth Shedday recently. Mother believes I will be fully black and white by the time I reach my hundredth. Then I'll have to go into government." He rolled his eyes, the green slit pupils narrowing. "Enough of that. Who have you found?"

"Well, I didn't exactly find her. I had this odd feeling while I was in Quargard B, so I left the world and came back to the Hall. I had to check with each of the worlds on my way down and of course, Mother knew the instant that I'd come home so I got stuck in Farinelm A for a while, but when I finally managed to..." Xanthe babbled.

"Calm down, Xanthe." Rilx gave her an amused grin, showing his peg teeth. "I swear you talk faster than Chirr when she's had too much firestone. What happened to make you come tearing down to the Earth Door?"

"Jenni's sister. She just stepped out of the Underworld Door, you know the one that we know is there, but we can't get through?" Xanthe's wings fluttered so fast that she shot up into the air over Rilx's head.

He caught her foot. "Steady, Xanthe, we don't know how far you might fly up there, remember? Now ground yourself, please." He hauled her down to his eye level and she descended the rest of the way down to the ground herself, taking deep breaths to calm down. He left one hand on her shoulder to keep her down while she relaxed.

When her wings were merely trembling slightly, Rilx let go of her. "So, Jenni's sister, Morgana has been in the Underworld? Does she know how she got there?"

"She hasn't said. All she's told us is that Arianrhod has warned her that the Crown Princess's life is in danger and that she is the only one that can save her. Something about potions from Lord Charon." Xanthe looked up at the Vir'Astillian pleadingly. "I have to help her, it's my turn on the Mentor Rota, but we have to tell her family about this and Madame Gilleé won't let me go to Llanirstyr. So, I was going to go to Earth Nexus, just through the door to contact them."

Rilx hissed. "No."

"Why not?" I know you said that I wouldn't look right, and my wings wouldn't work, but surely..." her voice tailed off.

"I told you an excuse. A truthful one, but an excuse. Lord Aderyn laid an enchantment that allows no altered human or sentient animal through the door. It would have driven you mad with pain." Rilx started walking up the corridor, his long heavy tail swishing against the marble floor. "I have to talk to Morgana and Denyse."

MORGANA SLEPT HEAVILY no dreams piercing her sleep, but when she awoke, snuggled up under a duvet in a room that could have been designed for her alone, she thought she heard voices in her mind.

"*She's not even awake yet.*" Her grandmother's voice sounded irritated.

"*I must speak with her, Madame Gilleé. She knows things that...*" the second voice was thick and had a strange hissing accent that made it difficult to understand.

As Morgana opened her eyes, she realised that she'd actually heard the voices, except the hissing one wasn't speaking English. *But it comes through as English in my mind. This place is so strange. What on earth is going on?*

She sat up in bed and turned the bedside light on. *Grand'Mere said that the white door had a bathroom behind it. I really want a shower, so any mysteries can wait.*

After her shower, she found clothes that had been set out on the small couch opposite her bed. After putting on the underwear left for her, she slipped a long sky blue velvet dress with white embroidery on the bodice over her head, marvelling at the fit. The sleeves went from fitted on the shoulder to wider than her outstretched hand, the point of each one falling almost to the floor and showing the white silk lining.

I feel like I'm going to a renaissance faire. Morgana giggled as she pulled on soft white leather ankle boots and stood in front of the full length mirror brushing her damp hair out.

There was a knock at the door. "Morgana, Cherie?" her grandmother's voice filtered through the wood. "Are you awake?"

Morgana resisted the temptation to give out a fake snore. "Yes, Grand'Mere." She called back.

"I have your breakfast ready, and you have a visitor. Come out as soon as you can, please." Madame Gilleé said.

Morgana brushed her hair until it lay flat and smooth, put on the silver chain and earrings that had been left on the dressing table and stood up straight, determined to show herself as strong to the newcomer. *It must be the owner of that odd, hissing voice. I wonder if he has a lisp or a cleft palate that makes him talk like that.*

She saw Xanthe first, fluttering by a cherry tree and stroking the flowers, whispering inaudibly. "Morning, Xanthe."

"It's afternoon actually. You've slept a whole day and a half of Earth Nexus time." Xanthe dropped lightly to the floor. "I love that dress, you look gorgeous."

"Thank you." Morgana looked around. "Madame... um, Grand'Mere said I had a visitor.

"Yes. Rilx is here." Xanthe smiled. "He looks a little scary, but he's a sweetie really."

What Xanthe actually meant is that he looks really scary. Look at those teeth. Morgana forced herself to shake the reptilian creature's hand. *He's warm and soft, like a snake. His world must be a hot one.*

"I hear that you came out of the Underworld Door." Rilx said as Morgana sat down across the table from him.

"So, Xanthe tells me." Morgana smiled as Madame Gilleé put a pile of pancakes in front of her, accompanied by fresh strawberries and cream. "Thank you, Grand'Mere."

Madame Gilleé sat down beside her, pouring out coffee. "You are welcome, little one."

"Were you really in the Underworld? How did you get in there?" Rilx fired each question off quickly as if he was scared, she might run away. She ate a few strawberries and part of the stack of pancakes. "Last we heard you'd tried to follow your sister to Llanirstyr. We were expecting you to be in the corridor somewhere."

Morgana sighed. *I'm not going to get any peace until I tell him.* She put her spoon and fork down. "Yes, I was in the Underworld. I walked in through a Black door because I wasn't sure which way Jenni had gone. Can I eat now?"

"Of course, sorry. Rilx grinned at the exasperation in her voice. "You sound just like Jenni when she thinks I'm acting crazy."

Xanthe giggled.

Morgana ignored them and concentrated on eating her breakfast. Only when her plate was clear did she look at Rilx again. "You said that like you know my sister well."

Rilx shrugged. "I was her Mentor when she came into the Hall of the Worlds for the first time. I helped her find and retrieve the Angel's Crown, then we fought the Angel to save Llanirstyr together."

"When was that?" Morgana wasn't too sure how to take the ordinary tone he used. She rubbed her palm with her other thumb nervously.

"What? Oh, time is a hard thing to work out when you're travelling between worlds and the Hall. It must have been at least five years ago by Earth Nexus Time." Rilx's tail swept back and forth. "Now we must get you to Llanirstyr. What is the danger that you told Xanthe about?"

Morgana told him everything that Arianrhod told her. "So, I need to get to Llanirstyr as soon as possible."

He frowned. "She said one Earth Day from that moment?"

Morgana nodded.

He turned to Madame Gilleé. "How long would that be in Llanirstyr?"

"Twenty days, give or take a few hours. But 'tis academic for there is as little time in the Underworld as there is in the Hall." The older woman shrugged.

"I still don't understand this time thing." Morgana complained. "How long have been I missing then?"

"I received the message from Jenni, with the addition to be on duty in the hall just in case you turned up there, about two hours before I met you, on my personal timeline." Xanthe said.

"It's been about ten days since I got it in Vir'Astil." Rilx said.

"I have known for a day on my own timeline, but as time is fluid here, it is of no moment." Madame Gilleé smiled at Morgana and laid one hand on her arm. "For your Père and Grand-Père, it will have been six hours."

Morgana sipped her coffee. "I don't think it's a good idea to tell my family that I am okay. I don't want to alert my sister's enemy." She picked up the satchel Charon had given her and rummaged around in it. "Arianrhod, Artemis or whatever she is called said the shield would guard me from sight." The shield slipped easily out of the bag despite its size and Morgana looked at it, tracing the animals on it with her finger.

"How?" Xanthe frowned. "It's a shield not an invisibility cloak."

"I'm not sure." Morgana admitted.

Something about the pattern of the tree branches as they wove around the animals made Morgana pause. "Does this look like writing to you?"

Madame Gilleé frowned. "Oui. One moment." She disappeared behind the bar and came back with a pad and pencil. "Hold it still, Cherie," she said to Morgana as she sat down. "And I will write what it says down." She scribbled for a long minute, then passed it to

Morgana who set the shield down on the floor beside her, keeping one hand on it to stop it rolling away.

"Amddiffyn y deiliad y Darian, O'r ddau arf a golwg oni bai eu cynnyrch." She read out loud. "It's Welsh. It means 'Protect the bearer of the Shield, from both weapon and sight unless they yield.'"

"Morgana." Xanthe gasped. "Where did you go?"

Morgana blinked. "I'm right here, I haven't moved."

"Morgana, cherie?" Madame Gilleé said, looking around the room, "Where are you?"

"I'm here." Morgana said, wondering if they were trying to play a trick on her. She smiled nervously, catching her lower lip in her teeth.

Rilx stood up looking around. "I smell magic of some sort involved here. Where did she go?"

Morgana tried to stop the amusement bubbling up, but it was too late. The laughter took over and she put both hands over her face, falling back against her chair helplessly.

Rilx stared. "Why are you giggling? Where did you go?" he said, sinking back into his chair.

Xanthe started giggling. "I think I know what happened."

"Please do tell us." Madame Gilleé said. "I for one, am unable to understand what just happened."

Morgana and Xanthe exchanged a look and started laughing harder, wrapping their arms around their waists.

Madame Gilleé shook her head smiling. "I fear we shall not get an answer out of them, Rilx."

Morgana fought the giggle urge back. "I had my hand on the shield when I read out what you'd written."

"It's an incantation. The shield made her invisible until she let go again." Xanthe gasped out.

"Do you have to say the words each time, cherie?" Madame Gilleé looked at the shield that had fallen onto the floor when Morgana let it go.

"I don't know." Morgana picked the shield up and looked at Xanthe who shook her head. "Looks like it."

"It's such a big thing to carry around though, even if you are invisible." Rilx said.

Morgana studied the tree branches again. They wound up into the interlocking knot pattern that wound around the circumference of the shield's edge. *There're more words here; well, it can't hurt to try reading the first half of them out.*

Holding the shield in both hands, Morgana said: "Crebachu o ran maint, yn dal i amddiffyn y cynhalydd i gyd." The shield shrank and after a moment, Morgana held it in the palm of her hand, the enamelled details making it look like a pendant.

"What if you need to use it as a shield?" Rilx asked.

"What I said was 'Shrink in size and still protect the bearer all." Morgana explained. "In theory, I should be able to just use the invisibility incantation and it would protect me from anything."

"Yes, but what if you end up in the kind of fight that you need a shield for?" Rilx persisted. He looked fiercely at her.

"Then I'll say the other half of that incantation; Grow and return to the right size." Morgana told him.

"Cherie, would you test this for us? We need to know that you are safe." Madame Gilleé smiled.

"Okay." Morgana thought for a moment then said, "Tyfu a dychwelyd i'r maint cywir." The shield grew rapidly until it was back to the right size for Morgana to use.

"Are there any other spells on there?" Xanthe asked, her wings fluttering in excitement and lifting her from her seat.

Morgana peered at the shield carefully. "I don't think so." She shrank the shield again and attached it to the plain silver chain she wore, by passing the chain through the arm holds.

"It doesn't matter, those will be enough, child." Madame Gilleé stood and disappeared into one of the rooms off the main bar.

Thirty-One

M organa's grandmother returned after about half an hour, with several items in her hands. "You will need these, my darling." She placed them onto the table in front of Morgana.

The girl picked up an expensive looking silver and sapphire cuff bracelet. "This is pretty. Jenni wears one like this; did you give it to her?"

Madame Gilleé shook her head. "No, she left it here for you, just in case you appeared here, like the dress you are wearing."

"The dress is hers?" Morgana stroked the soft material. "I didn't think she had such beautiful taste."

"Myfanwy designed it for you. She designs all Jenni's formal wear." Rilx held his left arm up. "Xanthe and I have cuffs too. They allow us through the enchantment Lord Archington placed on the door into Llanirstyr."

"So, it's like an identity card." Morgana slipped the cuff on, and her eyes widened as it tightened on her wrist. She tugged on it. "How do I take it off?"

"You can't." Rilx told her. "Jenni and Lord Myrddin are working on adjusting the spell though."

Morgana sighed and touched a bejewelled dagger. "I don't need that"

"What happens if this poisoner attacks you?" Madame Gilleé raised an eyebrow.

The girl reached into her bag and slid her sword out. "Mam gave me this while I was in the underworld. It was hers when she was alive."

Rilx whistled. "Nice blade."

"Carry it for luck then, the dagger was mine when I was your age." Her grandmother smiled as Morgana moved the dagger in front of her.

"It's a bit less noticeable than the sword." Morgana said by way of explanation as she put the sword back into her bag, then she picked up a white leather purse embroidered with a silver horse attached to a snake linked silver belt.

"Everyone wears those in Llanirstyr. There is some money in the purse for you from your sister and you can put whatever else you need on the belt." Madame Gilleé watched Morgana thread the belt through the loops on the dagger's sheath and put the belt on over her dress. "Now, you are all ready to go."

"I'll come with you, I'm invited to the Year End Celebration." Rilx stood up.

Morgana rose and moved to stand beside her grandmother who had withdrawn into herself and was stroking a stray wisp of hair. "Grand'Mere don't worry about me. I'll be fine." She put one hand on Madame Gilleé's shoulder.

Denyse sighed and looked up at her. "You remind me of your aunt, cherie. She was always confident in new situations." She laid one hand over Morgana's and patted her.

Morgana smiled, leaned down and hugged her grandmother. "I'll come back and tell you what happens."

"You'd better, cherie. Who knows what will happen to the tavern if I were to have to come after you!" Denyse laughed and hugged her back. "Look after yourself."

Morgana straightened up and raised her chin. "I will. Jenni won't know what's hit her."

Xanthe followed Morgana and Rilx as they left the Tavern. "Do you mind if I come down to Llanirstyr with you? I can't come in, but I want to make sure you get there safely."

"What on earth is likely to happen to me in the Hall?" Morgana frowned. "It's not as if there are wild animals."

"There are actually." Rilx looked at her. "They don't tend to come this close to the Earth Nexus Door, but past the Arachna corridor, you'll find Hall Sharks, birds and other animals. They live on the energy the hall produces as well as each other."

They passed a heavy, golden door that sparkled in the odd light of the Hall.

"What's through there?" Morgana slowed and looked at the intricate design scored into the gold.

"Chrysoldin. It's a world where the dominant race of humans was attached to the Egyptian Gods. I'm considered to be the physical manifestation of Sobek-Ra there. You'd probably be mistaken for Isis-Inara; Jenni was when we visited there the first time." Rilx hissed a little as he laughed. "You and your sister are identical so it might get a little confusing for your other aunt, Akila-Auset if we went in without her."

How much more family have I got that I've never heard of? Morgana shook her head a little. "Fair enough." She said out loud. "How much further is it?"

"Not far." Xanthe fluttered ahead of the pair to stand beside a pale stone archway. "Here it is."

Morgana followed Rilx into the corridor beyond the archway. The floor was tiled with blue slate and torches flickered in wrought iron holders on the walls. There was a faint scent of lavender as they approached the first door on the corridor.

"How do you want to do this?" Rilx asked, putting on a long blue and white robe with gold thread embroidery along the cuffs and the hems.

"Well, I don't want to be mistaken for my sister, so I think I'll be invisible until we are into the palace properly." Jenni touched shield from on her necklace. "I'll hold onto you as we go through."

"I'm not sure that will work." Rilx frowned. "It might be better for you to be mistaken for Jenni at first; she told me that Llanirstyri speak Welsh, so you should be okay."

Xanthe shook her head. "They don't speak the same form of Welsh as Earth Nexus do, Rilx. Invisibility is the better idea."

"Overruled huh?" Rilx sighed. "Alright then. Hold onto the back of my robe as unobtrusively as you can."

Morgana slid the strap of her bag over her head, wrapped the chain of her necklace around her free wrist with the shield held in the centre of her palm and whispered the incantation. "Amddiffyn y deiliad y Darian, O'r ddau arf a golwg oni bai eu cynnyrch."

Xanthe giggled as Morgana vanished. "There are so many fun things you could do with that ability."

"I'll settle for getting Morgana into the palace without any problems." Rilx snorted. His robe tightened on one side and turned to Xanthe. "Stay here. I'll come back out for you once we've dealt with the problem."

"Don't worry about me; I'm on Duty and I wasn't invited anyway." Xanthe fluttered her wings and returned to the archway leading out onto the Hall. "Good luck, Morgana."

"Thanks, Xanthe." Morgana said, her voice floating out from the patch of air beside Rilx.

The lizard man grunted. "Come on, let's get this over with."

MORGANA FOLLOWED RILX through the passageways on the other side. The Guards had passed Rilx through with a smile and a wave. After a few moments of manoeuvring herself through the crowded passage outside the entry room, trying hard not to touch anyone else, she whispered to Rilx: "Take me into a room with very few people in. I have an idea."

He nodded and turned into a side passage. At the end he opened a door onto a room full of books and looked around. "There's no one else in here. It should be safe."

Morgana sighed and as he shut the door, let go of the shield, reappearing next to a table. "That was hard work. I didn't think there'd be so many people in this place."

"It's a palace; a lot of people work here and with the celebrations happening, there are a lot of guests as well. Your sister is well thought of in Llanirstyr, so no one is going to slight her by refusing to attend." Rilx positioned himself in from of the door. "What are you going to do?"

"I'm going to check something." Morgana took her bag off and removed the box of potions. "I wonder..."

She sorted through the bottles, muttering to herself. "Blue are healing, Green help with tiredness, white are Lethe Water and red... are magic." Morgana grinned. "Looks like Charon anticipated this." She pulled a slim vial out of the box and read out the label. "Will distort appearance and voice. Shake well before drinking. Effective for one hour."

She pulled out the shook the bottle, pulled out the stopper and drained the vial. "How do I look?"

Rilx blinked, his eyelids crossing from right to left instead of up to down. "You humans all look the same to me." He stared at her. "Your hair has gone brown, and your eyes are green. It's changed your dress colour as well."

Morgana grinned. "Will it work?"

"You still look a lot like Jenni, but you could be a cousin rather than her twin sister now." He watched her put the box back in her bag. "That was a useful present; why didn't you use the potion earlier?"

Morgana shrugged. "Didn't occur to me to look until we got here."

"Well, I need to get down to the Great Hall or Jenni will be wondering where I am." Rilx opened the door. "Ready?"

Jenni slipped the bag over her shoulder and nodded. "I'll stay just behind you, like a servant or something."

Rilx snorted and left the room with Morgana hurrying to catch up.

Thirty Two

The Palace was crowded with people and Morgana found it difficult to stay behind Rilx. Despite the dress's change from blue to green, people still mistook her for one of Myfanwy's aides and kept trying to get her to stop and talk to them, make appointments. She extracted herself with muttered apologies each time, thankful that her knowledge of Welsh wasn't letting her down.

I have to find my sister. I have so much to atone for and to talk to her about. Morgana thought as she and Rilx negotiated a particularly packed hallway to gain entry to the Ballroom. They'd been in Llanirstyr for nearly forty five minutes and Morgana prayed to whichever gods might be listening that her disguise stayed put long enough.

In the antechamber before the entrance to the ballroom, she spotted her aunt and tapped Rilx on the shoulder. "I need to talk to Myfanwy in private."

"Okay." He strode through the crowd waiting to be announced toward the lady in question. Morgana followed a respectful distance, trying to keep her pose as Rilx's assistant in place.

"Ambassador Rilx, welcome to Llanirstyr." Lady Myfanwy greeted the reptilian as a friend, shaking his hand firmly and pressing a kiss to his cheek. "I see you have a new assistant..." she turned to look at Morgana and her eyes widened.

Rilx looked as well. "Damn, the potion is wearing off; your dress is turning blue again. Lady Myfanwy, we need to talk to you in private."

She nodded and led the way into a side chamber, shutting the door sharply as the potion wore off completely and turning to look at Morgana. "Just where have you been, young lady? Your family..."

"Is going to have to wait a little longer for news of me." Morgana interrupted, "I have a mission and if I fail in it, I'll be inheriting a throne that I really don't want."

"There's a threat to Jenni's life? How do you know? How did you change your appearance like that?" her aunt fired the questions at her rapidly, "Where exactly did you go?"

"Short answers: Yes. I was told by a Goddess. A potion. The Underworld." Morgana sighed. "Look Myfanwy, when would it be the absolute worst time tonight for a Poisoner to strike?"

"At midnight Jenni has to give a speech to welcome the New Year in from the royal dais. It usually ends with a toast, and she'd be expected to choose a partner for the next dance. Traditionally, she's supposed to announce her choice of husband through the partner she chooses for the Midnight Waltz. It's also the traditional start to the New Year Festival."

Morgana glanced up at the clock on the wall. It was eleven thirty. "In half an hour then. Either I need to take her place or be on the dais with her so I can take her glass from her."

Rilx did a double take. "Take her place? Why would you want to kill yourself?"

Smiling at him, she sat down. "I'm dying of Cancer, Rilx. Think of it as speeding up the process."

"Morgana, your mother wouldn't want you to..." Myfanwy began.

"Which mother? Our dead Birth Mother or the one who adopted us and then split us up when things got difficult in her relationship?" Morgana said, "How do you know what either of them would want?" her smile drooped, and bitterness entered her voice, "I've met Angharad. I know she wouldn't want me to do this, but I have to... or the only person in the universe that I truly love with all my heart will die."

Myfanwy sat beside her. "I understand your reasoning, but I could get the servants to replace the glasses or have one of them act as a poison taster. You don't have to risk yourself."

"I refuse to allow an innocent to do this. It's my mission." Morgana said.

"Do you know who is going to do it?" Rilx asked, pacing around the room.

Morgana shook her head sadly.

"There are a number of Noble Families that would come into line for the throne should she die." Myfanwy mused. "No one here knows about Morgana yet, tonight would have been your debut, so the poisoner wouldn't know that they had to remove you as well, but I can't think of anyone who would bear that much of a grudge."

Rilx stopped pacing. "Are all the guests here now? None outstanding?"

"I see where you are going. Bear with me." Frowning, Myfanwy stood and moved across to the door. She opened it enough to poke her head out and beckoned to the chief herald who stood at the entrance to the ballroom.

He strode through the empty antechamber and bowed before her. "Your Highness. How may I help you?"

"Have all the guests arrived and been announced?"

"All except Ambassador Rilx, your Highness." The Herald said, consulting his list.

"I have him with me currently."

"Then they are all here."

Myfanwy looked across at the Captain of the Guard, who stood at the entrance to the antechamber. "Captain, I need your help on a certain matter."

The captain saluted and strode over.

Morgana touched the shield and whispered the incantation to make herself invisible as Myfanwy let the captain into the room and dismissed the herald back to his post.

"What is the matter, Your Highness?" She asked, saluting again.

Myfanwy shut the door again and looked at Rilx who nodded. "I have had a warning that the High Princess is about to be poisoned. We have a plan in place to deal with that, but we need to keep the miscreant from leaving."

"When the last of the guests were ushered up to the antechamber, I sent word to the gate guards to lock down the palace, as is customary for the New Year's Ball." The captain said, "Not even the servants are allowed to leave the grounds until the High Princess gives the word."

Myfanwy smiled at her. "Excellent. Be aware that someone might attempt it though."

The captain saluted again. "Be assured, Your Highness, no one will get through." She turned toward the door, "If I may?"

Myfanwy waved one hand, "Of course, Captain."

Once the Captain had left, Morgana reappeared in a whisper of sound. "I feel a little better about this now." She opened up her bag and sorted through the contents. Then she frowned. "There isn't an antidote in here. I thought I saw one earlier, but it's gone."

"That doesn't change the fact that we have to stop Jenni drinking that toast." Rilx said.

"No. It doesn't change my plan either." Morgana said, standing up and taking a step toward the door.

"I can stop you risking yourself, child." Myfanwy laid either hand on her shoulders, "You've had no training. I can freeze you where you stand."

Morgana looked into her aunt's eyes. "I know, but this is my mission and my fate. I understand that now." She stepped sideways out of Myfanwy's grasp, touched the shield and with a whisper, disappeared.

Rilx rushed to the door, but it opened and closed before he could get there. He threw it open and was about to shout to the guards when Myfanwy tapped him on the shoulder.

"Leave her to it." She said s quietly.

"But..."

"I think I understand now." Myfanwy glanced back at the bag that Morgana had brought with her. "Bring that with you and let's go on in; we shouldn't delay the start of the festival."

JENNI THREADED HER way through the ball guests, greeting various different people and smiling at the rest. *I wish Morgana was here, I should be introducing her tonight.* Various young male nobles sent deep bows and hopeful looks her way. She acknowledged them but gave them no other indication of her feelings towards them. *I don't think they're going to like my change of tradition... but then Grandfather said that social change happens from the top down, so if I don't change it, who will?*

As she took the three steps up onto the dais, Myfanwy and Rilx appeared at the back of the ballroom. Jenni glanced up at the huge four faced clock that hung in the centre of the domed ceiling. *Rilx is late. That's not like him, even if he has gone up in status as Ambassador rather than Senior Hall Walker.*

There was a gentle tapping at the corner of Jenni's mind. She recognised her aunt's delicate touch, so she let Myfanwy link minds. *"What's the matter, Van?"*

"Start your speech on time, we'll join you shortly." She replied, waving one hand over the heads of the guests. *"Don't be surprised*

by anything that might happen. Just be aware that we have it under control."

Jenni nodded as Myfanwy's mind touch retreated, *"I understand."*

"Your Royal Majesty? Is everything all right?" the Court Steward said as she reached the front of the dais.

She smiled at him. "It's fine, just a little family matter."

He bowed. "The glasses for the toast are ready, shall we pass them out during your speech or after as is traditional?" he placed an emphasis on the last word.

Well, let's start as we mean to go on, shall we? Jenni took a deep breath, "Yes, pass them out during the speech."

The man's face clouded with anger momentarily, then his normal calm mask reasserted itself. "Of course, Your Royal Majesty."

Jenni raised one eyebrow slightly and he flushed as he scurried away. Then she turned to face the crowd, which took a few moments to become quiet. "Honoured Guests, welcome. This may be the sixth New Year Ball that I have presided over, but it is the first that I have ever hosted by myself as your High Princess."

The crowd cheered, applause rippling around the room. While she waited for it to die down again, Jenni noticed that there was a small knot of people who hadn't reacted to her words. Some of them seemed angry, some merely calm, but all of them stared at her with an air of expectation.

"This year to come will be full of celebrations and festivals, culminating with my Coronation on my twenty-first birthday. However, there will also be a number of changes that will happen in the Kingdom." The cheer that had greeted the news of the coronation, trailed away into a confused mutter.

Jenni soldiered on with her speech as the glasses for the toast were passed out.

More than one of the guests seemed shocked to be given them and the people who had been staring at her before, flatly refused to take them.

"Our government will be changing to bring it into a more inclusive mode and all of the kingdom will have a say in what is to happen." Jenni noticed the guards moving into new positions. They now covered the doors, which had been closed, and all of them held their weapons at the ready.

Unfortunately, the guests had also noticed and were looking upset.

Jenni looked around. *The dais has been surrounded as well. Where is Rilx and Myfanwy?*

A servant bearing a tray with toasting glasses mounted the steps. He proceeded to give them out, leaving Jenni until last.

She took the tall crystal goblet, beaded with condensation. The bubbles inside popped and fizzed, a faint golden glow from the liquid suffusing the glass. *I'm glad that I imported prosecco from Earth Nexus for this toast; Llanirstyri Vintners need a wakeup call.*

"The very first thing that is going to change is this; I will not be 'selecting' a husband through the outdated tradition of the New Year's Ball. There is no need for me to marry to secure my throne as yet, I have a younger sister that will remain as my Heir. Society shall listen to me on this; if you wish to marry, let it be for Love and not family ties, politics or wealth. This I decree as High Princess."

There was a gasp that travelled around the room. In more than one place there were mutterings and the group of people with no glasses in their hands began booing. Jenni looked directly at them as she raised her glass. "Therefore, I offer you all this toast; May the future year be as bright and happy for everyone in the Kingdom as I am with my family."

She brought the glass to her lips, only to have it snatched away from her. "Who did that?" There was no one near enough to her to have taken it, yet there the glass was, floating in mid-air. She reached out toward it to take it back.

"No Jenni. It's been poisoned. I can't let you drink it." Morgana's voice shouted inside her head.

Jenni winced at her sister's volume. *"Morgana, give me the glass. It can't be poisoned, I brought it from Earth with me."* She told her soothingly.

The glass floated away from her, and everyone stared at the bobbing crystal.

"I'm sorry Gwynnhafr, I can't let them get away with this." Morgana's mind tone was determined.

The Court Steward lunged at the glass, tripped over nothing and landed sprawling at Jenni's feet. The glass tipped up and the liquid inside disappeared.

With a whisper of sound, Morgana appeared as the last of the wine drained out of the glass. She smiled at her sister's shocked expression "Surprise!"

She felt the poison in the wine burn through her system, flooding her with pain that she hadn't felt since that fateful night in hospital, fighting off the Septicaemia the Meningitis had set off. Her legs weakened and she wobbled, the glass falling from her grip and smashing into sparkling shards on the floor in front of the dais.

Morgana watched as people seemed to jump out of the way of the shards in slow motion. *Why are they looking at me like that? I just saved my sister's life... shouldn't they be cheering?*

"Morgana!" Myfanwy stepped up onto the dais and caught her niece in her arms as the girl crumpled.

"'Gana!" Jenni dropped to her knees beside them. "What did you do? Why did you do it?"

"I drank the poison to stop them getting you." Morgana smiled, "You are the only person who ever mattered in my life, and I spent the last five years having a temper tantrum; I wasted my life when I could have enjoyed it with you, even blind as I was." She gasped as the feeling left her legs.

"But... we could... if you..." Myfanwy relinquished her as Jenni gathered her sister into her arms. "If you hadn't done this...

With her body rapidly giving out on her, Morgana managed to raise one hand up to touch the face above her that matched hers. "I have made too many blunders to be forgiven so simply. I have to die to be redeemed and reborn."

Her hand dropped back as she lost control of it. "Don't forget me, Jenni. Live your life the way you want to, not the way that all the stick-in-the-muds want you to. You need to be the real you."

Jenni hugged Morgana tightly. "I never stopped loving you or Mum or Dad; I never wanted us to be apart."

Morgana stared into Jenni's eyes for one long moment, then the poison reached into her face, and she could only see a blur. *"I'm sorry Gwynnhafr. I have to go now. I love you all."*

The blur became black.

Thirty-Three

Mara, Nex and Morbus stopped before the Earth Nexus door. "We can't go through here, Lord Thanatos." Mara said, "We're full daemons and the door won't let us through."

The God of Death laughed. "I go where I please and I am not human. I very much doubt that Lord Archington guarded against my presence, and it covers all of you." He placed his hand on the door, and it opened obediently.

"But what of the door into the Fire Realm? That too is guarded against us." Nex said.

Thanatos rummaged in the bag he carried and pulled out three black crystals on chains. "These carry the essence of my presence, hiding you from any observation whether physical, magical or technological and will allow you to step through the door to the Fire Realm."

Nex and Morbus took the chains and put them on.

Mara took hers and looked at it for a while before she put it on. "Thank you, Lord Thanatos."

The four of them stepped through the Nexus door and Thanatos led them out through the tunnels, exiting from them in a cave on the side of the Down above Drakord.

"The Fire Realm Door is on the other side of the valley." Thanatos pointed, "Follow the road through Drakord to Foreydon and you'll find the cave in the down behind it."

The three daemons nodded and began to walk down the path from the cave.

"However," Thanatos said, "Do any evil deed while wearing those crystals, and not only will I know about it, the crystals will crumble and you will be visible to all."

"We wouldn't dream of it, Lord Thanatos." Mara replied, "Thank you again."

Obviously mollified, the God disappeared back into the cave and the three daemons kept walking downhill.

"Are you going to obey him?" Nex asked her cousin.

Mara rolled her eyes, "What do you think? I have a mission to fulfil, and that foolish god has given me the means to not only get the Shield, but the Crown that Cousin Jezebeath failed to get. Once I have both, I'll be able to return to the Fire Realm without any need for the Blessing of the Reaper." Her eyes flared with a golden glow as she continued, "And should I be successful at this, the Dragon's Pendant will be within my grasp as well."

"What are you going to do?" Morbus said.

Nex was pleased to note that her brother was looking more than a little worried. *He's actually thinking for a change.*

"I'm not telling you. You two go home and say nothing of this to anyone. If our Lord Apollyon asks you, just say that the next part of my plan requires that I work alone, and I shall return soon." Mara smiled.

Nex sighed. "Come on Morbus, let's go."

"We can't just leave her." He objected, "Our orders were to guard her."

"You saw Lady Deumara fight in the Underworld, do you really think that she can't look after herself?" Nex turned and walked away from Mara.

Torn between his orders from Apollyon and Mara's order, Morbus hovered uncertainly.

"Go on Morbus. I'll come and find you when I return home, and we'll share a bath and talk." Mara purred, stroking his face.

Morbus blushed.

"Now go with your sister and don't worry about me." She turned back toward the cave.

Morbus stayed still, watching her walk.

When Mara reached the cave, she looked back, smiled at him and blew him a kiss. Morbus blushed again and hurried to catch up with Nex.

His sister took one look at his glowing face and shook her head. "Idiot."

They continued walking.

WHISPERS SURROUNDED her. Voices on the edge of her hearing called to her, familiar and strange. She walked forward ignoring them, the darkness around her going on forever.

Time as she knew it stood still.

She kept walking.

"NO."

"But your Royal Highness, she's been dead for nearly a week; protocol and tradition say..." the new Castle Steward stuttered to a stop as Jenni glared at him across her desk.

"I don't care. My Grandfather has assured me that the stasis field will keep my sister's body uncorrupted for as long as is necessary."

"We must have a state funeral before Midwinter, your Royal Highness." He repeated for the fourth time that day, "It's ill luck to have a dead body above ground on Midwinter Morning."

"I will not bury her. She is coming back, I can feel it." Jenni stood up, "And if you keep bringing this up, I will find someone who will do as I say, rather than what Tradition and Protocol says."

He nodded and backed away. "As you wish it, your Royal Highness."

"Go deal with the preparations for the Midwinter Festival. We still have to pick a Solar King for the parade and the celebration; there should be a file of the applicants in your predecessor's office. Select the five that you consider the best for the position, and we'll talk it over tomorrow." She dismissed him with a wave of her hand and turned her back to him, her shoulders rigid and tense as she looked out the window.

He left the room looking confused as Myfanwy entered.

"Are you upsetting the staff again?" Jenni's aunt said as she joined her, looking down at the copper roof of the pagoda where Morgana's body lay in state, surrounded by roses and held in stasis by the four crystal and gold field generators that Aderyn had brought in from Zonlasin B the day that Morgana died.

"They persist in trying to hold me to these traditions and protocols that they've learned. I thought my speech at the Ball made it clear that I would not be like the Queens who had gone before me."

"That's ironic." Myfanwy's mouth pulled to one side in a wry smile. "You're being just like Angharad. She discarded protocol and tradition left and right when she first became queen. Anything that she deemed too ancient or unenjoyable was discarded."

Jenni shot a look at her. "How many Castle Stewards did she go through?"

"I remember there being a new one for every festival, right up until she married your father." Myfanwy smiled properly at the memory. "A whole year and eight different stewards. The Staff didn't know if they were coming or going."

Jenni laughed and the tightness in her shoulders disappeared; sighing she rolled them around individually before stretching her arms high above her head. "I hope I don't go through that many!"

Myfanwy gestured down at the pagoda. "How long before you let them bury her?"

"As long as it takes to be sure that she is not coming back."

THE SAND WAS DEEP ENOUGH to make walking difficult, but she knew that she had to walk and keep walking until she reached the place that the three Kings of the Gate had told her to go to.

Eventually a landmark that she vaguely remembered appeared and with a sigh she stepped out of the sand and onto the frost rimed grass beside it.

The chill invaded her body and she hugged herself deeper into her cloak, trying to get back to the warmth that she remembered having. Her breath steamed as she walked further into the leafless forest. Moving around stopped the air temperature from making her shiver, but the occasional strong gusts of wind took away any chance of feeling warm.

From time to time, she saw other Judged amongst the trees. Like her, they walked to stay warm but when they grew tired of walking, they would huddle at the base of a tree in the long grass.

She wandered so long that she forgot why she was in the forest.

Sometimes she would emerge from the forest at the top of a hill to gaze across the underworld toward Elysium. Appreciation of the view was lost on her though; the cold stole any thoughts she had.

She entered a clearing beside an iced up stream that divided the forest from the Tiring Path. Four girls sat huddled together amongst the long grass, arms wrapped around each other's shoulders.

"Why are you four together? We are supposed to wander the forest separately." She said.

The girls gazed up at her.

One, with eyes the grey of the sea in winter, stood. "We had been close friends in life and died in the same car accident. Like you, we wandered the forest and shivered, but then I began to find the others and when I gathered us all here, we felt that we should stay together."

She nodded. "Does it work? Are you warmer?"

The grey eyed girl shook her head, "No, we are still as cold as our hearts were when we chose to ignore the laws of the land and drove while intoxicated, but it feels right that we suffer this punishment together." The girl sat down with her friends again, her arms snaking out around their waists and their arms wrapping around hers.

She fingered her thick velvet and fur cloak. "I don't know why I am wearing this, I died saving my sister but when I arrived here, I was wearing this." She looked down at the girls. Their skin was pale and lips blue; they wore thin summer clothing. Only the grey eyed girl wore a cardigan as well as her summer dress, another girl with eyes as green as spring leaves wore Capri leggings and a strappy top and the other two girls wore denim shorts and yellow t-shirts

"Maybe your body has been wrapped in it for your burial." One of the girls in shorts said.

"My sister probably would do something that illogical." She was surprised by how much emotion welled up, un-tainted by the iciness of the forest. A faint smile formed on her lips. "My sister is probably refusing to bury me at all."

"I wish my family had been able to wrap me in something so lovely." The girl in Capri leggings said wistfully, "Then perhaps I wouldn't be so cold."

The wind howled around the clearing, making the girls huddle together. She just pulled her cloak tighter around her body, but for the first time since entering the Hills of Treachery she wondered why she bothered.

"It doesn't make a difference what you are wearing, you know." She said, "You carry the chill of betrayal in your soul." The wind swept around them again and she let the cloak float away from her on it.

"What did you do to end up here?" The other girl wearing shorts asked, "Going by what you're wearing, you come from a wealthy family. Surely rich people get a free pass to Elysium?"

She looked down at the beautifully designed velvet and satin gown she wore, the gems and gold on her wrists and fingers. One hand drifted up to her face and felt the bejewelled earrings and necklace. It was the first time that she'd actually paid attention to what she was wearing.

"The rich are just as capable of betrayal and treachery as the poor." She replied.

"So, what did you do?" The girl insisted.

She stroked the sky blue fabric for a long moment. "I spent the five years before I died blaming my sister for everything bad that had happened to me. In my mind, she was responsible for our parent's divorce, the death of our blood parents and Grandfather... I even thought she was responsible for the septicaemia that damaged my eyes."

The green eyed girl laughed. "That's daft!"

She scuffed her soft white boots back and forth in the grass, listening to the icy crunch. "I know. I tried to fix it by drinking the poison one of her enemies had put in her wine."

"And that's how you died?" The grey eyed girl was confused. "Surely that makes you a hero?"

"That's what I thought at the time, but maybe I was wrong." She took a deep breath and shrugged, "I think I need to consider this a little more."

The wind blew her cloak out again and the girls in shorts whimpered. She undid the gold and sapphire clasp. "If you all get really close together, this should wrap around you."

"I thought you said it didn't matter what you wore?" the grey eyed girl said.

"It doesn't, but if you don't want it..." she held out the cloak toward them.

The nearest girl jumped up and grabbed it. "Thank you."

She smiled and walked away.

Thirty-Four

Aderyn and Myfanwy stood the other side of Jenni's desk wearing identical disapproving expressions.

"You yourself said that the stasis field will keep her uncorrupted indefinitely." Jenni said.

Aderyn nodded. "I did and it will, but I never intended for you to leave her on display like Snow White waiting for the prince."

"I won't put her in the ground until I am certain that she won't return."

"Jenni sweetheart, she died from that poison." Myfanwy said, walking around the desk to stand beside her niece, one hand resting on Jenni's shoulder. "We called in the best doctors we could find, from my School, Earth Nexus and some of the technologically advanced worlds on the Hall; none of them could save her."

"Besides which, if she did return into that body, she'd still be blind and in danger from the Cancer. Would you really want that?" Aderyn said softly.

Jenni stared at him.

"We have to move her inside at the very least." Myfanwy rubbed Jenni's back a little as her shoulders began to creep inward.

"Move her to the suite that we designated as hers then." Jenni replied, shaking off Myfanwy's hand, "at least when she wakes up, the surroundings will be nice."

Aderyn looked at his daughter and mouthed: *"Take it and leave her alone."*

Myfanwy sighed and shook her head. "As you wish, your Royal Highness."

Jenni said nothing.

As Aderyn shut the study door behind them, his sharply tuned cyborg hearing heard Jenni begin to cry.

SHE WANDERED THROUGH the trees once more. This time however, she didn't feel the cold quite as sharply. The path that she took felt familiar and soon she came across a young boy wearing a jacket that she recognised. His feet were bare, pale and blue in colour under the dried blood that was splashed across them.

"Where did you get the jacket?" she asked him.

"A girl gave it to me when she left the forest." He replied wearily, "She said that someone had given it to her, and she wanted to pass it on to someone else."

She blinked. She'd thought that that was a dream. It had to be a coincidence. "Why are your feet covered in blood?"

"It's blood from someone I knew at school. It reminds me of what I did." He began to cry, and she knelt down beside him, wrapping her arms around him. "He was a Geek and a smartarse. I hated the sight of him, so when someone from another school said that they had a bone to pick with him I agreed to help them."

She winced, somehow knowing what he was about to say.

"I chased him into the industrial estate where the other boy was waiting. He and his friends grabbed both of us. They made me watch what the other boy did to him, and I was close enough that his blood flooded over my feet" he broke down completely.

She said nothing while he cried, holding his shuddering frame tightly.

Eventually he finished his story. "They told me that if I said anything to the police, they would point the finger at me, so I stayed quiet, even after his body was discovered. The Judges at the Gate said I would bear his blood until I atoned for my behaviour."

She looked at his feet again, then moved away slightly, sat down on the ice covered ground and removed her white, soft leather boots. "Here. These might make you feel a little better." She handed them to him, "You look like you're the same size as me."

He took them. "What about you?"

She shrugged. "The chill is in our souls. It doesn't matter what we're wearing, we feel it anyway."

He looked confused.

"Put them on." She stood up, "I have a lot more thinking to do."

As she walked away, she glanced back. The boy was stroking the leather of the boots and looking at his feet. Then he crammed his feet into them quickly. The white leather remained that colour for no more than a few seconds before the bloodstains appeared.

The boy howled in anguish, scrambled up and ran into the forest in the opposite direction.

She kept walking.

THE MIDWINTER CELEBRATION was rapidly approaching. Myfanwy, Aderyn and Artair handled everything that they possibly could, only going to Jenni if they absolutely needed her signature or opinion.

Jenni spent as much of her waking hours sitting beside the bed in Morgana's suite as she could. She took all the unimportant meals in Morgana's sitting room and slept in the guest room of the suite.

Her family deflected all criticism and shielded her from the rumours growing in the Llanirstyri Court that their High Princess had gone mad from grief. Jenni was aware of all this, but there was something that called her to sit with her sister's stasis locked body. *I can still feel her. I don't think she's completely dead to me.*

So, she kept her vigil.

SHE FELT WARMER. THERE was no denying it. Even in sock covered feet with no cloak, she felt warmer than she had when she first arrived in the Hills. As she walked, she talked out loud to herself, in an effort to understand what was going on.

"I completed the quest for the shield and then used its powers to save my sister's life. Yet I still ended up here, because I betrayed her." She sighed and found an ice covered fallen tree to sit on. "I should be a hero because of that, not a Judged."

The wind whistled around her.

"Did I really have to drink that poison?" She said to it.

The wind picked up the sibilant in 'poison' and whispered it back to her through the lifeless trees. She listened and thought for a long while.

"I could have just kept it from her. 'Van was well aware of what I was doing and why. I didn't need to drink it; I could have just handed it to 'Van and have completed my mission that way."

The wind swept around her ankles and her dress billowed out like a sky blue velvet sea. Then the answer came to her in a flash.

"Why... did I feel I had to die?" she stood up and began walking again, "I had saved her, I would have been fine... except that I was still riddled with Cancer and Blind."

The hill steepened beneath her feet, and she lost her footing, sliding for several feet before catching a tree branch and righting herself.

"I was scared to live any longer. I was terrified of the Cancer treatment and the thought of the procedure to remove the implant as well as the tumours in my brain. I wanted to die to free my family of the burden of my care; especially Jenni." The wind returned to howl around her, blowing her skirts out to tangle around the tree trunk and her hair to snag in the low hanging twigs above her.

Unbidden, a memory resurfaced...

"TRUE, SHE HAS MANY friends, but only one sister. In one Earth days' time, in Llanirstyr Realm, a poisoner paid by the enemies of thine sister's rule shall attack her.

Thou art the only one who can misdirect his hand, for it is in thine powers alone. The Shield of Courage shall guard thee from sight and thine mother's blade protect thee."

"So, I have to go to Llanirstyr and save Jenni from being poisoned. What about my illness? And the blindness?" Morgana shivered at the thought of living as blind again. *"If I leave here, I'll be blind again."*

"Nay, sweet daughter. Charon hath given thee the way to heal thineself and thy sister, as well as banish thine sister's attacker unharmed." The light began to fade. *"Fare thee well, mine Chosen one."*

"ARIANRHOD TOLD ME THAT Charon had given me everything I needed." She muttered, untangling herself and plaiting her hair into a rough tail down her back. She used a ribbon from her bodice to finish the plait off. "But I was certain that the antidote in the box had disappeared and that the only way to save her was to drink the poisoned wine."

She started walking again.

"That was the wrong thing to do... I betrayed her again by using the poison to opt out of dealing with the problems ahead of me." The hill became a smoother incline and through the trees, she could see the Tiring Path. "I wish I could fix that."

The wind blew harder against her back, pushing her toward the path. It was a warm wind now and she began to perspire in the velvet gown as she fought her way through the trees.

As she reached the edge of the forest, a white raven dropped out of the sky to land in front of her. She recognised it.

"Charon?"

The bird shimmered and became the Ferryman in his feathered cloak. "Indeed, Morgana, it is I."

"I thought you didn't leave the rivers." She stopped moving and folded her arms.

"Only by my Master's request, and he has bade me escort you to his Palace." Charon bowed.

"But I thought I couldn't leave the Hills of Treachery." She gasped and tears welled up, "I wish I could; I'd go and be reborn in the hope that I could one day return my sister's love to her somehow."

Charon smiled. "That day may come sooner than you think. Come with me, Princess."

"I'M TELLING YOU, HER brain is alive. I can still feel her." Jenni insisted, "Call in who you want, test her again, I swear to you that she is still there!"

Aderyn wriggled his nose in thought. "There's one last person that I could call on, but it's going to be tricky to contact her. I'd have to go back to Earth Nexus at Full Moon and there's no guarantee that she'll answer me."

"Please Grandfather, do it. 'Gana is still alive. I know Dad and 'Van don't believe me, and the rest of the court think I am mad, but I am certain of it." Jenni said.

"I will do what I can." He sighed.

"Thank you."

Aderyn stood before the huge metal Earth Nexus door. *I've not had to use this function before, I don't even know if it's going to work.* He accessed the computer that controlled the door and checked the current time and date beyond the door. *It's the day after Guy Fawkes Night. The full moon was a week ago.* He thought for a moment and tapped in a date and time. Around the frame, a series of lights began to blink into existence. When they were all lit, the lights pulsed three times and the door lock clicked open.

He pulled it open and climbed through. After he'd exited the Folly, he climbed the Down as the sun dropped below the western horizon. At the Stone Circle he paused, one hand laid flat on the Keystone of the entry arch. "Lady of The Moon, Huntress Supreme. Hear my plea." He concentrated and his hand glowed white. When he removed it, the hand print stayed.

He walked away, then as soon as he was far enough that he wouldn't damage the stones with the shockwave, he switched to running.

One of the advantages of being an artificial man, is that I don't need to breathe when I am running. He thought as he sped past the Gallops toward the tower looming on the northern horizon.

Once there, he repeated his action, leaving a glowing handprint on the stone above the tumbledown tower's doorway. Then he sped south-east.

One by one, Aderyn visited each of the six towers that guarded the valley below them from dangers that the normal people of Arking Vale thought mere fairy tales. He finished his circuit at the Lady's Tower before walking over to the small stone circle in the centre of the park.

The moon had risen an hour or so ago and its light shone down onto the altar stone in the centre of the circle.

Aderyn entered the circle, laid his hands on the altar and repeated his plea.

"You called, my son?" A soft female voice entered his mind.

"I did, my Lady Goddess." Aderyn replied, looking around.

"What is it you want then? I'm more than a little busy at the moment." The voice became irritated.

"It's my Granddaughter... actually it's about both of them." He said.

"Give me a moment." The voice said after a small pause.

Aderyn waited.

The moonlight thickened and a woman with long, shining white hair and silver eyes stepped out of it. "What is the matter with Gwynnhafr and Morgana, Aderyn?"

He quickly recounted what had happened since Morgana had arrived in Arkingham.

"I know of Morgana's trip to the Underworld. I gave her the mission she needed to be able to leave." The Lady said, "But I am disturbed that she felt that she needed to die in order to complete it; that is something I never asked of her."

"Jenni believes that her sister is still alive. She can feel her through their mental connection." He took a deep breath, "Would you be able to come to Llanirstyr and see if she is correct?"

The Lady laughed. "Dear sweet Aderyn. Trust Gwynnhafr's instincts. All you have to do is remove the cancer and implant from her brain and give her time to heal."

"So, she is alive?"

The Lady's attention seemed to drift away like a cloud on the breeze for a moment. "She thinks that she is dead, but my siblings in the Underworld will deal with that. Give her a healthy body to return to, Aderyn."

He bowed. "I shall do my best, my Lady Goddess."

The woman smiled. "I know you shall, my son." And she stepped back into the light and disappeared.

Thirty-Five

Charon led her down to the river where one of the small boats that he brought the Judged into the Underworld with bobbed on the water. "This will take you to Lord Hades' Palace." He helped her step into the boat.

"I don't understand." Morgana said.

"All will be explained to you when you get there." Charon gave the boat a small push out into the water.

"Okay, but I didn't think being dead would be like this." She muttered as the boat began its voyage and Charon transformed back into the White Raven, flying back to his ship.

The boat sped along the waterways of the Underworld until it reached the white stone jetty behind Hades' Palace. Morgana found Angharad waiting for her.

"I know I said I would see you again, darling, but I didn't want it to be this soon!" Angharad said as her daughter threw herself into her arms.

After sobbing hard for a while, Morgana recovered enough to pull away. "I thought it was the right thing to do, Mama."

"It doesn't matter now, Morgana." Her birth mother said, "Lord Hades is waiting for you, so we should go."

Hand in Hand, they climbed up the hill toward the tunnel entrance, but before they got there, Xanthus landed in front of them. "I was told to bring you to the Palace, Morgana." He said, shaking himself a little.

"What about Mama?" she asked, holding to Angharad's hand tightly.

"I'll see you there, darling." Angharad smiled and faded away.

Morgana laughed a little shakily, "I forgot that she's only a spirit here."

Xanthus tossed his head. "Come on, I want to get back to the Moirae; they said that they'd give me some red apples when I came back."

"Still thinking of your stomach, Xanthus?" Morgana swung herself up onto his back, behind his wings.

"What else is there for me to think about in this place?" he grumbled as he took off, "It's been really boring since you left."

"What happened with the Daemons?" she said as he rose into the air and swooped elegantly toward the palace.

"Two of them took a bath in the Lethe and the other three took them back to their dimension with their tails between their legs." Xanthus let out a braying laugh, "I very much doubt that they'll try that again."

He banked and circled over the front court, landing neatly in the centre. "There you go, Lady."

Morgana slid down from his back. "Thank you."

The Pegasoi nuzzled her and trotted out of the court to return to the House of the Moirae. Morgana turned to mount the stairs into the palace.

"Princess, if you would come this way, please?" One of the servants materialised beside her, "Lord Hades and the Court are in the Garden."

Morgana followed her. *There's something odd this time. Last time I was here I was fully alive, and everyone treated me like a bomb about to go off. This time, it's so much more casual. As if I'm a regular visitor. Is that really how they treat the Judged once they've been released from their torment?*

They passed through a stone archway on one side of the Palace. The garden beyond was laid out as far as the eye could see, in so many different styles that Morgana wondered who could possibly have time to keep it all in good condition.

The part of the garden that was her destination was obvious as there was a lot of happy laughter and music coming from it. The servant led her into a large grassed area; one end of which was shaded by silk cloth suspended from white marble columns. Under the shade, large puffy cushions had been scattered across bright coloured cloths. In one corner a quartet played, while Hades and the Court listened.

The laughter came from the children who were playing an energetic game of tag on the grass, accompanied by a half dozen spaniel puppies. The adults were watching them and smiling.

"Ah, Morgana, come and seat yourself." Hades said, waving to her, "We were just enjoying the latest compositions from Tchaikovsky."

The Servant with her bowed deeply to the court and faded out. Morgana looked for a spare cushion and saw her mother hovering at the back of the Court behind Hades, so she sat on a yellow cushion with a black horse pattern near the Lord of the Underworld.

"Have you realised what has happened yet, Morgana?" Angharad asked quietly as the music began again.

"What do you mean, Mama? I'm dead aren't I, so I'm supposed to be here." She replied.

"Dear Sweet Child," Hades wife, Persephone smiled sadly, "Yet again you are just visiting with us."

Morgana frowned. "But I was Judged. I walked the Tiring Path and suffered in the Hills of Treachery's petrified forest."

Hades sighed and stood. "Come and walk with me, Princess Morgana." He held out his hand and helped her stand up again.

"But I only just got here." She protested.

"We'll come back in a moment." He replied, tucking her hand under his arm.

They left the music and laughter and strolled along a path between cherry trees that were both blossoming and fruiting at the same time.

"We sent you back to Llanirstyr to complete the mission you had been given by Artemis." Hades said, "And you should not have returned here for a long time."

"I thought that Time didn't matter here." She said.

"I wasn't referring to our perception of the time, but yours." He patted her hand.

"I thought I did the right thing."

They turned into an avenue of oaks that were wearing spring colours at one end and autumn colours at the other.

"You saved your sister's life at the expense of your own for selfish reasons." He said gently, "She is distraught and unable to function at a time when she will need to be alert. Your mission wasn't over after you saved her from the poison."

"What do you mean?" Morgana couldn't process what he was saying, her mind felt heavy, and fog bound for some reason.

"Having failed at the poisoning, Gwynnhafyr's enemy will try again at the Midwinter Festival Parade." Hades sat down on a marble bench between a summer leafed oak and an autumn one. Morgana sat too. "I don't understand. She's got plenty of soldiers to guard her."

"Perhaps your mother should clarify this. Angharad!" Hades raised his voice commandingly and Morgana's birth mother shimmered into being in front of them.

"How may I serve you, Lord Hades?" the former queen asked, curtseying.

"Morgana doesn't know anything about Llanirstyr's Midwinter Celebration. Would you please explain."

"Satyulemas begins on the 15th of December, Morgana. It opens with a huge firework show at midnight. On Yuletide, the 21st, the capital has a massive parade. Your sister will walk ahead of the float carrying the Solar King to the battle with the Holly King in the centre of Arking Town." Angharad paused.

"They'll be surrounded by soldiers, won't they? Nothing could happen to her?" Morgana felt the butterflies start up in her stomach.

"By tradition, the Queen (or High Princess) is unaccompanied, and anyone may approach her for a blessing." Her mother sighed, "There is also an obscure law that none of my family ever got round to changing that says that if the Queen (or High Princess) is killed without heir during the parade, the winner of the bout between the Solar King and the Holly King becomes King Consort of the Land in truth and selects his own bride to become Queen."

Morgana stared at her in horror. "I've left her unprotected. If I were invisible, I'd be able to walk with her and guard her from any attacks..." her voice trailed off.

"... and if you were there, even if she did die, you'd be there to become queen and continue the succession that Arianrhod decreed." Hades finished.

They returned to the garden, but now Morgana was too worried about her sister to enjoy the music, food and drink.

I really did do the wrong thing and now I can't go back. She thought, over and over again, tears welling up in her eyes every time she contemplated her sister's fate. She closed her eyes and took deep breaths in an effort to calm down.

The heavy feeling returned and between the music and the warmth of the air, she dozed off. She began to dream:

"THE REMOVAL OF THE implant went according to plan." The odd, blurry voice seemed to come from behind her, but she couldn't turn to see who was speaking. The room she was lying in smelled of disinfectant, the coppery tang of blood and something else that she couldn't Identify, but she couldn't see a thing. There were machines in the room as well, Morgana could hear the familiar bleep of a heart monitor and the whoosh of a ventilator.

Someone was beside her. They laid one hand on her cheek momentarily and spoke to whoever was behind her. "How many tumours?" the voice sounded muffled, and Morgana realised that the other person's voice was blurry because they were wearing a mask too. *I think that might be Grandfather.*

"Not many; its more their placement that is problematic." The other person said. There was a clatter.

I'm in an operating theatre again. I thought I was dead? She'd often half woken during the procedures to restore her sight, but there was always a nurse monitoring her who calmed her and sent her back to sleep.

The second voice sighed. "We have to get them all out. There are only a few days left to the parade and her sister is refusing to go unless Morgana is with her."

That's definitely Grandfather. She tried to get her eyes to work again and then remembered that the first person had said that they'd removed the implant. *So, I'm blind again.*

"The High Princess does realise that this may not work?" the person behind her said.

"It will work." Aderyn glanced down at her again, "Someone with a great deal of power has promised me that it will."

"What about recovery time? It could take her weeks to get over this." A third voice, female and vaguely familiar came from her right but it was so muffled that she couldn't' figure out who it was.

"We'll take her to..." Aderyn's voice became even more muted as he turned away for a moment, "When we bring her back, only a couple of days will have passed, and she'll be fully healed."

What is going on? Is this real or a dream? Morgana began to panic, and the bleep of the monitor sped up. The hand came back to lie on her cheek again and began to stroke. It was very soothing and soon, the panic had dulled to mere anxiety.

"Is she awake?" the female voice asked.

"The poison she drank has her in a deep coma, it's more likely that she's dreaming about something." The voice behind her said.

"That's another thing, how are we going to wake her to be sure that the procedure is a success if the poison is still in her system?" the woman said.

She's panicking about something. Morgana tried to send out her mind to find out what it was.

The hand on her cheek tapped twice. "None of that now, darling child. Sleep and trust us to heal you."

"Her mind is awake? Fascinating. Of course, that particular poison is supposed to kill instantly, but you Llanirstyri are nothing if not resilient." The person behind her sounded as if they'd like to do more than take tumours out of her brain.

"It shouldn't be though." The woman sounded like she was laughing. "Father, allow me to send her back under please. This next part is going to be difficult, and we can't be distracted."

Oh, of course, its Myfanwy. Who else would call Grandfather that. With a jolt, Morgana realised that she wasn't dreaming, and they really were operating on her brain.

Before she could react though, Aderyn said "Of course, 'Van. Put her back under." His hand stroked her face. "We'll see you soon, Morgana. Rest please."

"Morgana, you need to go back to sleep. We can't finish the procedure otherwise. Rest, little one." Myfanwy's mind surrounded hers and pushed her gently into the very depths of her own.

Sleep flooded across her.

MORGANA WOKE WITH A start and realised that her head was pillowed on Thanatos' lap. The handsome god smiled down at her. "Dream well?"

She ignored the question and sat up to look at Hades. "Did the poison put me into a coma rather than killing me?"

He nodded.

"Then why did I go for Judgement? Why did I go to the Hills?" she scrambled to her feet.

"All who experience the Lethargus come here. If they are lucky, they can be Judged and complete their time in whichever land they are assigned to." Thanatos said.

"Can I go back?"

Hades sighed and shook his head. "Not unless your body calls you back again."

Morgana stared at him and then broke into tears, running out of the garden through the Courtyard and toward the meadow.

Thirty - Six

"We've done the best we can." The Zonlasin Surgeon said in a quiet voice.

Behind him Morgana lay in a Healing Capsule which floated gently in mid-air. He, Aderyn and Myfanwy stood by the only door into the room and a Zonlasin Nurse silently monitored Morgana's vital signs.

"Your best is better than anything Earth could do," Aderyn said, "I just wish that she wouldn't still be blind."

"It may be a moot point; after all, she may never recover from the effects of the poison." The surgeon shrugged as if to say it didn't matter to him if his patient lived or died.

"We'll carry on as we discussed during the operation." Myfanwy said, "A Healer is waiting for us already."

"Where are you taking her?" a voice interrupted from outside.

They looked round.

"Artair, Helen, Jenni... we didn't know..." Myfanwy started,

"That we knew what you were doing?" Helen asked, tipping one eyebrow up, "Of course we knew, Jenni has been in contact with Morgana's mind and watching through her eyes."

Aderyn looked at Jenni who managed to look guilty. "I told you not to disturb her mind, Jenni. Were you watching during the operation?"

"I started to," The young woman admitted, "But something shoved me out and I couldn't' get back in, so I went to Mum and Dad and they suggested we come here."

"We were worried that something had gone wrong." Artair said.

"Everything has gone as well as we expected." Aderyn replied, "There is no need for you to worry, Artair."

"We're her parents; just because we have divorced, doesn't mean that we've stopped being concerned about our children." Helen snapped, "When were you and your daughter going to tell us what happened, Aderyn, before or after Morgana died?"

"Mum, stop." Jenni laid one hand on her arm, "This isn't helping." She turned back to her grandfather, "I assume that you're taking her to the Tavern to recover? So Grand-Mere can adjust time for her."

"That is the plan." Myfanwy said with a gentle smile.

"Then you won't mind if we come with you," Helen said.

Aderyn looked at Jenni. "Did you explain everything about the Hall when you brought them here?"

She nodded.

"Fair enough then, it is about time that you met my wife." Aderyn grinned.

Helen looked past them into the room. "Can we see Morgana first?"

"Of course you can." Myfanwy glared at her father until he and the surgeon moved away, then ushered Helen, Artair and Jenni into the room.

ANGHARAD FOUND MORGANA sitting under a copse of trees in the middle of the horse herd. Arion and Aurelia stood either side of her and Amira lay on the ground, her head in Morgana's lap, while the young woman finger combed and plaited her mane, weaving flowers into each one and tying the plaits up with grass

"Are you all right, Morgana." She asked.

"I've been so stupid, Mama. I thought that Jenni and Dad would be better off without me." She finished a plait and began another, weaving blue flowers into it from the pile beside her. "I didn't consider that I might still be needed."

Angharad sat down behind her and stroked her daughter's long blonde hair. "You'll always be needed by your sister, *Cariad*, even once she becomes Queen."

"But she has so many friends from so many different places; she won't want me around." Morgana leaned back, closing her eyes.

"When I became Queen, Myfanwy had similar feelings, so she went off to study Medicine on Earth Nexus." Angharad laughed, "But I sent her so many messages asking for her advice over the four years she was away, that when she finished her degree, she came home and became my First Advisor."

"What about Papa? Didn't he advise you?"

"Of course he did, but only my sister gave me truly honest advice." She pushed morgana back up into a sitting position. "You could be that for Gwynnhafr."

Morgana went back to weaving the flowers into Amira's mane. "But if my body doesn't call me back again, I'll be stuck here until it dies, and I can be reborn."

"Would that really be such a bad thing?" Amira snorted, "We'd be able to ride together all the time."

Morgana stroked the Arab's neck. "No matter how much I'd like that, Amira, I would be no good to my sister if that happens."

"Use this time in Elysium to hone your skills, Morgana." Her mother stood up, "I am sure that everything will be well."

Morgana took her mother's advice. She learned Llanirstyri custom and law with her mother, continued her warrior training with Scathach and Kuklayne and studied many different subjects with various different experts. She rode all around Elysium with Amira and flew over the Underworld with Xanthus.

"How are your studies coming along, Morgana?" Thanatos asked as he poured her tea. They'd been having a proper Afternoon Tea every seven days, and she looked forward to it as much as she did her visits to the Moirae's Cottage.

"I'm finding it difficult to understand politics, but other than that, it's an interesting way of passing the days."

"Politics never made much sense to me either." The God of Death smiled.

Morgana sighed.

"Is there something the matter?" he passed her a plate with her favourite cake on it.

She picked at it with her fork. "I wish I knew how much longer I'll be here." She put the fork down and picked up her cup.

"That's the problem with Lethargus, you can't tell when the body is going to call you back. It depends on a lot of things that are outside of your control."

Sipping her tea, morgana wished that she could contact Jenni and ask for her help. *She always knows what to do.* A phantom touch on the back of her hand made her drop her cup onto its saucer where it sprayed tea all over the table and her clothes.

What was that? Morgana touched her hand as the servants cleaned everything up. She looked up at Thanatos.

He was smiling again.

JENNI SAT BESIDE HER sister, holding her hand. *I wish you would wake up, I don't know what to do; you always did.*

"Your Royal Highness, I am fully aware that time in this place is completely different to that of Llanirstyr, but you must come back!" the Castle Steward ignored the looks that Myfanwy and Aderyn were giving him. "The Parade is only two days away and you must be seen to be taking part in the Satyulemas celebrations before it."

Jenni stroked her sister's hand and glanced up at the monitors on the other side of the bed. She did it once or twice a minute without really taking in the figures anymore. "I will not be attending anything without my sister. If I have to sit in the tavern for the next twelve moons, I shall, so that I am the first thing that she sees when she wakes up." She didn't look at him.

"But this is just a shell of the Princess, she isn't really there." He snapped, "Let it die, bury her remains, mourn and take up your responsibilities! Your Mother would be turning in her Grave to see such disregard of your position."

Myfanwy winced. "Lord Steward, if you wish to keep your own position, I suggest that you refrain from saying such things."

"Let him say what he will, 'Van. He knows where the door is." Jenni still didn't look at the man.

The Steward looked confused and glanced at the door leading into the Tavern Keeper's Residence. His mouth opened.

"Shut up." Aderyn said, "The Princess will wake up and her Royal Highness will return in good time to take part in Satyulemas. Go back to Llanirstyr, do your job and leave the worrying about the High Princess' and her sister, to Lady Myfanwy and myself."

The man's back became ramrod stiff. "Yes, my Lord Arkingham." He spun on one heel and marched out of the room.

Aderyn listened to the steward's furious footsteps and then chuckled as the door to the Tavern proper slammed. "Do you want me to look for another Castle Steward, Jenni?"

She said nothing, looking down at Morgana's face and stroking her hand.

"Jenni?"

"Hush." Jenni seemed oddly intent, then all of a sudden, pinched the fleshy part of Morgana's palm. Morgana flinched and the heart rate monitor went crazy for a moment.

Myfanwy moved closer to the bed and examined the monitors. "Do it again."

Jenni turned morgana's hand over and pinched the skin on the back. All the monitors went crazy.

"She's back." Myfanwy pointed at the EEG. "Is her mind there?"

Jenni gently pushed her mind against Morgana's. *I can feel her faintly, as if she's really far away from me.* She said as much and both Myfanwy and Aderyn looked elated.

"Try talking to her." Myfanwy said in Jenni's mind.

She nodded and pushed harder against Morgana's mind, *"Gana... are you there, Sis?"*

The EEG gave a leap and a chatter.

Morgana's eyes flickered.

"Morgana, come home, we need you. I need you." Jenni tried again.

The Heart monitor and the EEG both flared into life. Morgana's head, restrained so that she didn't damage the healing of her wounds, turned from side to side and her hands flailed.

Jenni withdrew her mind. "She's in pain when I do that. I can't cause her pain.!

Myfanwy said, "She'll return to us when she is ready, but I don't think it will be long."

Jenni went back to stroking her sister's hand.

"You need to get out of here and get some fresher air." Aderyn said, gently disengaging Jenni's grip. "Come and have something to eat and a nap."

Jenni let him pull her up but looked at Morgana.

"I'll stay with her, don't worry." Myfanwy said, moving round to take Jenni's place beside the bed, "You'll feel better after you catch some rest and relaxation."

"You'll call me if anything happens?" Jenni said reluctantly.

"Of course."

SHE SCREAMED.

Morgana clutched at her head and curled in a ball on the floor, surrounded by the remains of her cake and plate. *"Morgana, come home, we need you. I need you"* Jenni's voice in her head was faint, but the pain that it created wasn't. In a flash, the world around her morphed and she found herself in her bed in the Palace.

Angharad hovered anxiously. "Thank you for bringing her back, Lord Thanatos."

He bowed. "It is my honour. She is clearly still attached to her body, or she wouldn't be in so much pain and I know someone who will be able to help her."

He left the suite.

It took a long time for the pain to subside, and Morgana fell into a troubled sleep as it faded. Angharad stayed with her.

When the door opened again, Scathach stood there. "I'm here for t'Lass."

"She's asleep." Angharad said, clearly intending on standing in the warrior's way.

"Well wake her up, I hae nae got all day." Scathach put her hands on her hips. "Lord Thanatos bid me take her to Airmid."

"Until she wakes up, she's not going anywhere."

Morgana opened her eyes, yawned and stretched. "Mama, don't be silly, if Thanatos thinks I should meet someone, then I'm going, no matter how tired I am." She climbed out from under the light blanket that had been draped over her.

Angharad frowned. "You need to rest after that amount of pain."

"Lady Angharad, t'pain is why I am taking your girl to Airmid. She can do wonders with a few herbs and that spring of hers." Scathach said.

Morgana pulled her boots on and gingerly joined Scathach and Angharad. The latter looked worried. "Are you still hurting, darling? You look very pale and drawn."

"I'll be okay, Mama."

The warrior woman gestured to Morgana. "Come on Lass, let's be awae."

Despite Amira's best efforts to carry her carefully, by the time they reached Kuklayne's cottage at the edge of the forest, Morgana was sweating and gasping with pain again. She slid off Amira's back and stumbled over to the pond, lying face down to splash her face with water and drink several handfuls.

Kuklayne emerged from inside. "Here Morgana, take this. Charon gave me this for you." He handed her a small green vial as she rolled herself into a sitting position.

"That's just the thing." Morgana unstoppered it and downed it. The liquid tasted of chocolate and mint this time and as it hit her stomach, she felt better. "That won't hold me for long though. We'd better get to this Airmid quickly." She hauled herself back up onto Amira's back.

Kuklayne mounted his horse, and they rode on into the forest.

Thirty – Seven

Mara slipped back through the tunnels, into the Folly and back into the Hall of Worlds. *I can finally gain Apollyon's favour completely; I'll have the pick of Mates for my next Heat and maybe even... Lucifer...* she giggled a little as her childhood crush came back to make her heart flutter.

Inside the Hall, she looked for the Llanirstyr door. *If Thanatos is right, I should be able to just walk straight inside and as long as I don't do anything that he would deem evil, I'll stay invisible.*

She stepped down into the correct corridor and came face to face with a pair of Llanirstyri Royal Guard on the door to Llanirstyr Nexus; she gasped and held her breath.

They didn't blink or look at her.

Mara breathed out again quietly and slipped between them to stand in front of the door. They still didn't react to her presence. Taking a soft, quick breath, she pushed open the door and as soon as it was open enough, she slipped through.

The door shut behind her with a solid thud.

"What was that?" The guard on the right of the Door turned to look at it. "Did the Door just open and shut?"

The other guard laughed at him. "You're hearing things, Max."

"Well, who wouldn't in a place like this?" Max grumbled, "There's nothing here but these damnable eternal torches. I mean, have you ever seen one go out or need renewing?" he pointed at the torch on the wall opposite him.

The second guard shrugged. "It won't be long before we're relieved for the next shift. Calm down."

"That's another thing, Akex. How can you tell how long we have until shift change? Time doesn't seem to pass here, it's just one long endless moment."

Akek's stomach growled. "That's how. We always get a meal between shifts when we're on Hall Duty, so my stomach has learned to tell the time."

Max laughed. "You and your stomach."

"You wouldn't have it any other way, my Friend." His stomach grumbled again.

Mara slipped unseen through the corridors of the Royal Palace. Whenever she came to a group of people, she would stop and listen to what they were saying. *Maybe I can find out where the Angel's Crown is or where the Shield of Courage is being kept. I can't imagine that either of those dumb blonde princesses would think to keep them with them.*

None of the groups she listened to seemed to know where the High Princess was. They were all complaining about her absence and if she was going to miss the Parade and what that would mean for the kingdom's future.

As Mara got deeper into the palace, she began seeing more servants. Finally, she found one woman that was carrying a basket of bed linen.

Another servant stopped her. "Why are you bothering to change the High Princess' Bed? She's not coming back." He said.

"How do you know that?" she shifted the basket.

"I heard that she left the Crown in her rooms." He snorted, "If you're passing the responsibility to someone else, you leave it behind don't you."

"Don't be daft. She'll be back, you just don't trust her." The woman shifted the basket again, "Look I have to get on. Besides, why would she take the Crown with her to the Hospital? It's not like she's doing anything formal there."

He looked around. "Well, why don't you prove me wrong? See if the Crown is there."

"What would that prove?" she said. He looked confused and she shook her head. "Why don't you get on with your duties and I'll get on with mine."

The man stalked off muttering and the woman hid a smile as she walked away. Mara followed her.

The suite of rooms that the servant entered had all the hallmarks of royalty, but when Mara slipped into the bedroom behind the servant woman, she recognised a young woman that was not as comfortable with her position as she seemed.

Earth clothes were draped over the back of a chair, a pile of paperback books lay on the bedside table and a laptop sat on the small desk; a pile of folders and papers beside it.

Mara wandered around the room as the chamber maid remade an already pristine bed, gathered up the old linen and put it in the basket at the base of the bed. Then she turned to a large, solid looking cabinet at one end of the room, sorted through her keys and opened the doors.

A sparkle of light caught Mara's eye and she turned to watch.

"That's her everyday tiara, those are the seasonal ones..." the maid muttered to herself as she counted through the dozen or so tiaras, diadems and crowns in the cabinet.

Such an array of sparklers! Mara took a deep breath in appreciation of the display. *Hmm, maybe if I succeed in this, Lucifer will allow me to take over Llanirstyr? It's obviously a very rich dimension.*

"It's not here." The woman exclaimed, startling Mara out of her contemplation of the gems. "She must have taken it with her. Well, that should put that stupid rumour to rest." She closed the cabinet, locked it again and picked up her basket, striding out the door with a satisfied air.

Mara let out the breath in a whoosh as the outer door to the suite shut.

She looked around the room again. "If she hasn't left it in the cabinet, where would she leave it? I can't imagine that she'd take something that powerful with her, wherever she is." She mused aloud.

Closing her eyes, Mara concentrated, extending her mind out to see if she could find any glimmers of power in the room. *There are places where a powerful object has been placed temporarily, but I can't see anywhere that it might be kept. Hmm.* She opened her eyes again and left the bedroom, took up a position in the centre of the suite's sitting room and searched for power again.

"The fire place? Why would that have power radiating from it? No, not the hearth, the statue beside it." she muttered and strode over to the large, carved stone fireplace that dominated the room.

Beside it was a stature of a Dragon and it was this that gave off the glimmer of power. Running her hands over the carving, she felt something give underneath her fingers, there was a click as a wing twisted and a door opened in the wall behind the statue.

"Aha!" the daemon muttered in triumph and stepped through the door.

MORGANA HUNG ONTO AMIRA'S mane and reins, every step the mare made jolting her and sending pain throbbing through her head. The potion had worn off ages ago and it felt as if something was tearing at her brain. *Is it trying to get in or out?* She wondered in exhausted bemusement.

"Lass."

She turned to peer at Scathach.

"We be here." Her trainer gestured ahead of them.

Morgana forced herself to sit up and look around.

They'd come to a place where several streams met to create a large pool. An island rose from the centre of the pool and in the middle of the island, surrounded by smaller trees and brush, stood the biggest oak tree that Morgana had ever seen.

"The spring lies on the Island." Kuklayne said as he helped her down from Amira, "You have to go across by yourself."

Morgana took a moment to get her balance right, and then began walking toward the water's edge.

"Lass, there be a bridge to your right, but ye'll have to look carefully; Airmid hides it." Scathach called out.

Morgana looked around.

On the edge of the bank something sparkled like crystal, so she moved over a few steps. Beneath the water lay a transparent platform that looked so delicate that she didn't want to set foot on it.

A wave of pain swept through her, and she staggered forward onto the see-through bridge. It held, so Morgana continued walking, water splashing up to soak her leggings to the thigh. The pain subsided long enough for her to register that she'd made it to the island, then as she took a step up onto the grass, the pain returned, and she blacked out.

A cold, wet cloth on her face brought her back round.

Above her, a pair of bright green eyes crinkled at the corners as their owner smiled. Several thick red curls dropped across them, and their owner sat back, brushing the hair back from a heart shaped face.

"Welcome back."

Morgana pushed herself up into a sitting position. "Hello." She looked around, "Am I on the Island?"

The area she sat in was carpeted with lush green grass, dotted with wildflowers. Here and there were clusters of low bushes, some with flowers and others with berries. The oak tree that she'd seen from the other side of the bridge stood behind her, its wide branches forming a green and brown canopy above her.

"You are." The redheaded girl grinned, "I'm Airmid; how are you feeling?"

Morgana thought for a moment, mentally inspecting herself. "I'm not in pain at least."

"That's from the Water of my Spring. It's only temporary though; while you were asleep, I took the liberty of checking your health a little." She frowned.

"What did you find?" Morgana removed the now dry cloth from her head.

"Well, your soul is in good health, but from what little I could see through the soul link, your body is dying." Airmid took the cloth from her.

"What? Why?"

The Goddess sighed. "When they removed the black lumps from inside your head, they accidently let in a bug, and it has infested itself into your blood. Your body's link with your soul is very weak."

Morgana licked her lips. "Is there anything you can do?"

"Plenty. However, you would have to return to your body for it to work."

"I have a job to do anyway, so I need to get back anyway." Morgana winced as her headache returned.

Airmid soaked the cloth in the bowl of water beside her, "Lay this back on your head and lie down. You need to rest while I arrange a few things."

Morgana did as she was told. *I've had enough rest; I want to get back to my sister.*

IT'S BEEN NEARLY A week of my personal time since we brought Morgana here. Jenni mused, staring into the glass of wine in front of her. *I don't think that she's getting better though.*

"Are you going to drink that or just look at it?" Her father's voice jogged her out of her reverie.

She looked up at his drawn, shadowed eyes and sighed. "Look at it, I guess. How's Mum?"

Artair sat down. "Distraught, but coping."

"I wish there was more that we could do." Jenni twisted the glass round by its stem, making the wine in the goblet slosh a little.

"We have done all that we can do." Her father said, "It's in the laps of the Gods now."

They fell silent.

A waft of fresh air swept across them. It carried the freshness of the Spring woods, Wildflowers and trees with new leaves. Jenni could have sworn that she heard Blackbirds singing and soft spring rain pattering on dusty ground. *I can almost smell that odd scent that you get after rain as well.* She thought.

"You mean Petrichor." A soft voice told her.

"That's the word." Jenni grinned and looked up at the newcomer. *She can't be much taller than Caoimhe and I've never seen hair quite that shade of red before; it's like flames.*

The woman smiled. "You are Morgana's sister."

"You know my sister?"

Artair coughed politely. "Jenni, please introduce me to your friend?"

Jenni laughed, slightly embarrassed. "I'd love to Dad, but she's a stranger to me as well."

"I am Airmid, an ally of your sister and I'd like to see her please." The woman bowed.

"I don't know how much you know, Airmid, but my daughter is currently in a coma, recovering from a major operation." Artair said, "She is unable to have visitors."

Airmid smiled again and Jenni could have sworn she felt early summer sunshine on her face. "I know this, but I have come to help her in a way that no human healer would be able to."

The tavern door opened, and Aderyn entered from the Hall. He strode over to Jenni's table, ignoring Airmid. "The Daemon alarm has gone off in Llanirstyr. I don't know how they got there, but we have to repel them immediately."

"I won't leave here without Morgana, Grandfather." Jenni folded her arms across her chest.

"Morgana is dying," Aderyn said bluntly, "She would not want to see you lose your kingdom to the Fire Realm, just because of her."

"If you want it so much, Grandfather, then you can have it." Jenni pulled the thick sapphire and pearl cuff from her wrist and dropped it onto the table. With a shimmer of light, it transformed into a delicate looking tiara formed from a pair of wings made from pearl and diamond surrounding a massive sapphire teardrop.

"You brought it here?" He gasped.

"It's safest when it's with me. But if you'd prefer, you can take it and become King of Llanirstyr." Jenni shouted the last few words at him.

A gentle hand was laid on her shoulder and Jenni looked up to see Airmid beside her. "Calm thyself, Gwynnhafr. I can cure the infection that is stopping your sister from returning to you."

Aderyn appeared to notice Airmid for the first time and he had to struggle to keep his face calm. "Lady Airmid!"

"You know her, Aderyn?" Artair stood up and forced the older man to sit down in a chair.

"She is the Goddess of Healing that we worship in Llanirstyr and one of our family's ancestors." Aderyn sat down, "If she is here, then we can hope for the best again."

"Come with me, Gwynnhafr, I will need your help if this is to work." Airmid said.

Jenni stood up and so did Artair and Aderyn.

The healing goddess waved them back down. "The presence of men in this would not be conducive to the task at hand. Please wait here."

Jenni followed Airmid through the common room and into the private quarters, where Myfanwy and Denyse sat having coffee.

"Jenni, ce que le ...?" Denyse stood up.

"'Van, Grand mere, this is Airmid." Jenni said.

Myfanwy stood up, then curtseyed deeply. "Lady Airmid, thank you for coming."

"Morgana's soul is resting in the Glade of the Spring at the moment." The goddess looked around, smiled and made a bee line for the bedroom Morgana lay in. "We have very little time left before the link between her soul and body is destroyed."

Thirty – Eight

Amongst the soft grass of the Glade of Spring, Morgana dreamed...

The darkness surrounded her again. It wasn't as cold and frightening as the Hills of Treachery nor was it as warm and comfortable as Sleep. It surrounded her with a coolness that was familiar yet different.

Voices whispered around her, and Morgana realised that she was back in Limbo. "Something's different." She said aloud in an effort to drown out the whispers.

"She has been here before..." a whisper nearby said.

"A Returner..." a second whisper sounded from her other side.

"She knows where she is..." the first whisper said.

It was closer to her.

Morgana started walking.

"Tell us how to leave here!" The second one followed her.

"Take us with you..." a chorus pleaded.

She felt phantom hands grabbing at her arms and shoulders, even some at her legs and ankles.

Looking down, she realised that she was wearing a nightshirt. *"So, wherever my body is, I'm in bed."*

After a minute of enduring the hands, she broke into a run, the same sort of easy jog that she used to do when she was at school, no burning in her lungs or pain from her head when she placed her feet down hard.

"No pain?" she sped up and her body felt the same. "I can't feel any pain; it's all gone."

A point of light appeared ahead of her. As she ran toward it and it got bigger, she realised it was a door; a shining, silver door.

Morgana stopped in front of it. "It doesn't look like the door into the Underworld. This one only has a key hole."

A new voice began to speak. This one sounded as if it were coming from the other side of the silver door. *"Morgana, you have the key to the door. Unlock it, open it and step through."*

It was a familiar voice, soothing and calm with a slight gaelic lilt. It brought with it the smell of fresh grass and wildflowers.

Morgana placed her hands on the door. "It feels cool to the touch, like metal on a warm day."

"It's the only thing between you and life, Morgana." The voice was encouraging, and wound around the words, the sound of a tumbling stream tugged at her. *"Unlock it and step through."*

"How? I don't have anything." She felt tears starting in her eyes and dropped her hands from the door, then threw herself at it, trying to push it open or smash it with her shoulder. She only succeeded in making her shoulder and side sore.

"That won't help. Come on 'Gana, you can do this. Mam and Dad are here, Grand Mere, Grandfather, 'Van... they're all here, waiting for you to come back to us." Jenni's voice said, softly.

"All of you... waiting for me?" She couldn't quite believe that.

"They are." The other voice said, the one that reminded Morgana of lying on the grass in the park and looking up at the new spring leaves on the oak tree above her, *"You can open this door; only you have the key."*

Something caught her eye. Whatever it was, it gleamed in the same way as the door but with a warmer tone. She crouched down and picked it up.

It was a tiny, white enamelled raven, a pin badge. She turned it in her hands, stroking it's cold form, "Charon. I wish he were here now... or that I had his bag with me; surely there would be a key to this door in there."

The raven fluttered its wings, *"You are the key, Lady Morgana. You always have been."* Charon's voice echoed what her sister and the other voice had said, *"But if you do not hurry and step through, you will be trapped in the Underworld until rebirth this time."*

"I'm the key?" Morgana placed her right hand on the door and pushed. It rattled in the frame. She crouched and looked at the keyhole. Through it, she could just see her sister sitting on the floor in front of her, "Jen?"

"I'm here 'Gana." Her sister's voice and presence surrounded her, and she sighed happily.

The raven pin fluttered again in her left hand and Morgana instinctively clutched it to make sure she didn't drop it.

"Ow." Opening her hand, she saw blood welling up at the base of her thumb, "I'm the key... I wonder."

Dipping her right index finger into the bubble of blood, she touched it to the keyhole. A drop slipped into the hole and something inside clicked.

The door swung open.

The hands clutching at her faded away as they were touched by the light.

Airmid smiled at her, "Come lass. 'T'is time you returned home.

MORGANA WOKE UP IN a bed. She could feel the soft duvet tucked around her and the scent of lavender. *This is the Tavern. The bedroom in Arkingham smells of lemon and beeswax from Maebh's polish. I fell asleep in Airmid's Spring Glade and smells of water and growing flowers...What am I doing back here? I died in Llanirstyr.*

The room was dark and quiet. She pushed the duvet back and sat up. *My head doesn't hurt anymore.* Blinking, she couldn't see anything moving around her. *I'm still blind though. Am I still dreaming?*

A gentle knock at her mind's edge and the sense of spring rain, didn't help.

"*Airmid?*" Morgana almost whispered, letting the deity into her mind.

"*Yes, it's me. You've been cured of most of the cancer and the infestation that was draining your life. This, your family did, by taking you to another world. However, you are only what your aunt calls 'in Remission', Thanatos still has a hold on your soul.*"

She blinked again, "*And my eyes?*" She could feel tears rolling down her cheeks at the suggestion of having to return to the Underworld forever at some point in the future, undetermined.

"*There was nothing that they could do. And the draught of my Spring's Water can only bring it back slowly or destroy what is left of your cancer.*" Airmid sounded sad, "*I wished to give you the choice.*"

"*I can cope with blindness. I cannot cope with losing my family or the knowledge of the grief that losing me would give them.*" She replied.

"*Then take this.*"

Morgana felt a hand take hers, surrounded by the scent of growing flowers, where they lay on the duvet. A tiny glass bottle was placed in one palm and Airmid's hand cupped her other around it, "*Then drink and be healed...*"

She raised the bottle to her lips and drank, "*Thank you.*"

Airmid watched as the girl drank and caught both her and the bottle when she finished, dropping instantly into sleep. She put the bottle into one of her belt pouches and eased Morgana down onto the bed, covered her over again and left her to sleep.

Thirty-Nine

This time when she woke up, Morgana could feel the warmth of the sun on her hands where they lay on a soft, silky feeling cover. *Where am I? This isn't the Tavern, Arkingham or home...*

A door opened, and soft footsteps echoed from a wooden floor, moving toward her. They became duller as they approached her. *The bed must be on a large rug. There's a wooden floor beyond it and there are windows on my left, the warmth is stronger on that hand.*

The steps halted with a slight nudge against the bed on her right, and a soft Welsh, accented voice said, "Good Morning, Your Royal Highness. My name is Maebh, and her Royal Highness, the High Princess requested that I be your personal assistant when you are here in Llanirstyr."

Morgana sighed, "No she didn't. I know my sister. What she probably said was, "Maebh, can you go get my lazy sister out of bed and make sure that she doesn't bump into anything."

Maebh let out a giggle and stifled it with a cough, "It was something like that, I think. I'm sure she didn't mean it though."

"Oh, she meant it." Morgana smiled and pushed herself up in bed, "You sound a lot like Maebh in Arkingham."

"She's my Grand Aunt, I was named for her." Maebh said, "If it's too confusing for you, you could call me Mae instead. It's what my little brother calls me."

"Thank you. That means we're cousins of sorts then. So, you can drop the title in private." Morgana shoved the covers off, noticing that she wore a nightgown from the fabric covering her legs, "Guess I'd better get washed and dressed then."

"I'll summon your maid, she's just in the other room..." Mae moved slightly.

"Don't bother her yet. If you don't mind me mind linking with you, I can see through your eyes." Morgana said, holding her hand out, "Just take my hand if you'd be happy doing it."

"Her Royal Highness said you'd probably suggest that." A hand gripped hers, "I'm always happy to help my family."

After negotiating the walk from the bed to the bathroom, washing carefully and then walking from the bathroom to the dressing room, all using Mae's eyes to see what to do, Morgana felt exhausted. She dropped onto the large, cushioned chair in the dressing room.

"Ok Mae, go get the maid. I don't think I have the energy to do this myself."

Mae sighed, "Your sister said you'd try to do it yourself. She told me to tell you, "You've been seriously ill for over a month of your personal time line, so your body might be a little behind where your mind is.""

Staring up at her, Morgana sighed, "You could have led with that."

Mae grinned at her, "I could have, but her Royal Highness..."

"...told you not to?" Rolling her eyes, she leaned into the back of the chair, "I forgot, on this world, everyone does as they're told when Jenni speaks."

Discretely, Mae left the room.

Morgana raised her arms over her head, feeling the weakness of the muscles as they moved and the aches it gave her, then she laid them down on the arms of the chair. *How am I going to be able to protect Jenni like this? I can't even get myself dressed.*

A sharp chiming sound as if glasses were being clinked together attracted her attention and with effort, she pulled herself to her feet and took several hesitant steps toward it. She took a deep breath;

a hint of Jasmine and Lavender on the air suggesting that she was walking toward something with scented things on it or near it.

Moments later, Morgana came to an abrupt stop, as she walked into what felt like another chair, padded just as heavily as the one she had left, with a soft, fluffy fabric. Working her way round it, she sat down, bouncing slightly and catching something hard in front of the chair with her ankle. *Ow.*

Moving her hands forward until she touched the hard surface, which turned out to be horizontal; she explored it with her fingers, finding tiny bottles and jars arranged on the surface which had the faint feel of woodgrain to her fingertips. Behind them, a vertical hard surface, cold and incredibly smooth, suggested a Mirror.

Morgana laughed. *A dressing table, a mirror and fripperies for a blind girl.* Tears welled, and she distracted herself from the thought by moving her hands around the dressing table more. This time she found a pair of boxes. One had ornate patterns on it and when she gently lifted the lid, began to play music. She listened, *Moonlight Sonata by Beethoven, just the first movement though. I haven't played it since I went blind.* She sighed and closed the box again. *I won't be able to see again unless they can put the implant in again.*

Walking her fingers to the second box, she found that it was just plain wood, the woodgrain smooth, but obvious. One side of the box had neat hinges fitted to it and the opposite a simple hook and eye clasp.

Morgana smiled. *Charon's Box. I wonder...* She opened it and touched the vials inside. I remember sorting them into types. *The red was on the right and the green on the left, so the blue were in the middle. Green washes away fatigue, blue heals. Red is Magic.* Selecting a vial from the right hand side, she picked it up, stroking over the label.

A word appeared in her mind, *Summons.* Putting it back into the section she'd raised it from, she picked another at random, from the left. Stroking the label, she had *Fatal Fatigue* appear in her mind.

Another red vial gave her *Enclose* and an image of a thick green bubble surrounding a dragon. *A spell to enclose a dragon or to enclose the target? I'd need to be able to read the instructions.*

Checking the middle vials, she realised that the stoppers were different shapes. *Handy if you're blind, the red has flames for stoppers, the blue an equal arm cross and the green have what feels like a wrapped sweet on top.* She laughed aloud as she realised that it would also be handy if she had to keep her eyes on someone while she picked a vial. *I have to remember to thank Charon. He really thought of everything.* Then the laughter faded into silence. *This is what I should have used. My plan to drink the poison was flawed; I still could have saved Jenni from the poison, and we would have known who the poisoner was.* She closed her eyes and groaned slightly. *I was so wound up in my personal pain and suffering that I didn't see that, I saw only a way out of the whole situation.*

She lifted a green vial out, checking the label before she uncorked it. *Muscle Fatigue from Illness apparently, so that should work.* Having uncorked it and downed it, Morgana sighed with relief as all the aches disappeared from her muscles. *That's better.*

From the next room, Morgana heard the door open. She picked up a blue vial and touched the label. *Cure Disease.* She put it down and picked up another. *Cure Broken Bones.* The third she picked up was *Restore All Sight.*

She froze, the vial in her hand showing her a pair of eyes covered with cataracts becoming normal again. *It couldn't be that easy, could it?*

"Your Royal Highness?" a quiet timid voice said from a short distance to her left.

"Yes?" Morgana stroked the label again, hearing *Restore All Sight* echo in her head, over and over again.

"Her Royal Highness, your sister, she asks if you have given up trying?" the voice replied.

"And you are?"

"I'm your maid, Eavan, your Royal Highness. Do you wish to get dressed?"

Morgana smiled, "Yes, I'll get dressed. Something simple and easy to wear, so I don't trip over too much please." She passed the vial from hand to hand. *Have I given up trying what? What does she mean?*

She could hear Eavan walking around behind her, wardrobe doors opening and closing. *Jenni must have explored the contents of the box and knows I can cure myself with it. So, I'd better use it.* But something stopped her.

"Eavan, who put these boxes here?"

"I believe it was your mother, I was introduced to her when you were taken ill. The jewellery you had with you went into the music box, and the bag they were in is hung in the third wardrobe on the right, along with your scarves, belts and other accessories." The maid sounded a lot less timid now that she was working.

"Did my sister handle them at all?"

"No, your Royal Highness. After the Midwinter Ball and you fell ill, she refused to touch anything that you'd brought with you." The footfalls paused, "Are you ready to get dressed now? I can aid you, if you wish to see through my eyes."

The vial stopped moving. "No, it's all right, thank you."

Uncorking the vial, Morgana drank the contents in one gulp. She shut her eyelids and felt the liquid dropping through her into her stomach like an accidently swallowed ice cube on a hot day. The utter dark became a soft charcoal grey with red and blue lines that swirled and pulsed. Taking a deep breath, she opened her eyes.

As she opened them, the light reflecting off the mirror in front of her dazzled her painfully and she squeezed them closed again. "Is there a window in here?"

"Uh, yes, your Royal Highness, it's not open though." Eavan sounded confused.

"That's not the problem. Can you shut the curtains please." Morgana replaced the vial in the box and closed it, stroking it a little before she turned to face the maid.

"Of course, your Royal Highness." The sound of material flapping and the *shick-skrape* of metal rings on a metal pole told her what the maid was doing, "All done. Should I turn the lamps on?"

"Just one please, keep it quite low."

A whoosh and click happened and moments later, there was a subtle warmth from the direction of the maid.

Morgana cracked open her eyelids, blinking as the soft golden light made her eyes water. She smiled.

The maid had a completely confused expression on her face. "Eavan, put that on the side table please."

The maid complied.

Morgana blinked and looked around.

The Dressing Room had a large bay window on the longest side, with a couch, a table and a chair in it. At the far end of the room, next to the door that led to the bathroom, four wardrobes clustered in the corner. On the back wall, another wardrobe stood, beside a dais that had three mirrors on it, their gilded frames glistening in the light. The side table with the lamp stood on the other side of the dais and the large, padded chair stood in the middle of the space between the side table and the window.

"Luxurious." Morgana said, "I'd love to sit and read on that couch."

"Your Royal Highness.... Princess Morgana?" Eavan said, coming toward her, "I thought... that is, the High Princess said... uh..."

"That I am blind? I was. Thanks to The Ferryman, I have my eyesight back." She laughed, "Turn the lamp out and open the curtains slowly. I bet there's a great view from that window."

Forty

"The fact remains, your Royal Highness, that while your sister is disabled in such a fashion, she cannot be your Heir." The Minister of Finance stated his double chins wobbling.

"Blindness can be fixed, Lord Grattin." Aderyn Archington waved one hand, "My Granddaughter is perfectly healthy, and we can deal with her blindness once the Parade is over."

"How will she walk in the parade, Lord Archington? If she cannot see where she is going, she will embarrass the High Princess and the Family in the view of the whole country." Lady Vorthdan, the Minister of Culture said, shuddering, "And the Monarchy must never be seen to be embarrassed."

Jenni rolled her eyes and would have spoken, but Morgana's personal assistant entered the room. "Lady Maebh, have you news?"

Maebh's face was as stern as her Grand Aunt's would have been, "I do, your Royal Highness." She approached the head of the conference table and curtsied, "A note from High Princess Morgana."

Jenni took the paper, opened it and read it, trying very hard to keep her face straight. "I see. Return to my sister and tell her that all is in readiness. We will meet her in the Throne Room.

The young woman curtsied again and left.

"Well, how's Morgana?" Aderyn asked.

"She's fine, Lord Archington. She has heard of the doubts voiced by the royal council and wishes to put them at rest with a demonstration of her prowess." Jenni stood up and everyone in the room stood as well. "We will reconvene there in thirty minutes."

They bowed and curtsied, then everyone except Aderyn and Myfanwy left.

"All right, Jen. What did she say." Myfanwy asked, running her hand over her head. She appeared to be checking that the plaits that held her tiara in place, were still there.

"I'm not going to tell you." Jenni grinned at her aunt, "She wants it to be a surprise." She crumpled the paper and stuffed it into the pocket in her overdress. "Shall we go?"

Aderyn frowned at her, "Don't do this to us. What's happened?"

Jenni glared up at him as she stood up, "I'm your queen-in-waiting. Trust me, when I say that it's nothing bad."

"You're also my granddaughter and it wasn't that long ago that you were ignoring the repercussions of your actions." He said.

"Well, if you'd actually told me what I needed to know, instead of leaving me to guess it..." Jenni squared her shoulders and took a step toward him, "... perhaps I wouldn't have made those mistakes."

"Yes, you didn't exactly cover yourself with glory, Father." Myfanwy said, standing up.

Aderyn looked at his daughter, "You're going to side with her?"

She shrugged, "The facts speak for themselves. You didn't tell me or her about Akila-Auset, so she was forced to make decisions on the run. The subsequent political upheaval and creation of Chrysoldin Gamma was not her fault, neither was the destruction of the Temple on Chrysoldin Nexus."

Aderyn sighed and stood up, towering over both of the women, "I'm cursed with intelligent descendants; Akila-Auset said exactly the same thing."

"Well, let's allow Jenni to exercise her prerogative as Queen-to-be and keep her sister's secret." Myfanwy turned and curtsied to Jenni, "May we escort you to the Throne Room, your Royal Highness?"

Jenni grinned and inclined her head in answer.

Aderyn sighed again and stepped out of Jenni's way, bowing, "After you."

As they entered the throne room through the dressing room door, Jenni was surprised to see her sister standing in the middle of the space before the throne dais, wearing the armour, and carrying the shield and sword that she'd brought back from the Underworld with her. She also wore a mask made of gold fabric with the eye holes filled in with black mesh. Jenni recognised it as the one that she'd had made to hide her own identity during a Masquerade Ball a year ago.

"Your Royal Highness." Morgana turned toward her and inclined her head toward her, "I hope you don't mind my borrowing the mask. I didn't have anything suitable to hide my disability from those watching. I would not want my blindness to make them uncomfortable."

Jenni smiled, "Of course, your Royal Highness. I don't mind at all. You are my sister after all. Where are the rest of the Royal Council?"

"I refused them entry until I had talked to you. Mae is holding them at bay," Morgana gestured toward the main door, "Along with all the rest of the court. News travels fast around here."

Myfanwy laughed, "Oh yes, gossip spreads like wildfire amongst the Courtiers; I sometimes suspect that the masters and mistresses of the servants have them spying on everyone."

"You can talk! I know all about your little network." Jenni said.

"I have to keep you informed." Myfanwy said matter-of-factly.

Morgana laughed, "Of course. Well, sit down, sister, I would like to get on with this before poor Mae is lynched."

Jenni crossed to the throne and sat down, "Of course, High Princess Morgana. You may proceed when you are ready."

Morgana nodded and turned to look down at the two footmen standing by the main door, "Gentlemen, you may allow the Royal Council and the Court to enter."

The footmen bowed deeply, straightened, then opened the doors.

Lady Maebh entered, just ahead of the Royal Council. She walked down the red carpeted aisle. A step behind her was Eavan, the maid that Jenni had picked for Morgana. The two of them curtsied to Jenni and then to Morgana who shook her head slightly, so they moved to stand on the left.

The Royal Council strode purposefully to their usual seats on the right hand side of the throne dais, each of them genuflecting to Jenni before they took their seat. The rest of the court, the courtier's servants and a large number of city-folk filed into the remaining space, chattering like jackdaws and magpies.

"Looks like word spread further than just the palace," Jenni murmured to Myfanwy, "I recognise a few merchants' aides."

"Your Royal Highness' sister is a huge source of curiosity. Remember they didn't know she existed until your announcement and then she 'fell ill' the same night. The rumours and gossip have spread like water through a soft towel dropped in a muddy puddle." Her aunt replied.

MORGANA WATCHED THE people enter dispassionately. *I would have preferred a smaller audience, but I suppose the more people who know, the faster the rumours that Eavan and Mae told me about fade away.* She glanced at Mae and mentally tapped at her cousin's mind, *"Did you arrange what I asked for?"*

Mae didn't answer, just nodded.

Okay. Morgana looked around and assessed the crowd the way that Scathach had taught her. *There's no malice to be felt, just curiosity... fair enough.*

The crowd quieted as the room filled, then the footmen stepped into the doorway, blocking anyone else from entering. Morgana could see people behind them, trying to peer over their shoulders.

"Time to start." She muttered to herself, took a deep breath and then stepped up onto the throne dais, turning to face the crowd.

"Royal Court of Llanirstyr, listen to me now." She called out, silencing the last of the discussions. "I am High Princess Morgana, the sister of High Princess Gwynnhafr, your Queen-in-waiting."

"Hah!" A deep voice from the Royal Council seats boomed out. "You're wearing a mask. You could be anyone under that." The speaker, a large man with double chins stood up, "Take it off and verify your identity, stranger."

Morgana looked straight at him, "No."

Aderyn stepped forward from his position at Jenni's right, "Lord Grattin, I know my granddaughters, and I can assure you that this is High Princess Morgana. I swear it on my life."

"Hmph. Very well, Lord Archington, I accept your oath." Lord Grattin glared at him and then at Morgana, "But if this... person... tries to harm our High Princess..."

"I forfeit my own life. I know the rules, Lord Grattin."

"No lives will be taken today." Morgana snapped, "Least of all, my grandfather's." she touched his mind softly as she said, *"Sit down, Lord Grattin!"*

The portly lord sat down with a look of surprise on his face.

Morgana hid her satisfaction at the effect of the trick that Mae had taught her, "I have heard that many of the people in the city and no few amongst the court, believe that I am incapable of succeeding my sister. That my blindness, *my disability*, makes me less of a person. That I should be put away into some country house, so that my sister will marry and produce a *proper* heir."

With each phrase she saw different members of the council flinch. From the Court came the noises of both shock and agreement.

Typical human society then. She sighed.

There was a rustling toward the back of crowd, gasps as people were shoved aside and four armed figures burst into the clear space in front of Morgana. The six guards that were on the dais, moved rapidly between the edge and Jenni, whose face dropped into an icy glare for the intervention.

"What!" Lord Grattin roared, "Guards! Protect the High Princess!"

"Which one, Grattin?" Morgana laughed at his confused expression, then as the figures approached her, began drawing various weapons, "What do we have here? Assassins for me or for my sister?"

The figures remained silent, just moving forward menacingly.

The front rows of courtiers murmured fearfully and shuffled backward, compressing the crowd and adding to the general hubbub. Morgana glanced at Mae and Eavan; they seemed uneasy, and Mae frowned at the figures. *Something's wrong with our plan?* But before she could ask, a fifth figure strode forward, and Mae's face became pure shock.

Morgana blinked at the new figure. *Obviously female, red hooded cloak, black armour... not of any style I've ever seen.*

After a soft knock, Mae's mind voice said, *"We asked for two disguised guards from the palace captain, not four. And that woman is wearing Fire Realm colours. How she got into Llanirstyr, I don't know."*

"Tell my sister about this quickly. I may need back up." Morgana said, drawing her sword and moving toward the woman, "Hold your advance, Stranger."

The woman pushed her hood off her head, the helm underneath hiding all, but the glow of her bright red eyes, "I may be a stranger to you, High Princess Morgana, but you are not a stranger to me. I have followed you through many different places. You have my shield." She gestured at the shield Morgana held.

"This was gifted to me by Kuklayne himself." Morgana said, "After I defeated him in a challenge."

"I, too, have fought and beaten Kuklayne." The woman said, "I am Lady Deumara of the Fire Realm."

"I highly doubt that." Aderyn said from the Dais, "All entrances to Llanirstyr are warded against those from the Fire Realm."

"Do you ward against Thanatos too?" Deumara smiled, stroking a shining black crystal encased in and hung from a silver chain.

Aderyn frowned, "No mortal mage can ward against Thanatos."

"Then you have no choice, but to trust my word." Deumara replied. "I am of the Fire Realm."

Aderyn's frown deepened.

Morgana took a deep breath, "In that case, you would have to challenge me for the shield."

"Oh no." Deumara shook her head, "I am not that stupid. I bought my proxies here."

"Don't you mean brought?" Lord Grattin snapped.

The Daemon shook her head, "I paid good money for these... gentlemen... on Xandin before I came here. They are mine, body and soul."

One by one, the armed figures pulled their scarves off, showing a thick gold chain sealed tightly around their throats.

"Slavery is illegal here." Lord Grattin roared, "No matter what they practise elsewhere, in these halls, those men are now free."

Morgana rolled her eyes behind the mask, "*Someone tell him to shut up, so he stays shut up.*" She said to her sister in a tight channel to her mind, "*We do not need those fighters running amok.*"

Jenni didn't' answer, but the slight jump Lord Grattin made in his seat, did.

Morgana grinned.

The armed figures looked at each other, their eyes wide. They began to edge backward, but Deumara turned her head through a hundred and eighty degrees and growled "Stay put."

The three men stopped moving, their faces pale under their tans.

Morgana stifled the shudder from witnessing the manoeuvre. *That's impressive as well as disgusting.* Aloud, she said, "What of it? The Challenge of the Shield is one on one, Challenger to Shield Holder."

The Daemon smiled, "I don't want to challenge just for the Shield."

"Oh?" Morgana raised an eyebrow, even though she knew no one could see it, "What else are you after?"

"I've been in the city for quite a while, *Princess.* I've broken bread with people both high born and low born, and in that time, I've heard all sorts of things." Deumara reached up and took her helm off. Two long black plaits tumbled out and she rotated her head a little, stretching her neck out.

Morgana heard whispers of shock from the Royal Council. *"Sounds like a couple of your council recognise her, sis. Better make note of them. I can't risk looking round."*

Jenni's mind acknowledged the suggestion.

"And are you going to tell me what you found out?" Morgana asked, "Only I wasn't expecting off-world company, so I haven't prepared a proper welcome or anything." She sheathed her sword and took up a less aggressive stance.

"I can have tea and cakes after the battle, when I'm Queen and you're my prisoner." The daemon shrugged. "After all, you're disqualified from ruling because of your blindness and your sister up there isn't even a proper queen yet."

Ahh. There it is. How did I know this would be coming? Morgana sighed audibly, "So how do you think you can become Queen? Just have my sister killed and take over? I hate to tell you this but if we go, there are at least ten cousins in direct line. You going to kill all of them?"

"Oh, but I don't have to. I just have take the Angel's Crown and that automatically makes me Queen." Deumara grinned at her, and Morgana felt fear wash over her at the thought of this woman being Queen here.

"It's not as easy as she makes out, 'Gana. The Crown is sentient, and it burned Jezebeath when he tried the same thing." Jenni told her.

"Hmm. Somehow, I don't think you understand this world the way you think that you do." Morgana said, thankful that the mask hid her expression. *Looks like she is taken in by the mask too. Good.*

Deumara put her helm back on, "It doesn't matter. I'm challenging you for the Shield, and once you're immobilised, I'll challenge your sister and kill her. Then I'll be Queen." She stepped backward and gestured at the three men to move forward. "Get on with it."

Forty - One

C haos.
The crowd screamed and scrambled back toward the main doors. The Guards that mae had arranged for were caught up and dragged backward in the crush, and the guards from the antechamber were prevented from getting in. Morgana could hear someone shouting orders in the antechamber, which reassured her that there would be back up coming soon, so she concentrated on the daemon and her fighters.

The daemon's men did as they were told, but every line of their stance told Morgana that they didn't want to. She didn't take her eyes off them though. *"Mae, keep an eye on Deumara, I can't risk dividing my attention from the men."*

"Yes, highness." Mae said, her mind tone worried, *"try not to die."*

"No fear of that, I've had enough death for a lifetime." Morgana took a deep breath and unsheathed her sword, "Lady of the Moon, hear me. Protect my family and bring me victory."

"Praying to that bitch won't help you." Deumara sneered.

"I wasn't praying," she replied, raising her sword, "Just reminding her of her promise."

One of the fighters, a man with bright green hair poking out from under his helm, rushed forward, aiming a slash at her shield arm, behind the shield. Morgana pivoted and parried, knocked him backward and dodged another attack from one of the other two, who had a neatly trimmed black beard.

"Get in there and hold her!" Deumara screeched.

The third fighter, who wore a light blue tunic under his breastplate, ran in, his sword sheathed, and made a grab at her.

Morgana slipped out of his grasp and smacked him across the back of the head with the flat of her sword. This sent him flying into green hair, who seemed determined to incapacitate her shield arm.

Morgana used the time that it took the two to detangle themselves from each other to distract Blackbeard, "You know, Lord Grattin is right. Those gold chains are just an accessory here." She began to circle him.

"I owe the King a very large debt. If the Lady doesn't get what she wants, the King will keep me fighting for him until I die." He said.

"Was the debt to do with your family?" she asked, dodging a swipe from Greenhair, and a grab from Blue Tunic.

"Tell her nothing." Deumara ordered.

Blackbeard shrugged and attacked.

Morgana parried Black beard's attack, ducked Greenhair's sword and briefly struggled against Blue Tunic's hold then stamped down on his toes, elbowed his stomach with her shield arm and pulled herself free as he gargled and let go.

"Seriously Gentlemen... I assume you are all gentlemen. We can work this out, you don't have to fight me." Morgana took several steps back and risked a quick look around the room.

The crush at the door had gone and the guards from outside were moving towards the front of the room. *The daemon hasn't noticed yet though.* Morgana thought, careful not to look at any one particular point behind the woman, *neither have the fighters.*

The three men had stopped attacking her and were watching her carefully. Deumara was staring at them intensely.

Giving them telepathic orders or some kind of spell perhaps. Hmm. Morgana began to move away from the men, toward the daemon. The three men watched her but didn't move with her. *Something odd is happening here.*

She moved back toward the dais, not taking her eyes off the four invaders.

Deumara quirked an eyebrow at her, "Running back to the bosom of your family, princess? I didn't think you'd be a coward."

"I don't care what you think, *Cythraul.*" Morgana replied, "I'm not backing out of the challenge, just thought I'd make room for my back up."

Deumara looked behind her and shrugged, "Them? They'll be taking orders from me soon enough."

There was a scream from Blue Tunic. He'd dropped to his knees and as Morgana watched, his sword clattered onto the marble and the hand that had been holding it, changed, the bones lengthening and the skin blackening. The other two men began to change as well, their limbs thickening and clothing splitting into rags.

A spell then. Changing their forms. "I take it that you're dissatisfied with their service." She said, trying to not wince at the sound of snapping bones and ripping flesh.

"Well, they seem incapable of following simple instructions as humans." Deumara shrugged again, sounding bored, "Maybe they'll be able to do as they're told now."

Morgana shuddered. *"Jenni, this is diabolical. Can anyone around here do anything to stop her spell?"*

"No, I've already asked Van to do something, and she says that the spell changing them is using energy from a source that the daemon is carrying. She also can't penetrate the Daemon's mind shield, or the personal shield she has erected around her." Jenni replied.

"So, we can't do anything to save them from her?" Morgana felt sick. *I didn't even think of trying to attack her directly. I'm so stupid!* Out of the corner of her eye, she saw her sister shake her head. Then she had an idea. *"Mae. You know the box with all the little bottles on my dressing table?"*

"Yes?" her personal assistant sounded as nauseated as Morgana felt.

"*Send Eavan to get it. She'll be able to get out if she uses the door on the dais.*" Morgana hoped that Deumara wouldn't notice the maid's exit. "*I suspect that the outer halls are packed with people, so she'll need to use the private staircase from the dais antechamber up to my sister's sitting room and then go to my rooms.*"

"*Good idea to get her out of here, but why bring the box?*"

"*I need something from it. She'll need to get a pair of goblets and some red wine too. I'll tell you more once she returns.*"

A howl from the direction of the mutating fighters ensured that everyone else's eyes were locked onto the agony they were going through, and Morgana saw eavan climb the dais and slip through the dais door.

The three fighters had obviously finished mutating when Morgana focused back on them. Deumara was smiling proudly at them, as if they were her children. "Beautiful aren't they. When I found them on Xandin, I could feel that they had Daemon genes in them, it just needed coaxing out of them."

Blue Tunic was a half scaled, half furred Daemon hound, black with a long blue stripe down his back. Black beard had changed into a black maned manticore, vaguely leathery wings folded back and his scorpion tail with a huge barb dripping venom. Greenhair had become a long, low-slung scaled creature, a cross between a bright green, Komodo dragon and an octopus, long tentacles waving from his back. The only things that hadn't changed were the gold chains around their necks and their eyes... human and terrified.

Hold on. I'm almost certain that what I need to save you is in Charon's Box. Morgana sighed unhappily.

"Don't you like my pretties?" Deumara's eyes glistened with amusement, "Maybe you should inspect them up close!" she snapped her fingers and the three creatures looked at her. "Go and show her how lovely you are, my pets."

Morgana brought her shield and sword up into guard as the three approached. Greenhair's tentacles whipped out toward her, trying to grab the shield, her sword arm, and her body all at once, but only succeeded in pulling the mask off her face, breaking the ribbon that held it in place.

"Well, that's an improvement at least." Deumara said, "I don't know why you were hiding behind it."

Morgana refused to answer, slapping away a questing tentacle with the flat of her blade. On her left, Black beard's tail waved threateningly, but from the look on his face, she could see he was trying to stop it from striking.

"I can still help you." She said to him. "I can work out how to break this spell and free you from your slavery, you just have to stop doing what she tells you."

A question began to form on his lips, but before he could push the words out of his lion like mouth, Bluetunic howled from her right and attacked, forcing her to spin and fend him off, catching his leap on her shield and pushing him away as hard as she could.

The hound turned a somersault and landed on top of a pair of guard that had been trying to sneak round the side. It turned on them and tore them to pieces; shreds of flesh, material and metal flying around them. They fought back valiantly but the screams told Morgana all she needed to know.

"Fascinating, isn't it?" Deumara drawled, "That particular beast has claws and bones of solid Wolframite Carbide. Have no idea where that mutation has come from, but my Prince will be most interested in breeding him."

Swallowing and trying to ignore the daemon's voice, Morgana forced herself to scan the area for threat. The guards had stopped trying to outflank the daemon and her beasts and had settled for keeping the space between the fight and the door secure. Deumara was stood watching the hound eat and the other two creatures had separated from her and the manticore was curled in a tight ball, gripping his scorpion tail to his chest with his front paws. The betentacled Komodo was backed up against the wall, his face twisted into a grimace and his tentacles writhing and changing colours around him, black ink pouring out from under his tail and pooling.

"Deumara, Stop." Jenni called out from the dais. "Let's negotiate rather than fighting."

Morgana saw eavan return with the box, wine and goblets. The maid moved silently to Mae's side.

"Mae search through the box and pour the contents of the bottle marked 'Banish' into the wine carafe." She told her.

Mae nodded.

"You wish to negotiate, Your Royal Highness?" Deumara raised her face plate on her helm, "I respect a ruler that would sacrifice themselves to stop harm coming their people." She snapped her fingers and the hound growled, then bounded back to her side, sitting to attention. "I'm happy to call a ceasefire while we discuss my ascension to the throne."

The other two creatures didn't respond to her. She looked at them and sighed, "Oh dear, clearly those two weren't strong enough in mind to withstand the change. Morgana, be a sweetheart and give them mercy, please. They've gone mad."

Morgana glanced at the hound, "You have that one under control?"

"Oh yes. He likes his change." She stroked the blue stripe and the hound writhed ecstatically under her touch. "I have no idea what the other two will do to you though."

Forty-Two

Morgana sheathed her weapon and laid the Shield on the dais, as she reached out with her mind to the manticore. She touched his mind and felt the swirling turmoil inside. *He's fighting the animal side. If I go blundering in, the animal will win, and I'll have a fight for survival on my hands.*

She pulled back and touched the mind of the other creature. There was nothing there. *No animal instinct, no human spirit? I'll have to check.* She slipped into its mind. *It feels a lot like when I was in Limbo, but without the voices of the waiting Dead.*

A light sparkled deep inside and as she approached, it reached out to her, *"I don't want to be like this. I want to die. Kill me. Please."*

The simplicity of the request shocked her. *"I could find some way to change you back."*

"I will be a slave still if you do that. I took slavery because there was no other way to clear my debt. My wife and child will get saddled with it if I die or run away before it is paid off. But I cannot exist like this, and I refuse to remain in bond to her."

Morgana pulled out of his mind, and turned to look at Deumara, "I cannot in good consciousness, destroy either of these creatures. They are your property under Xandin rules, even though those rules are an anathema to all good Llanirstyri citizens."

"They mean nothing to me. They were a means to an end, so I don't care what happens to them." Deumara shrugged.

Morgana had an idea. She pulled the pouch off her belt and fished around in it while asking Jenni, *"Jen. Which of these coins is the most valuable."*

"The very largest ones. They have a raised diamond in the centre of them." her sister replied. *"One is worth about the same as the cost of a well bred horse on Earth Nexus."*

Morgana smiled and pulled six diamond coins out of the pouch. "Deumara, I will offer you 3 of these, for all of the creature's bonds."

A gleam appeared in the daemon's eye, and she shook her head. "That's less than half what I paid for them on Xandin."

"Four then? You said they aren't worth anything to you." Morgana glanced at the Daemon Hound who had whimpered and moved away from Deumara. "It's better than me killing them and you having nothing."

"Hah! I paid the King of Xandin in false coinage. It matters nothing to me either way." The daemon laughed.

"False coinage is treason on Xandin. Gold is rare there and every gold chain the slaves wear represents the debt that person is in slavery for." Jenni told Morgana.

"Good to know. Thanks." Morgana replied, mulling the information over as she considered what to say next.

"False coinage you say? So, to sum up, you've committed Treason on Xandin, invaded the Llanirstyr Royal Palace and murdered two Llanirstyri people by proxy? Have I got that right?" Morgana played with the coins in her hands, the metal chinking.

"I suppose so, if you want to use such negative language." Deumara folded her arms.

"Your Royal Highness, how would you rule if you were trying such a case as this?" Morgana called to her sister, without taking her eyes away from the daemon.

"In a case with such a set of crimes, it would be the maximum sentence available for each one. We do not have the death sentence here." Jenni replied, "So she would be confined to the Underground Prison to the North."

"If it were tried in Xandin," Lord Archington said, "The murders would be automatic slavery to the tune of two lives; the invasion and threat to the crown, behanding; and the debasement of the coinage would be beheading."

"But I will never return there, so it bothers me not. And as your beloved Heir is about to step down to save her people, the crimes here will become moot." Deumara examined her nails without looking up at the dais.

"Such evil as described and done upon this world will certainly consign you to Tartarus after death." Morgana said.

Deumara frowned, "Evil? You really consider those deeds evil? In my world, they would be misdemeanours." She pulled the chain out from around her neck and looked at the black crystal hanging from it, clearly considering something.

"And that is the reason that the Fire Realm are banned from various other realms as well as the Hall of Worlds." Lord Archington said with a grimace, "The Evil that Lucifer and Apollyon insist on committing causes harm to all the worlds, realms and living beings. Until they can show they have changed and will abide by the Laws of other places, they and their people are confined to the Fire Realm.

Deumara gasped as the crystal on her palm crumbled, "No!"

"Her shield is gone." Van said.

"Problem?" Morgana asked, as she put the coins away.

"No, silly girl, not for me." Deumara took a deep breath, and a green flame wreathed her hand.

"I can see her source. It's the jewel on her breastplate." Van said. *"Crack it and the power will drain, then I can overpower her."*

"I have a better idea. Jenni. Back me up." Morgana replied. She tilted her head and looked at the green flame, "So you lose your shield, and you abandon negotiation? Not particularly honourable."

Deumara looked embarrassed, "Good point." She shook her hand and the fire winked out, "So, negotiation. I believe your young heir was about to hand the Angel's Crown over to me."

Morgana rolled her eyes, "Not quite that fast. Before we get anywhere near that point, you must go through three trials, just like the ones my sister had to."

"Really? Oh, very well. If a weakling like your sister can do them, they must be easy." The daemon woman made a 'come here' gesture, "Let's go."

Morgana shook her head, "No. First you have to give over the bonds of those creatures to me. They could be used to circumvent the challenges."

Deumara sighed, "very well." From a large pouch attached to her belt, she produced three pieces of parchment, "Here are their bills of sale. Take them."

Morgana strode across, took the parchment and turned to the daemon hound, stretching out her mind to his. *Take a place next to the Manticore. Harm no one, stay silent and still.* She added a touch of command to her mind tone, and the hound bowed to her, then did as she asked.

Morgana walked back to her place before the dais, turning to Mae, "Bring goblets and the three wines for the first trial." Then she added, directly to Mae and Eavan's minds, *"One white, but add a drop of orange food colouring, one blue with two drops of red food colouring and the red you put the potion in."*

Mae curtsied and she and eavan went into action.

A Table and two chairs were brought. A small side table was furnished with six glass goblets and three carafe's of wine.

"Okay, Morgana, what's going on?" Jenni asked her on their private channel.

"It's called 'thinking on my feet'. I had something else planned for the red wine initially, but this will work much better. Just go with it."

Morgana bowed to Deumara, "My Lady Deumara of the Fire Realm, please take a seat."

"*Hmm.*" Jenni said.

"I refuse to drink anything that you have had brought out without poison testers." Deumara said, "I heard what happened at the New Years Ball."

"Of course. The Trial wines only harm those who are evil of heart and mind." Morgana replied, "I shall be one tester, my sister shall pick another, and you may pick a third."

"*I need to pick a tester? What are you doing, little sister.*" Jenni frowned.

"*Please Jen! Nothing in the wine will hurt you or anyone else in this room... other than her as far as I know.*" Morgana turned to the dais, "Your Royal Highness, please nominate a taster."

Jenni nodded. "Lord Archington."

"Very well. Will the two of you join us down here, please?"

Lord Archington inclined his head and extended his arm to Jenni. Together they stepped down from the dais.

Morgana turned to Deumara who stood behind the chair with it's back to the Royal Council, "Lady Deumara, please nominate your taster."

The daemon didn't look round, merely said "Lord Grattin."

"*That explains a great deal.*" Jenni said, anger tinging her mind orange.

"*At least you know who to discuss this with later.*" Morgana replied.

Lord Grattin stood up. "I have no idea what you are doing, young woman, but I refuse to join in with this farce." He sat down again, muttering to himself.

Deumara sighed and turned to look at him, "But Lord Grattin..." her voice softened and Morgana could feel a spell being woven, reaching out toward him, "... Ashve... you promised that you would love me forever if I could become queen and make you King."

The Minister of Finance flushed an unattractive purple, "Uh... um..."

"That explains why he was so adamant that you are not confirmed as my heir, sis." Jenni said as Lord Archington seated her at the table. "Come on Lord Grattin. I give you permission to put your life on the line for my opponent." She spoke in a soft tone, but Morgana could feel steel in her sister that she'd never seen before.

Grattin's face drained of colour completely. He nodded, stood up and walked over, wobbling slightly. He reached Deumara and seated her opposite Jenni.

Jenni turned to the Captain of the Palace Guard, "Captain, if you would serve the wines?"

The woman saluted, "It would be my honour." She moved to the side table.

Morgana stood with her back to the dais between Lord Grattin and Lord Archington. The latter looked down at her with a quizzical expression on his face but said nothing.

"First the White. For Purity of Intent." Morgana announced.

The captain poured three glasses of wine from the vaguely orange white wine.

"That's an odd looking white wine." Deumara remarked.

"We have some unique vineyards in our world." Jenni told her.

The captain handed the glasses to Lord Archington, Lord Grattin and Morgana.

"Gentlemen, I hope your hearts are pure." Morgana said, raising her glass to her lips and taking a long sip. Lord Grattin sounded like he was choking as he drank. Lord Archington chuckled and drank the portion in one go.

Deumara watched them carefully. Jenni seemed bored with the whole proceedings, only morgana could feel her sister's apprehension.

When they'd finished and nothing happened after five minutes, Deumara said, "Fine. I'll drink." She pointed at the glass Morgana had, "But only from that one."

Jenni inclined her head, "Then I must drink from Lord Grattin's glass."

The captain took the indicated glasses, poured more white wine and handed the glasses to Deumara and Jenni.

Both drank, finishing at the same time.

"Ah, that's the Somerset Vintage. Always has a slight note of apple to it." Jenni said, smiling.

A round of applause from the watching Royal Council and Guards made Deumara grimace and growl, "Next."

"Next is the blue wine. For the Heart with only love in it." Morgana announced.

Deumara watched the captain pouring the wine, "That's more violet than blue. I've never had blue wine though, so what would I know?"

"Blue comes from a vine imported from Dracisealm. The Vineyards there and here are fertilised with Dragon manure, and it tends to be a robust wine, not for the faint of heart." Jenni said, smiling at her.

Morgana bottled up her laughter and took the glass the captain handed her. "To the Future Queen." Lord Archington raised his glass as if she'd proposed a toast, then three of them drank.

This time, Deumara took Lord Archington's glass.

Jenni sipped hers slowly, but Deumara swallowed it down in one. Then she coughed, "robust is right. That's stronger than I expected." Then she grinned, "But actually very pleasant, a good burn to the brain."

She doesn't suspect a thing. Morgana thought as the captain poured out the red wine. *"Jenni, I'm not entirely sure what will happen next. This is the one I prepared earlier."*

"What did you use? Poison?"

Morgana sent her an image of the little bottles in their box. *"Charon gave these to me. It's a Banish potion."*

Jenni blinked, *"I thought they were perfume bottles. Well, this is going to be interesting."*

"The instructions said it would banish anyone who drank it back to their own world. I also don't know how long it will take to work." Morgana said.

"Let's hope it doesn't send you or grandfather anywhere!" Jenni watched the captain bring the wine round to Morgana. *"Good Luck."*

Morgana smiled at her, took the glass, and said, "Red. For the Spirit that will sacrifice itself for all others." She drank.

Lord Archington and Lord Grattin drank.

Morgana felt Charon's mind touch hers, so she let him in, *"Why have you drunk the banish potion? It's only supposed to be used by one person, yet you've fed it to three."*

"I had no choice, Lord Ferryman." She replied and showed him the recent events.

He laughed. *"Well, I suppose you were justified in wanting to banish the Daemon. I'll send Thanatos to collect the fat one shortly. He's going to have to appear in person, so I suggest you keep the room calm."*

"It's a poison?!"

"No. He's just going to have a heart attack from the wine he's consumed." Thanatos' voice said. The two deities minds left hers.

She handed her glass to the captain. "Thank you for your service, Captain."

The captain nodded and took the other two glasses.

Deumara chose Grattin's glass, "Time to trust my taster I suppose."

Jenni smiled at Lord Grattin who was looking rather uncomfortable, "My minister of finance is always reliable in everything he does."

Lord Grattin smiled at her.

The two women drank. The room was as silent as a classroom with no children in it, everyone watching intently, somehow aware that something was about to happen.

Morgana spotted a pale shape appearing beside Grattin. *That's what they meant. I hope it doesn't alert Deumara.* She prodded Jenni who despite trying to look unaffected, was leaning back in her chair. "Jen. Don't be alarmed, but Grattin is going to die shortly."

"I thought you said it wasn't poison."

"It isn't. But Deumara is about to get a surprise. Look at her."

Forty-Three

Deumara had begun to glow like a firefly. She looked at her hands. "What's going on?"

Grattin dropped to his knees, coughing harder. The Captain of the Guard moved to his side, supporting the portly lord and helping him to lie down.

Thanatos arrived, his golden curls bouncing slightly as he popped into existence beside Grattin. "Greetings your Royal Highness." He said, bowing to Jenni, "You seem a little worse for wear. Let me help you a second." He snapped his fingers and Jenni sat up, looking alert.

"Thank you... ah...?" She said blushing.

"Thanatos. Angel of Death." He bowed and turned to Morgana. "Congratulations on your success, Lady Morgana."

She smiled at him, blushing a little. "Which one?"

"Discovering what you are meant to do in your life." He replied.

"It took a lot of Death to do that." She sighed.

"But you overcame the odds." He bowed.

Deumara cleared her throat, "Can I just interrupt this little flirtfest to ask; What in Balorn's Name did you do to me and Grattin?"

Morgana turned to her, "I put a potion in the red wine meant to Banish the drinker to where they belong. As you and Grattin are the only people reacting, that suggests that you have somewhere else to be."

"What?" the daemon looked at her hands and arms, yellow glow sparkling slightly.

"You're going back to the Fire Realm, Daemoness." Thanatos replied, "Sadly, your unremitting evil destroyed my gift, something meant to aid you to return home; thus, you must return via a Gift of Charon. However, as the potion was diluted, it is not strong enough to complete its work. You are suspended between the Fire Realm and this one."

Morgana winced. *Whoops. Please read label before use.*

"Worry not. I shall aid it's work in a second. However, first I must take this poor soul to the Black Door." Thanatos bowed and stepped across to Grattin who was gasping for breath, attended by the captain and a green sashed physician.

"So, you kill one of your own, in an attempt to kill me?" Deumara sneered at Jenni, "What happened to honour, High Princess?"

"I trust my sister implicitly. And Lord Thanatos has confirmed that the potion was not a poison, therefore honour is satisfied." Jenni shrugged, pushed back the chair and stood, "High Princess Morgana, I shall leave the rest of this in your capable hands. Lord Archington shall remain with you as an adviser, and my voice. I have much to do."

"Your finance minister lies dying by your sister's hand, and you sweep away, bloodless? Oh, no. I came here for the Angel's Crown and Shield of Courage, and I will leave with them!" Deumara lunged around the table and grabbed the crown off Jenni's head.

Jenni gasped as the move tore strands of hair from her head, from the hair grips that had held the crown in place.

Deumara backed away, tucking the crown into the pouch on her belt, then changed direction and ran for the shield. Lord Archington stepped between her and the dais, "I'm afraid I cannot allow you to do that, Lady Deumara."

She smacked into him hard, bounced backward and hit the floor with a sound like an ironmonger's stall falling over. "Huh? What... who are you?"

He bowed, "I am Lord Aderyn Archington, Advisor to the Queen of Llanirstyr."

She narrowed her eyes, "You... you're a construct!"

"Android, please. I'm still human even if my body is constructed. Now go and sit down or I shall make you." He smiled pleasantly as he helped her to stand as effortlessly as if she were wearing silk.

Morgana laughed and said, "Dewch ata i." holding her hand out. The shield lifted into the air and flew to her hand, avoiding anyone in the way. As soon as she was holding it, she said, "Crebachu o ran maint, yn dal i amddiffyn y cynhalydd i gyd" it shrank, and morgana attached it to the chain around her neck.

Deumara stared, "It responds to Welsh?"

"Only for the true bearer" she replied, "Your Royal Highness, you may leave this in my hands. I shall make sure Lord Grattin's body is dealt with in all honour."

Jenni nodded, "Thank you, sister."

"I've still got the Angel's Crown!" Deumara crowed.

Jenni paused as she reached the dais and smiled, pulling back her sleeve, "That trinket? Just a replica. Take it. I have about seven others." Around her wrist glittered a blue and white cuff, "This is the true Crown, and it never leaves my side." Then she dropped her sleeve, turned and swept out of the room without looking back.

Morgana walked across to Lord Grattin.

His body was still.

She stared at it. *Did I really kill him? Do I have to add his death to my tally sheet?* He didn't look like he'd suffered in his whole life. He wore velvet robes, thickly embroidered with flowers and leaves, and his skin was smooth and unlined. *I don't feel anything. Does that make me evil?*

Thanatos had disappeared and the captain and the physician were talking. "Do we have an official cause of death?"

The physician bowed then sighed, "It wasn't whatever you added to the wine, I know that. More than likely, it was his lifestyle. I've been telling him for years that his over consumption of luxury foods heavy with fat, and the accompanying alcohol would kill him eventually."

Morgana glanced back at the table where a glowing Deumara sat with Lord Archington stood behind her. "That tallies with what Charon and Thanatos have said. Make sure that it is properly documented, please. Captain, ensure the body receives due reverence for his position, and clear the Hall." She stretched, joints cracking, "I'll remain with the prisoner and Lord Archington until Thanatos returns to take her to her world. Carry on, Captain."

The captain saluted, "As you wish, your Royal Highness."

Deumara sat staring at the crown she had taken from Jenni when Morgana sat down opposite. The glowing daemoness was running her fingers over the smooth pearls and glittering sapphires.

"Was it worth it?" Morgana asked.

Deumara looked up. "Hmmh?"

"All of this," Morgana's gesture took in the three creatures who were still by the wall, Grattin's body and the wine goblets.

"Well, it could have been worse. I could have come with more than three slaves. You really ought to get your captain to check the security of this place, it tends to be very lax when there's a big event on." She replied, sounding tired.

"I'll remember that. Why did you do it?"

"Pride. Greed. Lust. All the usual emotions that send your mind crazy." Deumara laughed, "In my world, those are considered positive. I wanted Lord Apollyon to notice me and make me his next Mate."

Morgana couldn't help shuddering, "Apollyon? I had some education in the Underworld while I was there the second time, and I was told that he's Balorn's Son. Doesn't that make him ancient?"

Deumara laughed harder, "Oh he is. But time moves differently in the Fire Realm and while he's a couple thousand years old in his personal time line, he looks about fifty. He's a real silver fox."

Morgana made a face. "Whatever floats your boat, I suppose."

"Oh yes."

"Will he punish you for failing?" Morgana wasn't sure if she wanted an answer.

"Oh, I do hope so..." she replied breathily, then blinked, "uh, you're serious." She shrugged "Probably, but the punishments for women are lighter than the ones for men. We're more valuable as breeders." Deumara sat back in her chair, looking more like a queen than a defeated enemy.

Morgana blinked and stared at her. *She's not serious about that is she? I'll have to talk to Grandfather I suppose.*

They lapsed into silence, the noises of the guards clearing the hall and the servants dealing with Grattin's body.

After a while, Deumara asked, "What are you going to do with the slaves? They could possibly return to human form as long as they accept what they've become, but I think the Komopus won't let himself do that."

Morgana looked across at the creatures. The hound had curled up and gone to sleep, the Manticore was licking its paws, and the other was completely still in its pool of ink, only it's breathing showing it was still alive. "I'll find some way to change them back."

"Good luck with that. The spell I used activated their latent Daemon genes; it's a part of them."

Morgana took a deep breath and let it out, before she stood up and began to pace. *Where is Thanatos, I want her out of here.*

"I can't come. There's a massacre in China on Earth that I have to deal with. Someone else is coming." Thanatos' voice said in her mind abruptly, *"She'll be with you now."*

Morgana stopped pacing. "Finally."

On the dais, a beam of light appeared through the window. Deumara looked at it and the blood drained from her face. "Oh please, not her. Apollyon will kill me."

Morgana was confused. *How will light get the daemoness back to the fire realm, and why is she scared of it?*

"Sweet one, it's not the light she's scared of, but me." A familiar voice said.

A gasp echoed around the hall from the remaining servants and guards, all of whom dropped to their knees, mumbling prayers.

Morgana frowned. *I recognise that voice, but last time she was more formal.*

"Lady Moon. I thank you for gracing our world with your light." Lord Archington bowed deeply.

The woman who stepped out of the light beam looked a little like Jenni and a lot like their birth mother. "Thank you, Aderyn, but I'm just here to take a misplaced Daemon back to where she should be." She frowned at Deumara.

"And you are?" Morgana asked.

"Well, for a start, I'm your great-great-great-to the umpteenth power Grandmother. For another, I'm the Goddess of the Moon and Hunt in Llanirstyr. I believe they still use my oldest name, Arianrhod." The woman tilted her head to the side and smiled.

Deumara squeaked and fainted onto the floor.

"Well that makes it a little easier," Arianrhod said, gesturing. Deumara's unconscious form floated up from the floor, through the air above Morgana and the table to the goddess standing on the dais. Arianrhod gently cradled her in her arms, "Don't worry, I won't hurt her, and I won't let Apollyon hurt her either."

"Okay. Uh, what do I do about them?" Morgana asked, pointing to the creatures, then looking back at the goddess.

Arianrhod looked at them and sighed, "Well, for a start, you need to pay off their debt and then return them to their families."

"But they're..." Morgana began turning, then she blinked. Where three monsters had been sat, were three men in ragged clothing with gold chains around their necks. "How?"

"I'm a deity. I have much more power than you might think." Arianrhod smiled, "I'll be off now."

Morgana turned back, just in time to see the two women disappear into the light, "Thank you?"

"*You're welcome. Now make the most of your new body and enjoy your life for a while. It won't be long before you'll be in mortal danger again.*" Arianrhod's voice said in her mind.

The light faded back to normal, and Morgana sighed, "That felt oddly anti-climactic."

"Deus Ex Machina always does, Morgana. Shall we go and find your sister to celebrate?" Lord Archington said.

Morgana nodded, suddenly too tired for words.

The End

Don't miss out!

Visit the website below and you can sign up to receive emails whenever Kira Morgana publishes a new book. There's no charge and no obligation.

https://books2read.com/r/B-A-SVI-WYGID

BOOKS 2 READ

Connecting independent readers to independent writers.

Did you love *The Second Door*? Then you should read *Curse of the White Tiger*[1] by A. E. Churchyard!

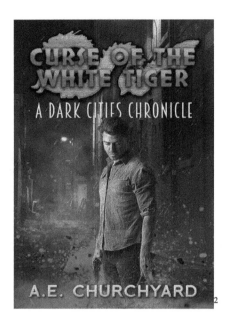[2]

Turn a city upside down and shake it - what falls out? The Treaty that binds the Vampires, Werewolves, Humans and the rarely seen True Dragons is over 1000 years old. It provides stability and safety for all the citizens of the city of Te Ling. Triads and Yakuza are not welcome here and Tourism flourishes amongst the bright lights, Night clubs, Temples and leisure facilities. But many lights cast a multitude of shadows and they just get darker as you get deeper. Li is as deep into the darkness as you can get: cop by day, shadow by night, he eats and drinks the lifeblood of the city. A threat to the current Te Ling Triang Leader is a threat to the City and The Black Dragon cannot be risked.

---

1. https://books2read.com/u/mBw11k

2. https://books2read.com/u/mBw11k

Handed the responsibility of tracking down and removing the threat, Li soon realises that knowing too much can be a curse... Read more at tpsworld.wordpress.com.

Also by Kira Morgana

Terrene Empire Tales
Blossom & Kitsune: A Brief Tale of Earthquakes and Nine Tailed
Foxes
Snow & Kitsune: A Long Tale of Wild Weather and Tanuki

The Dragon Flower Saga
Hat or Tiara?

The Secret of Arking Down
The Angel's Crown
The Dragon's Pendant
The Second Door

The Tower and The Eye
A Beginning

Standalone

The Necklace of Harmony: A short story collection

Watch for more at tpsworld.wordpress.com.

About the Author

Kira thought she was a Teacher, until Life pointed out to her that she is actually a writer. As her Cats, Kids and Partner (in that order) approved, she decided to agree with Life.

Currently she is working on a seven book Science Fantasy series, with several accompanying spinoffs and as "A.E. Churchyard" on several Science Fiction projects.

As if that weren't enough to do, she also sings in a Chorus Line, takes Tap lessons, and is delving into the world of Illustration and Graphic Novels

She does all this from a body in South Wales, UK. Where her mind is, she hasn't yet worked out, because apart from seeing a lot of fantasy creatures, she hasn't actually managed to find someone with a connection to a map app...

Read more at tpsworld.wordpress.com.

About the Publisher

Teigr Books is the official Publisher of all Kira Morgana, A. E. Churchyard and Mandy E. Ward books.